about the erupti   f
he'd said nothin   e
crowd of dark suits and dresses rising in standing
ovation, as I remained seated in a special state of
confusion. *What? Who was he calling an amazing
woman he could not live without? She did his dry
cleaning? I did his dry cleaning and hand-pressed
many-a-dress shirt. What was she doing touching his
shirts?*

I sensed an obvious discomfort at my banquet
table. The wife next to me raised her eyebrows and
gave me an open-mouthed, super-smile, which said,
*"Yes, that was inappropriate for him to say, and yes, we
all noticed."*

All the color must've drained from my face as I
remembered locking eyes with Mitchell amid the
applause before he darted behind the big black curtain.

She was only his assistant, right? Was I
overreacting? Was he genuinely indebted to her or was
he purposely trying to disrespect me?

My ears were ringing now and my head was going
to explode. I'd had migraines before, but this was the
mother of all migraines. I shut my eyes and splashed a
little water on my face, trying to quell the fire in my
head.

When I opened my eyes I saw a woman.

I wasn't alone.

Pretty Dolls and Hand Grenades

by

Cara Reinard

This is a work of fiction. Names, characters, places, and incidents are either the product of the author's imagination or are used fictitiously, and any resemblance to actual persons living or dead, business establishments, events, or locales, is entirely coincidental.

Pretty Dolls and Hand Grenades

COPYRIGHT © 2016 by Cara Reinard

Cover Art by *Kristian Norris*

The Wild Rose Press, Inc.
PO Box 708
Adams Basin, NY 14410-0708
Visit us at www.thewildrosepress.com

Publishing History
First Crimson Rose Edition, 2016
Print ISBN 978-1-5092-0584-4
Digital ISBN 978-1-5092-0585-1

Published in the United States of America

Dedication

To my wonderful husband
for supporting me
on my long, bumpy road
to publication.

Acknowledgements

A special thanks to the early readers on this series: Hope Cox, Jennifer Monasterio, Virginia Pierce, Justin Reinard, Vickie Reinard, and Janice Sniezek

And, thank you so much to the Mars Library Critique Group, who every other Monday act as my extra pair of eyes for the blips on the page and an extra pair of ears when I need someone to listen. Even though we only meet twice a month, you ladies inspire me everyday: Dana Faletti, Nancy Hammer, Lori Jones, Cathy Omulac, Carolyn Menke and Kim Pierson.

Chapter 1
Dollhouse

I always imagined I'd live in a dream dollhouse when I grew up. It didn't have to be pink, but it should come complete with big shutters, four bedrooms, two children, and the perfect husband. The nuclear family, the American dream, a precedent set by the lollipop and rainbow fantasies of little girls everywhere.

I had the American dream. At least for a little while.

****

This old dream house was an oven upstairs, the downstairs a constant breezeway. The million-dollar renovation I'd so carefully planned and supervised, transformed it from a turn-of-the-century charmer to a rustic-contemporary masterpiece; but the uneven temperature left me dissatisfied.

My mascara began to sweat as I finished putting away the laundry in my daughter's upstairs bedroom. Josie's sweater appeared shrunken as it dangled from my fingertips.

"Come here," I insisted, holding the sweater up to Josie as she sat rear-faced on her bed listening to her iPod, and thumbing through her phone.

She waved me off, her vertebrae jutting out of her slouchy tee like a peekaboo skeleton. She didn't have to stand up. I could see all I needed from sizing up the shirt to her body. "Honey," I mouthed, asking her to remove the ear buds with my hand gestures. She looked at me with dark circles beneath her sunken eyes. Her ballet practice yesterday had been grueling, so I decided to let her rest.

My hands trembled as I shoved the sweater into the drawer, wondering whether I'd hand-washed it like the others or if it had somehow snuck into the dryer with the dark-colored shirts.

Maybe I shouldn't be leaving the kids tonight. There were obviously some issues I had to address. But Mitchell needed me on his arm this evening. To be a supportive wife and a loving mother was a careful balance to master.

As I surveyed myself in Josie's floor length mirror, I noticed the bottom of my dress was a bit tight around the hips.

As if she could hear my thoughts, Josie sniped, "Your dress is way too tight."

I wrinkled my nose in dismay as my thirteen-year-old daughter eyed me from behind.

Why hadn't Liz, my personal shopper at Barney's, told me it was snug when I'd tried on the knee-length, black Chanel dress? Smoothing down the wrinkles at my hips and over my slightly soft belly, I sighed and stared critically at myself in the mirror. Liz said it was "Cecelia-stamped", meaning it was perfect for me. There was nothing I loved more than *perfect*. My brain ticked and tocked for *perfect*.

"Where is it too tight, Josie?" I asked. She didn't answer me.

"At least, I have great shoes," I said, intending for it to be a joke, but she rolled her eyes.

They were great shoes. Brand new black Louboutin four-inch heels to be exact.

Josie groaned and tossed her hair back, "Whatever," she sighed, already bored.

"Josie, honey, we're going to need to discuss what your idea of too tight is when I return," I said, settling on her bed. I reached out to brush her cheek but she flinched away from me.

"What-e-ver, Mom," Josie replied again, preparing to reinsert her ear buds. It was her answer for everything these days.

Mitchell's parents would be here any minute. I needed to put away all of the laundry and fix the towels in the guest bathroom. As I folded Josie's last pair of jeans I heard the doorbell ring.

Shit!

I needed to touch up my makeup. This upstairs was killing me. I heard the heavy door click open. Peering outside, it was no wonder they let themselves in. It was a howling, growling snowstorm out there.

"Deb, Cliff, I'm up here, make yourself at home, I need to finish up," I hollered down the stairwell, carrying my empty laundry basket to the upstairs linen closet.

"Come on, Cece, we've got to go!" Mitchell yelled from the foyer.

Somewhere in between my in-laws' arrival and my daughter's tirade of scrutiny, my husband had entered the house. I descended the stairs too quickly in my high heels nearly barreling into my mother-in-law on the landing.

"Hello, dear," I heard Deb say softly with an annoyed edge to her voice. The modest woman had

3

never liked me. Women who didn't wear makeup would never understand women who did, and it was a truth I'd come to accept as fact.

"Right now, Cece. We're going to be late!" Mitchell shouted.

As Mitchell exited the house, he left the mahogany door wide open, sending a chill throughout the already icy room, leaving his black coattails flapping in the wind. The fur tickled my fingertips as I grabbed my coat off the rack and followed him. I stood at the top step of the porch, contemplating the best angle to get down, searching for my husband's strong arm to hang onto. But when I looked up he was already in his Mercedes, fiddling with the heat and radio. He'd pulled the car up our governor's drive, leaving me alone on the stoop in my stilettos to fend the glacial steps and ice-skating-rink-for-a-driveway.

When I slid into the passenger side of Mitchell's car the cool leather bit into my thin pantyhose. Mitchell didn't look at me as he drove away from our Montclair, New Jersey suburb toward the city. Through the drifting snow, he navigated carefully to the Marriott Marquis in Manhattan.

"You could've put my heated seats on too, yeah know," I complained.

"You want to start on me, Cece? We're half an hour late because of you," he bickered.

"Mitchell, please. I was just trying to look my best for my husband. What's your problem?" I asked.

"I heard you asking Josie about your dress," he said in an accusatory tone.

"So."

"So, what do you think asking those kinds of

4

questions does to Josie's self-esteem, Cece?" Mitchell sighed like he was *Father of the year*. He was far from it.

"My stalling wasn't really about the dress, it was about her," I answered.

"Right, because it's never about you. You can't tell me you weren't up there checking yourself out in your skin-tight dress," Mitchell argued.

Skin-tight sounded bad.

"I am worried about Josie. But on the subject of my dress, are you agreeing with her it's too tight?" I asked, biting my lower lip.

"First of all, there's no good way for me to answer that and you know it. The question is a trap. Second of all, if that's the only thing you heard from what I just said, you don't deserve an answer," he said coldly.

It wasn't the only thing I'd heard. The truth was, I knew there was something wrong with our daughter, but I also understood what it was. Josie was her mother's daughter. We were creatures of compulsion, born to serve our craft, hungry for the rush of excellence. Josie would turn her head when she'd witness me scrubbing something until my fingers were bloody. She'd go ho-hum when I'd work tirelessly on a home project until I'd practically collapse into my obsessive pool of perfection, because she understood it too.

"She's a dancer. How many times have I told you ballerinas need to maintain a low body weight? It's her coach who's putting pressure on her. You know her dream is to go to Julliard and if it's what she really wants, then I'm willing to help her. That's me being a supportive mother," I reasoned.

5

Mitchell's face twisted. *"A supportive mother?"* His focus on the snowy road shifted to me for the first time since I entered the vehicle, but I peered out the window instead of facing him. He'd never understand. Mitchell hadn't seen Josie pirouette with the grace of a Trumpeter swan or lift her leg with the efficiency of a professional athlete. I had. I'd been to every performance.

"A good mother. By helping your teenage daughter count carbs? You're insane. She should be having sleepovers and pizza parties not counting grams on the side of cereal boxes. You're creating a monster," he argued.

Things had gotten a bit out of control in my household, but I didn't have all of the answers, and I didn't know how to fix it. Me, accepting Josie's faults in pursuit of her dreams, her accepting mine in pursuit of my sanity, my younger son oblivious to it all locked away in a room somewhere playing video games.

"You're her father. Feel free to step in, if you're so concerned. I've tried to get her to be less stringent, but it's what she thinks she needs to make her dreams come true, and it's my job to help her reach those dreams."

"I've tried to intervene, Cece, but when you allow her to eat like a bird it just cuts my damn balls off," he said, "God damn traffic!" Mitchell laid on his horn outside the Lincoln Tunnel.

"Eat like a bird, Mitchell? So, she's eating chicken and fish instead of Happy Meals and sugar, and you're complaining?"

He didn't answer me. Mitchell didn't realize how hard it was for me to deal with Josie's eating habits either. How she'd only eat boiled chicken breasts to avoid the oils and grease from the pan. If I didn't make our meals devoid of salt, she wouldn't touch them.

"Sodium makes me bloat," she'd say.

"That's more than four ounces, measure it please," she'd demand in regard to whatever protein I was serving for the evening meal.

Mitchell blared his horn once more.

"We've been waiting outside this tunnel to get into the city our whole lives. What's your hurry? The damn thing never starts on time anyway."

"Not that you'd care to remember, but I am winning a big award tonight for being top producer of the company and I'm supposed to give a speech to open the ceremony," Mitchell snapped.

"Oh yeah," I muttered.

The sad part was, I had forgotten. I was so tied up in picking out my dress, worrying about Josie, and getting the house ready for my in-laws, I had completely forgotten. I sat there turned in the opposite direction of my husband for the rest of the drive. We used to be so good together. We were the perfect pair, and I couldn't help thinking about how much things had changed.

Mitchell and I were the matchy-matchy couple in college. The ones people gushed over saying how adorable we were with our brunette, wide-smiled likeness. My slender body fit perfectly into his, measuring just right to rest my cheek on his chest when we slow danced, or to lay my head on his shoulder when I donned heels.

And my fixation with my family, whom I demanded yearly photos from to everyone's dismay, was one of my great obsessions. My husband hated our yearly photo sessions most of all. I actually had to give him a blowjob the night before the last one to ensure he would smile the next day. The great lengths I went to make my husband smile.

But it wasn't only for show; I loved my family. Well, I guess some of it was. Is loving your family so bad? Is it so terrible to do everything you can to get it just right?

Squealing tires broke me out of my trance. We arrived at the hotel with fifteen minutes to spare. Mitchell bolted out of the car and started walking ahead of me, leaving me tripping behind him in my newly cut shoes.

"Jesus, Mitchell, slow down! What is this, the Nobel Prize you're winning?" I asked.

I barely made it into the elevator before the doors shut. His fury of dark eyes caught me in a way, which made me question whether I would make it out alive.

"You have no idea how hard I've worked to win this award. All my money you love to spend and you don't give a damn how hard I've worked to earn it." His voice was even-keeled and eerie, as if he was talking right through me.

"I know you work hard, honey. Every weekend I've spent alone reminds me. Believe me, I know," I snorted.

Mitchell threw back his head in silent laugher, looking at the mirrored ceiling like he wanted to jump right through it, his dark billow of hair swaying from side to side as he shook his head. I used to love to run my hands through his thick mop, but looking at it now, I couldn't remember the last time I'd touched it.

"All you can think about, Cece, is how everything

in the world affects *you*. It's your world, I'm just living in it," Mitchell mused.

"Well, you should be well-practiced for your big speech tonight, Mitchell. You've certainly got the drama part down pat."

Mitchell shook his head at me again, red-faced and rendered speechless. When the door opened, he took off, not bothering to take my hand, staying a pace ahead of me once more.

"Can you please be civil and at least walk with me? You're being a child," I hissed.

Mitchell either didn't hear me or wasn't listening anymore. Likely the latter. I watched him huff into a standstill as he was greeted by a line of people waiting to get into the event, which forced him to wait for me after all. I scurried beside him, anxious to hold up appearances as I searched the lobby buffet table for our place cards.

"Look dear, I found our table," I said gently.

Mitchell glanced back at me looking like a poster child for high blood pressure, his reddish face and lips pressed firmly shut. I knew then it would be a silent evening.

We'd been having more and more silent evenings lately, where we would coexist for the sake of whatever event we were forced to attend, not talking to one another because one of us was perturbed with the other.

This evening would be one of *those* nights. I cringed at the thought of having to sit through it.

As soon as we reached our table and began greeting Mitchell's colleagues, he was whisked away by tech support and fastened with a microphone for his big speech. I watched as the sweat brimmed on his forehead. Mitchell was great one on one, which made him a stellar salesman, but sizeable audiences unnerved him. I suddenly felt terribly guilty for my behavior, realizing his stress was elevated because of his impending speech to his colleagues.

"Mitchell," I called out before he was taken back stage.

Irritation flitted across his face as he hesitantly looked back over his shoulder. I felt like an unwelcome gnat flapping in his ear; a pesky bird chirping every time he tried to focus.

"Good luck, honey," I mouthed.

"Right," he muttered. My heart burned in my chest. He was *really* angry.

A few people who thought they were important appeared on stage to announce the thirty-something annual award banquet for one of New York City's premier real estate agencies. The ceremony always kicked off with the most distinguished honor, *The Top Sales Producer Award*, immediately followed by dinner. Then, there would be a few honorable mentions, and afterward we were thereby released from our seats and allowed to crowd the open bar as a live band played to whom no one bothered to listen. Dancing was out of the question.

Mitchell had been with the company for twelve years and this was his first time on stage. I sat on the edge of my seat in anticipation, much like the way I composed myself for one of Josie's dance reviews. Proud mother. Proud wife. I positioned myself at the table facing the stage, so I could make direct eye contact if Mitchell glanced straight down the middle of the crowd. But I had a feeling he wouldn't. The nervous inclination building in my belly told me I wouldn't get the chance to properly congratulate him tonight either.

I watched him strut to the podium with confidence, knowing he was a nervous wreck on the inside. He looked handsome and had aged so well in the last decade, despite being overworked and keeping up with our active family. The corners of his sideburns had started to lose their color, and I imagined him as one good-looking gray fox. I was always attracted to his strong square jaw, his large, get-lost-in-you dark brown eyes topped with come-hither, naturally arched eyebrows.

And he had one dimple on his left cheek, which popped out when he smiled, and I found it irresistible. Mitchell often half-smiled when he was trying to be crass, pulling at the cute, dimpled cheek, defeating his purpose—too cute to be crass. The half-smile appeared now, as he fished out his notecards. It was also the same look he wore when he was nervous.

Come on honey, you can do it. Sorry for being difficult.

"Thank you colleagues and friends. It has been a long, hard year in the unsettling world of real estate with the economic downturn and all the challenges of a buyer's market. All of us in this room have had to work twice as hard to keep our heads above water and sell through an unsellable market, fighting for every client and every dollar...."

He went on to express the hardships of being a real estate agent, as everyone in the room nodded in agreement. The speech depicted tales of waiting in the rain, sleet, and snow and getting up to meet clients before seven a.m. and after midnight to make the sale.

Not to mention being expected to bend to the buyer's needs in ways that would make an agent would throw up their hands in prior years.

That's funny. I didn't know any of his job woes. Mitchell had been keeping me in the dark, sheltering me from the grim details. I knew he was working extra hours, but he said he was pulling in the same seven-figure income despite the housing climate, so I didn't bat one single, mascaraed eyelash. I never realized it was so hard on him. I winced as I thought of the scolding I gave him when we got home from Camdyn's soccer game, calling him a bad father. It was a terrible fight. I didn't really mean he was a *bad* father. I had been upset because he'd missed Camdyn's goal, and I'd used his hot button to piss him off. We both had been way too eager to push each other's buttons lately.

Mitchell was doing a great job on stage carrying out his well-prepared speech and my pride for him swooned as he began his closing remarks. After zoning out for a few economic facts and figures, I was back in the moment when I heard him thanking various people for his successful year. The corner of my mouth perked up at the last few sentences waiting for his final words.

"I want to thank Herbert Weinstein and Jason Lowenthal for splitting harder to sell listings with me, only to bring in the perfect buyer and complete my year. And most of all, I want to thank one special person. Without her, I could've never kept my calendars organized, my dry-cleaning pressed, my phone messages in order or my head on straight. Thank you so much to one amazing woman," he paused.

I looked up at the stage beaming, waiting for him to say my name, forgiving me for all the silliness of the evening, retreating to where he belonged, so we could celebrate this huge moment in his career.

"A big thank you to my personal assistant, Katelyn McCallister, who I only hired a little over a year ago, and who I can already not live without," he finished.

Chapter 2
Amazing Women

The hotel bathroom seemed like a safe enough place to hide. The red and pink hues of the wallpaper matched my splotchy face, the metallic zigzag pattern making me dizzier than I was all ready.

My reflection was a flushed yet pleasing almost forty. Nice, neat, thin and trim, with barely a wrinkle on my unblemished face. But *assistant* sounded like a young word. And young was something I was not. I fought for air, as I often did when I was nervous, reassessing the situation.

Panting now, I couldn't help thinking about the eruption of clapping at Mitchell's words as if he'd said nothing wrong. My mind retreated back to the crowd of dark suits and dresses rising in standing ovation, as I remained seated in a special state of confusion. *What? Who was he calling an amazing woman he could not live without? She did his dry cleaning? I did his dry cleaning and hand-pressed many-a-dress shirt. What was she doing touching his shirts?*

I sensed an obvious discomfort at my banquet table. The wife next to me raised her eyebrows and gave me an open-mouthed, super-smile, which said, *"Yes, that was inappropriate for him to say, and yes, we all noticed."*

All the color must've drained from my face as I

remembered locking eyes with Mitchell amid the applause before he darted behind the big black curtain.

She was only his assistant, right? Was I overreacting? Was he genuinely indebted to her or was he purposely trying to disrespect me?

My ears were ringing now and my head was going to explode. I'd had migraines before, but this was the mother of all migraines. I shut my eyes and splashed a little water on my face, trying to quell the fire in my head.

When I opened my eyes I saw a woman.

I wasn't alone.

She leered into the mirror over my shoulder.

"Oh!" I jumped. "I didn't hear you come in," I explained, and then pressed my fingers to my temple again to stifle the pain.

Her reflection was so stunning; I didn't dare turn around to face her in my current condition. A blonde bombshell in a crimson and black holiday dress, which would've looked vintage with its dropped waistline, if it wasn't for her killer body. There was nothing vintage about her physique.

"There's no one in the stall," I mentioned, attempting to nudge her away. I tried to concentrate on my reflection instead of hers as I dabbed my face dry, reapplied my makeup, and willed my headache to cease.

"I need, uh, how do you say touch ze' makeup?" she said in what I thought was an Eastern European accent of some sort.

"Right, I'm sorry," I apologized, gathering my items and throwing them back in my purse.

"Quite ze' speech, yes," she commented.

I clamped my eyes shut in horror. Other people *had* noticed Mitchell's affection for his assistant in his speech. It wasn't my imagination.

As the mystery woman neared the counter, she pulled her red scarf-like shawl tighter around her shoulders. Even though she was the one who was apparently cold, I got a chill.

"Yes, well…" I attempted to explain.

I nervously patted at a stray droplet of water on my neck before I relinquished the countertop to her.

"If it were my husband, I'd be throwing water on his face," she hissed.

She was absolutely right. Why was I hiding in the bathroom feeling sorry for myself? I should be confronting my husband.

"Yes, well, maybe he was very excited to win the award and for everyone who helped him along the way," I reasoned, trying to save face.

She was scowling at me with uncertainty. Who was this woman? She was probably a spouse, like me. A little sympathy wouldn't hurt.

"Okay then, have a good night," I said hurriedly as I exited the ladies room.

Now, I was boiling mad. Mitchell had made a fool out of me. He'd asked if I wanted to hear his speech last night to make sure everything sounded okay, saying how he was unsure about certain parts. Maybe I should've listened. I was wrapped up in a very in-depth Pinterest project on our new bathroom remodel and told him I was sure anything he wrote would be great. Was telling everyone he couldn't live without his assistant part of his original speech or something he threw in at the last minute to hurt me?

Another button. He'd pressed a giant, hot button with the words: *Cut Your Wife's Heart Out* plastered on it.

When I returned to the party, I found him at the bar, back-slapping his colleagues with his crystal award and hefty bonus check in one hand, scotch on the rocks in the other. I quietly maneuvered my way into his social circle without him seeing me.

"Congratulations, honey," I said, with my best smile.

"There you are," he responded, although he didn't look me in the eyes. He hid behind the clinking of ice cubes, barely acknowledging my presence.

"Yes, here I am, and I need a drink," I announced.

Mitchell motioned with the wave of his hand to the bar, signaling me to get it myself. When I returned with my gin and tonic, he already had his back to me. He had turned to greet a young woman. She shuffled over to congratulate him. Shuffled. That's how I would describe the movement of her feet. Clunky boats tromping across the floor, her steps too close together, ankles wobbling a bit, like a girl who didn't know how to walk in heels.

Mitchell and the woman exchanged a brief hug and my stomach knotted. But it was a non-lingering, very business-like, congratulatory hug. I quickly interrupted their exchange, extending my hand and stepping in between them.

"Excuse me, I'm Cecelia Laramie, Mitchell's wife. I don't believe we've met," I declared.

"Oh hello, I'm Katelyn McCallister, Mitchell's assistant," she responded with a demure smile.

A fan of blush spanned her freckled cheeks as she

shook my hand. Mitchell didn't care for women with freckles. My fears subsided. Mitchell and I were a pair of beautiful, golden-meets-olive-skinned people. Katelyn's face was littered with brown spots. I found myself trying to count the little dots as my eyes bored right through her.

"Well, I guess I should thank you for making my husband's year so fruitful," I commented, flashing my teeth.

She blushed again, reminding me of a little girl. A mark of immaturity. Every woman should be able to gracefully take a compliment by at least age twenty. *Stupid twat.*

"Oh, Mrs. Laramie. Simply doing my job, and trying to work my way up to agent," she said. *Yep, trying to work your way up MY agent.*

"I'm sure with hard work, you'll get there," I encouraged.

"Oh, we've been working hard," she said, arching her eyebrows. "Princess Dietrich's been no treat," she added, patting Mitchell's pinstriped shoulder. He smiled. I was revolted.

"Well, when you have to find rooms for horses and dogs too…" Mitchell started.

Katelyn erupted in an awful guffaw startling me. I watched her nervously tuck a stray ringlet of strawberry-blonde hair behind her ear from her messy updo.

I remembered us scraping by when Mitchell was an assistant. We were newlyweds, crammed in a two-bedroom apartment in Hoboken, living off tiny Chinese noodles and dreams. I was employed by our alma mater, New York University, as an admissions counselor shortly after receiving my degree in Business Administration. It was the year Mitchell decided he would never make enough money with his accounting degree and started over in real estate. It was also the only year I would ever make more money than my husband.

"I remember Mitchell's days as an assistant. Oh, the struggle with what they give you to start out with, but it's all worth it in the end," I said, giving her a condescending head-to-toe look.

I couldn't help letting the new, amazing woman in my husband's life know I thought she looked cheap. Cheap from her bargain basement, velvet dress that clung to her young curves to her plain, multi-string of tiny fake pearls hanging from her long neck. Cheap from her non-descript, platform pumps, which made her too tall to be elegant, to her her straggly, red hair, too thick for the clip she tried to wrangle it together with.

"Well, as long as I have enough to pay my cell phone bill, I'm good. Email and Facebook, the staples of life, yeah know? Oh, what am I saying? You're probably not even on social media, right, Cecelia? My mom doesn't have a clue how to work it, and insists it's a ploy to hack your bank info."

Was she comparing me to her mother? Was she calling me old?

Katelyn exploded into another obnoxious laugh. It was like a sinister *Bawaha* gone all shrill and wrong. If that was her sexy kitten laugh someone needed to kill that cat quick.

Mitchell let out a playful laugh next, and I was over the inside jokes and flirty giggles.

"Well, it is New York. Shame to have to sacrifice

drinks out with friends for your, um, Facebook," I said with distaste.

"What would you know about struggling, Cece?" Mitchell asked.

"Short memory, dear. We practically lived off nothing when you first started here," I reminded Mitchell.

Mitchell furrowed his brow and his eyes shot sideways, as if he couldn't remember whether or not what I'd said was true.

"Well, Mitchell, you were brilliant tonight," she intervened, touching his pinstripes again, and I really needed her to stop touching him. "It was a pleasure meeting you, Cecelia, I have to run," Katelyn remarked.

"So soon, Kate?" Mitchell asked.

He sounded more disappointed than I would've liked and I didn't enjoy hearing his nickname for her. I realized then "Kate" was short for Katelyn, but the warmth in his tone made me wonder if he'd been the one who'd given it to her.

"Yeah, I have a new puppy. My roommate is watching him, but I feel bad strapping her down with my dog on a Friday night," she explained.

She has a new puppy. Isn't she so sweet? She's a little girl. A little girl with a brand new little puppy.

"Oh yeah, how is Dexter adjusting to his new home?" Mitchell asked.

"He's good, chewed a pair of my heels already though," she complained.

It might explain the ugly pair of shoes she had on tonight, but probably not. I suspected she just had bad taste.

"Oh no! I love dogs, but Cece's not a fan. My boy,

Camdyn, really wanted one, but gave up on asking about two years ago," Mitchell added.

And now I am the evil, dog-hating wife who keeps their son from the only thing he truly desires. Thank you for painting me black, Mitchell.

"Mitchell, you know a dog would destroy our hardwood floors and all the hair isn't worth the time it would take me to keep up with it," I explained.

"My wife has OCD," Mitchell announced.

Katelyn's cheeks turned bright red.

"Well, dogs are a handful. Have a good night," Katelyn said.

She hurriedly exited, leaving us to suffocate in our awkwardness. I watched her walk unsteadily out the door. She seemed innocent enough. Who would want to screw a woman who couldn't even properly walk in high heels? We left shortly after without saying much to one another. It was a silent evening, and now I had more reason to keep my mouth shut than he did.

Outside, the snowfall had turned into a blizzard. The hotel was under construction and we had to walk on a grated floor to get to the parking garage. The holes in the grate were not large enough for a regular high heel to get stuck, but just wide enough to snag a stiletto. My foot caught and I went down. Mitchell swung around to break my fall. He saved me from face planting into the crisscrossed metal plate.

"Jesus, Cece!"

"My heel caught," I said, steadying myself. "And broke! Damn it, I just bought these."

"And how much did those cost you to wear them for one night?" he asked.

I didn't answer him. He didn't care I'd almost

21

smashed my face on the floor, only how much it was costing him in the process. I took my shoes off and walked the rest of the way to his car barefooted through the parking lot.

"Gross. There could be crack needles on the ground. At least, watch where you're stepping," Mitchell barked.

"Well, I can't walk in one four inch heel and one flat heel and you sure as hell aren't going to carry me!" I yelled.

"Got that right," he sniped back.

As soon as we were seated in the car, Mitchell's phone buzzed and I began to scrub my feet through their stockings with the Clorox wipes I'd stashed in our glove compartment.

"Herb wants to know if we want to meet him and the missus for a night cap in Hell's Kitchen." Mitchell read his text.

"What part of, I have only one shoe do you not understand?" I asked.

"We don't get out in the city much, Cece. I could throw you over my back until we get to the front door," he joked.

"It's a blizzard, I only have one working shoe, and it seems as though you have a new, amazing woman in your life. Maybe you should ask her to go to Hell's Kitchen with you. If she's not too busy babysitting her puppy dog," I snapped.

"I knew it," he grumbled.

Mitchell skidded out of the parking garage as he veered his car in the direction of the Lincoln Tunnel, heading for home.

"You knew telling everyone you couldn't live

without *Kate* would piss me off, so you decided to publicly humiliate me? Just because we have a private disagreement does not mean you need to lash out at me in front of the whole world," I fumed with indignation.

Times Square buzzed all around us. Mitchell might as well have put his speech on one of the lighted teleprompters. A big neon sign with: *This is How You Disrespect Your Wife in Public.*

"That's why I asked you to listen to my speech last night. But you were too busy Pinkerting," Mitchell commented.

"It's Pinteresting! So that was the question you had on your closing speech?"

"Whatever the hell it's called. And, yes. I needed to give her my thanks, but didn't know how to word it. I wanted your input, but you didn't care, so there yeah go," he griped.

"Mitchell, if you would've told me what exactly you needed help with, I might've reacted differently."

"You're impossible. And jealous of my poor assistant," Mitchell said disapprovingly.

"I'm not the only one who noticed. Some woman in the bathroom said she was embarrassed for me."

"Don't be ridiculous. What was her name?"

"I don't know. I was so mortified I didn't ask her. Some gorgeous foreign blonde woman."

"Well, that narrows it down in the world of real estate wives," Mitchell sniped sarcastically. "She was trying to get a rise out of you."

"Mitchell, you told a crowd of people your assistant was an amazing woman you couldn't live without!" I screamed.

"Well, she has been instrumental to my success.

How would you've worded it?" he asked seriously.

"Well, let's see," I said smacking my lips together, "The part where you said you couldn't live without her was a bit strong. How about, a special thanks to my personal assistant, XYZ, who significantly contributed to my success this year."

"Well, now there's some feedback I could've used last night," he said, shrugging me off.

I threw my hands up in surrender. My headache had worsened from fighting all evening, and I leaned back into my seat and closed my eyes. Mitchell didn't disturb the inevitable quietness. It was time for our silent evening to continue until we could make it home and climb soundlessly into bed, not touching each other or speaking until the morning. So much for never going to bed angry. That rule didn't apply in our dream house.

Chapter 3
Fashion Show

It was two months later and Fashion Week in New York City—an annual occasion my girlfriends and I lived for. This year the show had a dollhouse theme, featuring real life dolls throughout the ages. I'd been a huge collector since I was a child, so this was a special event for me. My desire for the more valuable ones, still in their boxes, was another hobby Mitchell tolerated, despite the bang to our bank account.

Each doll was carefully preserved in its box and encased in a special room in our house, which was painted in ivory and pink. Mitchell referred to it as *The Ivory Tower*, irked the dolls were still trapped in their boxes only to be placed in another glass box—an ornate, lighted, custom, display case. My special room was kept under lock and key and rarely exposed to anyone. As my mother always said, *"Keep your cuckoos in their clocks, not everyone needs to see them."*

Minsk dolls, the European divas used by undercover informants during the early years of the Cold War, fascinated me the most. The fact that classified information was encased in the cavity of their hollowed out bodies gave me a thrill. Stunning beauty on the outside, stealthy filler on the inside. She was the perfect doll.

I'd had my eye on the number one Minsk doll for quite some time, but the opportunity to get my hands on her had yet to present itself. The number one Minsk doll was the very first of its kind. She wore a red and black swing dress, fitted on top, then hanging loosely from her hip to her knee in true fifties fashion. Her face was painted in overly-seductive-for-the-times make-up, accentuated by her blonde hair, and pulled back in the signature Minsk babushka.

All of the ladies in the neighborhood labored over their ensembles for the show, calling in their personal shoppers and makeup artists to complete their look. Fashion week was a big deal, made grander by the fact, today also happened to be my birthday. The stars were all aligning in my favor. My birthday plan was to attend the show with my friends tonight, dine in the city tomorrow evening with Mitchell, then cake with the kids on Sunday.

I sashayed in the mirror, thrilled for my elaborate celebration. I chose a black and hot pink, color block dress by Stella McCartney. I had on black tights to shelter me from the winter air and black, high-heeled Michael Kors booties.

My regular crew of four other Montclair housewives picked me up for our night out. Robin was driving since she owned a minivan and the rest of us didn't want to play bumper cars in the city with our expensive rides. After Robin had her identical twin boys through IVF treatment, and then triplet girls after her second round, her large minivan was the only vehicle roomy enough to support all five of them.

"Just step over the crushed goldfish and baby spit up. I had time to get the car seats out, but couldn't clean up the rest, and then Marcus came running after me for something, so I just pretended like I didn't see him and reversed in full speed down the driveway," Robin joked, but we all knew she was serious.

"Five in diapers. And you left him alone? I hope he survives," I said with a cackle.

"You laugh. My stylist almost walked out on me after Quinton tried to eat her makeup brush. My days of being pampered are definitely over," she said, as her chestnut curly hair trailed haphazardly down her back in a messy-hot way only Robin could pull off.

Robin was always laced with the finest jewels, and won the prize in our group for the best accessories. Her parents owned a prestigious jewelry store she'd help run until she met Marcus a few years ago.

My cheeks puffed out in stifled laughter as I elbowed Maeve, pointing to the stray Cheerio bobbing at the end of one of Robin's curls. Maeve arched her immaculate eyebrows and shot me a small grin.

"Superb ruby earrings," Maeve commented to Robin.

"My three girls will have to fight over these!" Robin shouted.

"Now why would siblings fight?" Julie asked, jabbing her sister with her elbow in the rear of the van.

"Ouch," Callie complained.

Mitchell referred to Julie and Callie as the Bobbsey twins, because they did look almost exactly alike with their blonde bobs and oversized blue eyes, Callie being slightly taller and leaner than her less feminine-looking older sister.

"I told you not to wear your black and silver dress because I was wearing mine," Julie snapped.

"Who died and made you my fashion warden?" Callie asked.

"You both look equally fabulous in your very unique black and silver dresses," Maeve said in her cool, suave voice.

And then there was the fabulous Maeve, (pronounced Mave, with a long A), an ex-model who was married to a plastic surgeon, and clearly not in need of his services. Maeve's long, blonde hair flapped in shiny glory down the center of her emerald sheath dress when she moved her head. She had three children, a super flat stomach, and the envy of every lady in our neighborhood. I tried giving my freshly curled, shoulder length brown hair a toss, mimicking Maeve, but she looked so much cooler doing it.

"Okay darlings, what is the game plan?" Maeve asked.

"I thought we would head straight to Bryant Park, use our parking pass, and walk around shopping until the show begins," Robin explained.

"Sounds like a good plan to me," Julie agreed.

"So are you salivating over the special doll premier this year, Cece?" Callie asked.

"Can't lie, I'm pretty excited girls," I beamed.

Everyone laughed with me or at me, I wasn't sure. We were a group of gals pushed together by our neighborhood and our kids' activities, and I'd felt like a blessed woman since the day I'd met them nearly ten years ago. I'd spent a decade raising babies and sharing beauty secrets with these ladies. They were the arc that completed my social circle.

We headed toward midtown, and the madhouse had already begun. Apparently, I wasn't the only one who had a special place in my heart for collector dolls. As doll-themed decaled tour buses lined the sidewalks, little girls in their best pink tutus skipped excitedly down the walk with their parents.

As we started through the entrance of the looming white tents, which housed the extravaganza, I felt the rumble in my belly and the burning in my ears from all of the excitement. The entrance was amazing, with a large five-foot fountain and six lighted pillars; a different structure representing each decade of fashion with little dolls inside of it. There had to be somewhere around four hundred dolls inside each pillar. Floating inside the grand entryway fountain were over two thousand shiny red apples acting as a tribute to the Big Apple.

There was also a life-size mannequin number one Minsk doll, the same one on my wish list. I had a sick thought I would like to take the giant lady home with me and hide her in my special room.

As we found our seats, I watched Maeve give a double-cheek kiss to one of the fashion designers who'd dressed her for so many years. I didn't want to seem giddy like a doll-crazed child, so I remained poised, but anyone who knew me could see the excitement percolating at the corners of my mouth.

The tent was jam-packed this year with more people waiting to get in. The event was apparently oversold with more tickets than there were seats. I was glad we got there early. It would be pure torture for me to peek my head through the tent to observe the glorious pink, sparkly decorations and not be able to see what was on the other side.

As we sat down, Maeve grabbed my hand

delicately and gave it a light squeeze saying, "Happy Birthday, Cece."

"Thank you, Maeve," I gushed.

The show started and my heart palpitated as they played a video opening with an animated doll stating, "I want my dream house."

See, Mitchell, it's not only me who thinks that way, you stick-in-the-mud. He should know all about it, he tries to sell people their dream homes every day.

I tried not to let my thoughts trail back to the argument I'd had with Mitchell over my credit card bill the previous evening. I swept the thought out of my mind. He would not ruin this day for me. I heard the announcement: *Mercedes-Benz Fashion Week presents the first ever dollhouse runway show! Whoosh*—and just like that, my husband was out of my head, like the ever-growing numbers on our credit card bill—out of sight, out of mind.

The show itself was a fantastic display of models showcasing women's fashion throughout the years, starting with the number one Minsk doll in her red and black swing dress. A model followed her wearing a fifties-style, deep green, Christian Dior, chiffon, halter dress. Model after exquisite model in outfits highlighting the iconic dolls throughout the ages pranced onto the stage. There were a few showstoppers that caused me to gasp out loud, embarrassing my friends a little, but I couldn't help it. There was a series of vintage party dresses, a Marilyn Monroe style, white, belted ensemble, and to end the evening, the big stunner was a Cher-worthy, gold-beaded, cutout gown.

I exhaled deeply at the perfection of the final dress and the absolutely stunning model fitted into the tiny frock.

I nudged Julie who was sitting on the opposite side of me and whispered into her ear, "I own the doll version of the one in the gold dress." I'd spent $1,200 on my one and only Minsk doll, making it the most expensive of all my doll purchases. She was the spy disguised in a masquerade ball gown—splendid.

"So nice," Julie said as she nodded, a big fake smile fixed across her petite cheeks. She was trying so hard to be enthusiastic for me.

To top it off, each of the models sported hot pink Louboutin shoes. The show could not have been more perfect. It was like it had been planned with me in mind.

When the show ended, droves of people hit the streets for after parties, charity events, and other doll demonstrations. This was the best birthday party I could have asked for.

We dispersed into the large crowd. At one of the impromptu tents there was an auction with Minsk dolls on the roster. Maeve had run into old friends in the industry, and those old friends had introduced my girlfriends to the male models who had worked the show. The ladies were enthralled with the super-hot beefcakes, a far cry from our over-worked husbands who were hard-pressed to keep us happy, let alone dedicate the type of gym time necessary to look like these guys. Having different agendas, we all agreed to separate with a set meeting time and place closer to where we were parked. I wasn't angry, seeing the obvious appeal of ogling over a real life doll with perfectly chiseled abs, rather than watching me fight the masses for a glimpse of my plastic, female one.

****

The bidding began with many fabulous finds, but I only had eyes for her. I tried to be monetarily conservative after my nasty spat with Mitchell the previous evening. I was disappointed because I assumed they would announce her first if she were there, being the number one doll and all, but some antique dollhouses and tiny home interior accessories trumped the first half of the show.

But then, toward the end of the bidding, I saw a pop of red and black and a drawn up blonde ponytail and I knew it was her. I bid one thousand dollars, knowing there was no way the amount would stick. Two thousand and three thousand dollars passed quickly. *It's a lot of money, but it's my birthday! If I get her at this price Mitchell will see it as a great investment, because I can resell her for at least eight thousand dollars.*

When they called four thousand dollars, my hand shot up without thinking. I had to have her. It was meant to be. These special tickets would've never made it into my hands. This auction wouldn't have been right in my line of vision leading me to the event if I wasn't supposed to have her.

Then the man with the black scarf and the microphone announced, "Five thousand dollars."

I saw a woman with a little girl throw up her hand and bid, her child's hopeful eyes wide with excitement. *Sorry kid, learn now life isn't fair. What's a nine-year-old need a five thousand dollar doll for anyway?*

When "Six thousand dollars" ratcheted out of the auctioneer's mouth the fast way it does, I put my hand up again in response. It was insane to let a little girl ruin a collectible doll. She would probably play with it, rough it up, and make it worthless. Then, seven thousand dollars came and went as the nervous heat tingled up my face. I was in too deep. The doll was valued at eight thousand dollars and I told myself it was my absolute ceiling bid. Then eight thousand dollars came and went and I still didn't have her.

****

I returned to my group of girlfriends forty-five minutes later, not even using half of the two hours I thought it might take to get what I wanted. They were in the same spot behind the stage, tossing back glasses of pink champagne with the hunky models. My hairline was still buzzing from the stress of the auction. Everyone turned to look at me, losing their smiles as I approached.

"Cece, you look pale. Are you okay?" Robin asked.

"Oh yeah, I'm fine. I-uh got my doll," I stammered.

"The number one doll?" Julie asked.

"Yes, I won her in auction," I proclaimed, a little more proudly, but still distressed.

I grabbed a flute of champagne off the nearby tray and took a sip to put out the flames. We all clinked glasses and I tried to join the party, but the anxiety of my purchase was weighing me down. By the change in tone of my acquaintances, I clearly had ruined the mood.

"Great. You look a little shocked. Did you get a good deal because it was on auction?" Julie asked.

"Well, I've only ever seen two of them in the states before, so it should resell higher than I got it for. Unfortunately, you won't get to take a peek at her until she's delivered to my home next week," I stated.

I took a big gulp of bubbly hoping to diffuse the conversation. The ladies all exchanged wide-eyed glances.

"So, how much was the broad?" Callie asked, her extremely slight frame already feeling the effects of the champagne.

"She's a bit high maintenance," I answered.

"Oh Cece, how much did the blonde bitch cost you?" Julie asked.

Laughter erupted amongst my tipsy gal pals.

"Ten thousand, two hundred dollars. And I had to crush a little girl's dreams in the process," I said. The rest of the champagne stung as I gulped it down whole.

"Holy shit!" Robin yelled.

"It went to a good cause. The auction, I mean," I said in my own defense.

"Wonderful then, what charity?" Maeve asked, all cheeky, batting her ridiculously long eyelashes. Maeve could say, *I just took a dump,* and make it sound beautiful.

Shit. Shit. Shit. What was it called? Young Women of American, Young Mentor or something...

"You don't know? Oh who cares, Happy Berfday to you, Cece," Callie slurred.

The ladies all giggled again and tapped glasses once more. I knew it was all in good fun and I should be laughing along with them, but I was embarrassed and suffering from some serious buyer's remorse.

"Ladies, thanks for your support. I actually left my cell phone in the car and need to inform Mitchell of my purchase. Do you mind if I take the keys and hang out in the van until you're ready to go?" I asked.

"Are you sure you want to ruin your birthday so early, dear?" Maeve asked.

I'd never actually come right out and told the ladies about my fights with Mitchell over finances, but I had dropped subtle hints, and he'd dropped some not so subtle hints to their husbands.

"Oh, he'll be fine. He knows how long I've wanted her," I lied.

"The girl you couldn't live without," Robin said, as she winked, tossing me the keys to the van.

I took the keys, but my stomach curled as I remembered the last time I'd heard those same words, *girl you couldn't live without*.

****

It was a hike back to forty eighth street from midtown. Maeve had hooked us up with killer parking passes, but the six-city block trek in high-heeled boots had seemed much shorter and warmer in the company of others. I needed air, space, and time to think about what I was going to say to Mitchell to justify my purchase. He had to understand this was important to me. And it was my birthday, after all. Maybe if I didn't shop for six months that would suffice. But then I would have to ostracize myself from my friends, and that wasn't fair. My cheeks felt tingly and flushed again and I wondered if I was catching a cold. It was probably from the adrenaline rush I often got after an extravagant purchase, coupled with the excitement of the day, but I needed to check my reflection and see if I looked as bad as I felt.

I tried to catch a glimpse of myself in the window of a French restaurant close to the parking garage called, *Le Bernadin*. I pretended to be looking at a posted menu in an attempt to check myself out in the glass. I must have been burning with fever, because instead of seeing my own reflection, I thought I saw Mitchell's. No, it couldn't be him, he was out with a male client tonight, not a young lady. Yep, it was definitely him; standing in front of the maître's station with a female guest. I would know his snarky laugh and swaying head of thick, brown hair anywhere.

I inhaled deeply and ducked behind the door. It was a Saturday and he'd told me he had to go into the city to show a property to a client flying in for the weekend. He occasionally took clients out for lunch, but it was dinnertime now, and it was a rarity for him to spring a large amount of cash on a prospective buyer, especially at a swanky place like *Le Bernadin*. The woman he was with was not his client, and they weren't shaking hands in a business agreement. Instead, he had his hand on her ass, and she had her head on his shoulder.

The *Gut Wrench*, is what I called the feeling you get when you are caught in total surprise and your insides feel like they're being wrenched from your body. At the moment, it felt like a full force tug on my intestines.

The realization of my last few months in solitude, alone with Josie and Camdyn in our crazy house, came to fruition with every playful flip of this young woman's hair. He hadn't stopped touching me because he was tired. He'd stopped touching me because he was touching her instead. It was evident in the endearing way he brushed her arm. He used to caress my skin the same way.

The twilight hue of the restaurant shone a

yellowish shadow down the back of the lovebirds, giving the scene a nightmarish glow. She pulled him closer to her, head nuzzled into his shoulder, whispering things to make him smile, popping out his dimple—my dimple. He looked carefree and happy, and ten years younger in her company. I swallowed the lump in my throat.

No, she wasn't a client. I knew exactly whom those spiraled, rosy, locks belonged to without seeing her face.

I pounced inside the restaurant, taking charge as they were escorted to their table.

"Ma'am. Ma'am, do you have a reservation?" the hostess asked.

Her little French voice was like a whisper. The couple I'd stepped in front of was eyeing me with disdain. I hadn't noticed, but I'd started to silently weep, my mascara streaking down my face in drippy clumps, crumbling to pieces like my marriage.

"No, no," I whispered back, answering the French woman and protesting at the same time. My feet moved backward toward the exit, my hands working wildly to balance myself, rubbing at the tears, smearing black down my face like war paint.

The encroached upon couple leaned back in the doorway, letting me through as I stalked back outside, practically running to the parking garage. As much as I wanted to confront Mitchell and Katelyn, I couldn't face them. Not yet.

If I were flushed before, I was on fire now. A roaring, hot headache erupted across my forehead as I worked my way through the February night. My black tights felt frozen to my legs, which was strangely inviting as the rest of me lit up in flames. As I entered Robin's vehicle, my breathing became ragged, a few small puffs from the night air catching in the rearview mirror. As I banged my head off the back of the leather seat in agony, the thoughts kept coming faster than I could process them.

He was ruining our perfect foursome, which had always looked so deliciously impeccable in family photos—our rich, brownie-topped daughter and son completing the picture.

What had been running through his head to prompt him to destroy our happy life? I needed to wrap my head around it. I closed my eyes and pictured the moment he'd met her. I envisioned her walking into his office for her interview and Mitchell thinking she was different and exotic-looking with her wild, curly, red mane, wondering to his nearly forty-something self if the drapes matched the carpet and if she might be interested in an older man like himself. The long-legged temptress waltzed in, glinting her blue eyes in his direction, handing over her under-qualified resume, hoping her looks could make up for her lack of experience and then was elated to accept the assistant position to her extremely handsome, older, new boss.

When I'd met her at the Christmas Party, I'd dismissed her. Sure, she was young and pretty; pale, blushed, freckled cheeks and a black, plain velvet dress hugging every twenty-something curve on her body. But my husband wasn't into pale and redheaded. He preferred women with dark hair and olive skin, like me. In college he displayed pictures of Carmen Electra on his wall, not Nicole Kidman. So that was it, I'd dismissed her.

We hadn't had sex in months, and I'd wondered why he'd stopped badgering me for it. How many months had it been? Three? Four? Mitchell wasn't the type to handle two women at once. A swindler with words, although rather inept in the romancing department. There could only be one person to demand his attention at a time, and right now it sure wasn't me.

So, their courtship had to be new. New and raw. Fragile and breakable.

This couldn't be. She couldn't have him. He did not belong to her.

I was the one he'd chased all through college, turning him down over and over before I finally said yes. He loved the thrill of the chase, but I always had the upper hand. I loved him, but he always loved me more. He'd always needed me. Until now. Lucky for me, there were lots of reasons new relationships failed.

If their relationship were new and raw, I would pick it apart until it bled and died. Like a young animal given the chance to breath, then stomped out before it could move on its own. If their relationship were fragile and breakable, like my fine china, I'd toss it off the hardest surface until it broke into a hundred pieces making it worthless.

They would not ruin me.

The makeup remover in my Bottega bag did wonders in scrubbing the scary lines off my face, but my red eyes and blotched skin mirrored my hell in the rearview mirror, reminding me of Anita Botson. Anita was a woman in our neighborhood who'd recently gone through a nasty divorce after she'd discovered her husband was cheating on her with the nanny. She'd looked like my reflection each and every day on her daily drag to the mailbox.

Shamed. Shamed as the day is long, not wanting to reach out, but in need of a nanny in a bad way, so references were imperative.

"I'd prefer if they weren't, um, young. Young or foreign, yeah know," she'd quiver into the phone receiver.

Anita wasn't a part of our immediate social circle, but she was a fellow woman in the community. The one no one wanted to be. Damned in a grand old home with three young children and no one to rake the leaves.

It was fall when her husband left her. She'd tried to rake the foliage, dressed all stylish in her fur-lined boots, until she must've gotten overheated and frustrated, tossing the toasty footwear onto the lawn and screaming wildly at the overflowing black garbage bags. She'd gone off and screamed at the leaves like everything in the world was their fault, kicking the bag with her white socks, sending crunchy pieces flying outside the bag she'd tried so hard to tie. "All the beautiful colors! You love your girls in all their beautiful colors!"

She'd tromped around screaming and crying, browning her socks until she had mud caked to her ankles. When Anita tried to put her boots back on, the sludge completely soiled the inside of the fur. The public display garnered her the nickname—"Bootsy".

The thing was; Anita Botson got to buy all of the new shoes she wanted. Because she took Theodore Botson to the cleaners. And not the kind to launder her boots.

But, no one wanted to end up like Anita Botson. No one called Bootsy to shop or lunch. No one invited

Bootsy to dinner parties or asked her kids to sleepover, because she'd been shamed. It was too uncomfortable to have her around, even though she'd done nothing wrong.

Katelyn and Mitchell would not shame me. I wouldn't allow it. I'd stomp this thing out before it really begun.

Chapter 4
Birthdays and Bombshells

Birthdays were for celebrating, but tonight I felt old and broken. It was more like my death day. As in—the death of my marriage.

Now at *Jean Georges,* our favorite restaurant in the city, Mitchell would be footing the bill two nights in a row for the most elite French restaurants in New York City—one for his mistress and one for his wife.

I hadn't told him yet about my purchase, not sure how to say it exactly. *I spent ten thousand dollars on a doll, and by the way, I know you're diddling your assistant*, was the speech I wanted to give him when I got home last night, but instead I took a hot shower and curled up in bed, pretending to fall asleep.

Questions swirled around in my head like the lost voices of every woman who's ever been cheated on. *What's she have that I don't? Why her? What's so damn special about her? What's so insignificant about me?*

These women's voices weren't like mine though. They were the desperate pleas of women who'd let themselves go; women who didn't take good enough care of their home or their man to warrant respect. Boring, unadventurous, spinsters who'd denied their men sexual pleasure, so their husbands had to go looking for it outside of the home. These are the women

men cheated on—not me.

I couldn't stop chewing on the harsh reality, gnawing at the nasty scab until it interfered with my every thought and movement, tearing me apart so viciously my mind couldn't conjure the mental strength it needed to sort this out.

My pride—shot. My heart—ripped open. I didn't put the usual effort into getting ready for my birthday dinner. I wore the same black, Chanel dress from the dreadful Christmas party. I didn't bother with my hair; leaving it hanging straight and uncurled to my shoulders, stray hairs freely gracing my aching eyes.

"Are you still not feeling well, Cece? You look so tired even though you went to bed early last night. I didn't even get a chance to ask you about the big show," Mitchell commented. It'd been a silent ride to the restaurant, despite his attempt at small talk.

You look tired. Why don't you just say I look like shit? Don't worry, she'll look like this someday too after she pops out a few kids and finds out you're a cheating bastard.

"It was fine," I said.

I grabbed the wine menu, looking for something to numb the pain.

"Just fine? You were looking forward to the grand dollhouse show for a year and it was just fine?" he asked.

"Not really," I answered.

"Something happen at the show? Did you get into a fight with one of the girls? Let me guess. Someone had on the same dress as you did. Oh, gasp."

This was a personal blow because Maeve and I had worn the same Missoni dress to one of Julie's charity functions last year, causing a bit of riff between friends and a blowout between Mitchell and me. The dresses were different colors, at least; mine was the designer's signature weave of blues, greens and purples; hers a mix of oranges, yellows and reds.

But at the time, I'd felt undone, as I'd imagined guests gawking at me like a pig parading around in peacock's clothing next to her. As my eyes floated over different cabernets on the menu, my mind drifted back to the dreaded evening.

****

"Don't you see why I'm upset, Mitchell? This is so embarrassing," I whined.

"It's not so big of a deal. It's a dress. You're acting like a teenager upset someone wore the same prom gown as you," he argued.

"You don't understand. I looked like a fool next to her. It's a social tragedy."

Mitchell pulled over the car and turned it around.

"Where the hell are you going? Home is the other way and we're not going back to the party," I argued.

"You need to get your head out of your pretentious ass. You want to see social tragedy? I'll show you social tragedy."

"It's embarrassing, because she looks like her and I look like me. Surely, you have to understand, even being a man," I reasoned.

"Get over yourself! She's a model for Christ's sake. No one expects you to look like her. The dresses looked so differently on each of you, I would've never noticed they were the same unless you told me," Mitchell said.

"That's the problem. They are ornate dresses.

Anyone should've been able to make the connection, but because she's Maeve, they don't even look like the same dress. So you're saying she's better looking than me and you're more attracted to her?" I asked.

Mitchell didn't answer me and gave me his *you're-being-so-fucking-stupid-I-can't-even-answer-you* look. This was another one of our silent treatments. Before there were entire silent evenings, there were the brief moments we would simply not respond to questions, alluding to the fact the question was not worthy of our response.

I was doubly embarrassed for my needy question and exhausted from the stressful evening. I drifted off and ten minutes later woke to the fog lifting over the city. Where the hell were we going at this time of night?

"Mitchell, Josie's watching Camdyn, we're not supposed to be out late. Where're you going?"

No response. Twenty minutes later we were headed over the George Washington Bridge.

"Okay, Mitchell, can you please tell me where we're going now?" I asked.

"Just sit tight and think about your social tragedy."

I had nothing left in me for another argument. I dozed again only to wake up in what looked like the projects.

"Mitchell, where the hell are we?" I whispered.

"The Bronx," he whispered back, in a mocking tone.

"Are you trying to get us killed? It's dark. We have a Mercedes. We're going to get jacked. Turn around now," I said.

"Don't worry, I'm not going into South Bronx, this

part isn't so bad. It's Allerton, lots of working class folk here. Reminds me a lot of where I grew up. There's a restaurant I want to take you to," he said.

"You can't be serious?" I asked.

Mitchell kept driving to his destination. It didn't appear like a rapture of gunfire and killings, the vision of the Bronx I was used to watching on the news. But it wasn't exactly the type of place I wanted to find myself alone at night either.

"I'm not getting out of the car, Mitchell. I'm way too overdressed for this place anyway and I don't think we should even park our car here. What're you trying to prove?" I asked.

"Trust me. There's something you have to see."

I flashed big, worried, brown eyes at him, becoming more nervous by the minute.

"I don't need to see anything bad enough to get out of the car. And I'm not hungry, I ate at the party," I pleaded, frustrated by my husband's relentlessness.

He was not giving up and found a parking space in front of a restaurant, which was completely empty with only a single light on inside the place. It had a plain, white, brick storefront and a green and white awning out front. It didn't appear to be a nighttime venue.

"Oh no, looks closed," I said.

"It's open, trust me," he said as he got out of the car.

Mitchell grabbed the passenger door for me and I slid out shakily, checking my back for predators. He grabbed my shoulders and motioned me to the front door, walking us through the entrance with ease. The owner looked at him with familiarity, as if to say *Hey son, grab a broom and help me clean up, will yeah?*

"Got a crowd out back tonight, Tony?" Mitchell asked the small, balding man as if he were a regular.

The establishment was obviously a deli, judging from the glass-paned display cases of meats, cheeses and breads spanning the length of the store. Tony looked like he was getting ready to close, wiping down the few tables and sweeping the floors. What crowd, I wondered?

"You betcha. Every Saturday night, chief. You two don't look like you're in need of a free meal though," he said suspiciously.

"Oh no, we're here to help. Thought I could volunteer my services tonight and show my wife what your gracious operation does for the people in the community. I helped you out a few months back. It was the Saturday after Thanksgiving. You made a special meal for all of the folks who didn't have enough money to get their turkey dinners," Mitchell said.

"I thought you looked familiar. You're a little overdressed for the occasion, but come on back," he said.

The man opened up the alley door and there was a line of people, adults and children, waiting for a hot meal. I assisted my husband pouring leftover soup and handing out plastic-wrapped sandwiches.

"Our first hot meal all week, Tony. Jimmy still hasn't found work," one woman said, as she grabbed soup for her two children.

"Well, where the hell is Jimmy then?" Tony asked, as he handed them each a sandwich.

"Too proud to take free food." She laughed.

"Here's one to go," he whispered. Tony shoved a sandwich in her raggedy, cardigan pocket. Her messy, side-knotted brown hair got caught on a button as she smiled and turned to leave with her brood.

She gave him a shy wink and said, "Thanks," then darted around the rest of the people with her paper bowls and wrapped sandwiches.

The hungry families pulled at my heartstrings. The worst was the single mother who arrived late. She was an ethnic woman, dragging her two toddler boys along as they playfully tried to run away from her. We'd run out of food and Tony's service was *First Come First Serve*. He had a set amount for the evening and once it was gone he closed up for the night.

My eyes welled up as he told her, "No more. I'm sorry."

Her little boy rubbed his belly and said, "Mama, hungry."

The woman's face broke down into a tired frown. Her impoverished grimace was so worn, and I could tell their trip to the deli had been a rough one. By the looks of her children's red, chapped cheeks they'd walked many blocks in the cold for nothing.

"I tell you, we leave earlier and you no get out the door," she scolded the younger boy.

She turned to leave, her little ones more agitated now than on the way to the deli. I pulled two twenties out of my wallet.

"Excuse me, ma'am, please, take this and buy your boys some dinner," I said.

She turned back around slowly, curling her mouth like a woman with soured milk on her lips.

"We don' need your charity, pretty lady," she grumbled in an accent I didn't recognize.

We made eye contact and the hatred in her eyes

shredded me. The woman wore tired bags under her eyes, which were wrung dark in her sallow skin. Her sharp-looking, stained teeth pulled into a tight opened-mouth smile.

"Please, I have children too," was all I could think to say.

She looked down at her son with his hand swooning over his belly, eyes longing. Her expression changed and we suddenly had something in common. We were both mothers who loved our babies. She walked back toward me and gently snagged the bills from my manicured fingers. The woman said a quick, "Thank you" before briskly turning around, pulling her kids in tow.

"Better watch out, lady. If people hear you're giving out free twenty-dollar bills, they're gonna overrun this joint," Tony said.

"I don't know how you can stand to turn away a hungry child," I said.

I didn't mean for it to sound harsh, but it did.

"I do this as a courtesy. I could save the extra soup and lunchmeat and sell it for profit tomorrow, but I choose to do this instead, one day a week. I can't afford to feed the world. I'd go broke, lose my business." His friendly disposition hardened as he turned away from us grumbling something into his coat. I could feel Mitchell's eyes scolding me.

Tony gathered up the extra scraps of saran wrap scattered on the ground and threw them away in the dumpster behind the store, tsk-tsking at the fact some of his customers would leave such a mess in exchange for his generosity.

"I know, I know. I'm sorry. I think what you do is

wonderful. In fact, we were at a charity tonight and I didn't get to make a donation before we left. Can I write you a check to help fund your operation here? I think it's wonderful," I insisted, feeling horrible for my blunder.

"It's not necessary. I do it because I like to give back to the community," he said.

"Here, take this," I said. I wrote him a check for one thousand dollars.

"Tony, and, what's your last name?"

"Sabitini," he said, giving in with a sigh.

I handed over the check and his eyes widened in shock.

"You better watch this one, son. She's handing out money left and right. Better keep her on a short chain," he joked, letting out a jovial belly laugh.

Mitchell and I exchanged a playful glance, as we both knew Tony's comment was all too true. I didn't say much on the ride home. Point taken, but I still wasn't happy with Mitchell. He wore a smug face all the way home. It was the same look my parents gave me when they told me not to eat too much Halloween candy, then found me doubled over on the couch with a belly ache, Kit-Kat wrappers strewn at my feet. They should've known better than to leave me with a bag of chocolate, because in my world of obstinate discipline, sugar would always be one of my only unwavering weaknesses.

"How in the hell did you even find out about Tony's place?" I asked.

"You stumble upon lots of things when you're in my line of work," he answered gleefully.

"The Bronx isn't your territory."

"Doesn't have to be. I can sell anywhere I want as long as I'm licensed in the state."

"So, you're telling me you sold a property in the Bronx this past November?" I asked.

"No, I'm telling you I found out about the place last November, randomly through work," he explained.

"Why didn't you tell me where you went the Saturday after Thanksgiving?" I asked.

"Because you were shopping."

"Maybe I would've liked to have gone with you."

"And miss the sale at Barneys? I wouldn't dare pull you away."

"If I would've known you were doing something like this, I would've gone."

"Bullshit."

"Mitchell, I'm not as bad as you make me out to be. I enjoyed helping those people tonight. I still have tears in my eyes from seeing those two little boys." I sighed.

"You can't throw money at people and expect to make a difference," he argued.

"Please don't get all philanthropic on me. You drive a Mercedes not a Prius, you wear expensive leather shoes and custom tailored suits to work every day and you have a flat screen television in every room of the house!" I yelled.

"I never said I was a saint. But do you see what social tragedy is, Cece? Social tragedy is a little boy almost going to bed hungry, not Maeve Delange wearing the same dress as you tonight," he said in the same Kit-Kat tone.

"I get what you're trying to say and I know poverty exists, but here's my point. Everyone's perception is relative to his or her own reality. I don't live in the Bronx. I live in Montclair. So a poor woman's definition of tragedy is going to be different from mine," I reasoned.

Mitchell let out a long drawn out sigh of defeat. The smugness fell and was replaced by something else—sorrow maybe. I hadn't seen him look this way before. He had given up the fight.

"Never mind, Cece. You don't get it. I thought seeing it might work. It was my last ditch effort to get you to see, but this is how you really are and you aren't changing, are you?" he asked the question in a low voice, almost as if he were asking himself and not me.

"You think I'm shallow, I get it. But there are lots of things I get right too, Mitchell. Please don't focus on the bad stuff. I do a lot for our family, to make our household run smoothly. I'm not perfect, but you're not perfect either. Your absence does not go unnoticed by your family," I said.

"Our household runs smoothly? You make us sound like a corporation," he said in the same dejected tone.

"Well, running a family is like running a company. There are lots of things to keep straight. And what did you mean, last ditch effort? Last ditch effort for what?" I asked.

"It doesn't matter," he said.

****

Looking back, I realized it was the moment he decided it was over between us. He was probably looking for the woman he married who'd been happy in our two-bedroom apartment living off soup and Chinese noodles, not caring about anything else as long as she was with him. But he couldn't find her anymore. And, neither could I.

The disparity of his newfound outlook was unfair. He'd been the one to spoil me with lavish presents, introducing me to flashy brands I hadn't known existed, fostering my extravagant tastes with expensive trips and showy gifts.

On our fifth wedding anniversary, after he'd scored his first multi-million dollar deal, he'd uttered the words, *"Do you know what this is? It's a Cartier."* He was referring to the sparkly diamond watch, which begged me to stroke it, beginning my insatiable thirst for all things brand.

Now, he was chastising me for the very lifestyle he'd promoted. The one I'd never necessarily needed, but he'd insisted I have. He was the fake, the phony, not me. He'd lobbied for the title of the man with the largest swinging cock on the block, and now he suddenly wanted no part of the scene. Enchanted all of a sudden by everything pure and good. What a joke.

"Cece. Hello, Earth to Cece. Did you pick out a wine yet? You've been staring at the menu for an eternity," Mitchell asked as the server waited patiently.

I pointed blindly to a Cabernet on the menu, barely reading the name, but recognizing the horned deer on the front. After our elaborate trip to Napa, I'd come to know it by its label alone.

"You're acting weird. Do you want to go home? I'll make you some chicken soup or something? Make my wife reappear?"

"You can't make soup. You don't know how to cook anything, let alone soup," I griped.

"I was talking Campbell's," he joked.

"Why would I pass up this delicious French cuisine? I haven't eaten at a place like this in so long. How about you?" I asked sharply.

"Um, haven't been here since last year, with you," he answered.

"I didn't ask you about this place. I asked about French food," I snapped.

"I had French fries for lunch yesterday," he remarked, not catching on.

"Very funny," I sighed, as I buried my head in the dinner menu.

"So, are you going to tell me what the hell happened at the doll show to put you in such a foul mood? What was the fight about this time?" he asked.

"There was no fight. However, I bought myself a birthday present," I announced.

There was a long pause. "How much, Cece?" Mitchell asked.

"Let me explain."

"I don't care, simply tell me how much," he insisted.

"I found the number one Minsk doll on auction, Mitchell. It will resell higher because it was purchased at the dollhouse event," I reasoned.

I met his eyes this time. In most arguments involving money, I knew I was guilty and averted his gaze. But he had so much more to be guilty about tonight. Our dark eyes met in a long stare-off. He looked away first. I won.

"How much?" he asked again.

"Ten thousand," I said firmly.

Mitchell's mouth fell open so far I feared it would hit the tablecloth. It was the longest moment in time, as his skin turned ashen and his arms fell slack, pulling his shoulders down into a defeated slump. I didn't know if he was going to scream or cry. Mitchell choked on his words as they tried to come out.

"Mitchell, you know how long I've wanted her. She's rare. And European. I've only ever seen two others like her," I said quickly, hiding behind my menu again, feeling unapologetic.

"European? I don't care if she comes to life and gives me hand jobs. You must return it," he stated through gritted teeth.

I shook my head in blatant defiance.

"Cece, you have to take it back," he whispered.

"It was an auction item, all sales are final," I chirped from behind the menu.

"My sales are down this month, I can't pay for it," he choked.

This alarmed me. Never in our fifteen years of marriage when I overspent did he tell me he couldn't pay for something.

But all I said was, "You'll figure it out."

"You have to sell it, Cece," he whispered again.

I peeked over the menu and Mitchell looked downright petrified.

"You'll sell something soon. It's winter. The market always turns around in the spring," I encouraged.

"I only have enough to pay for the debt you racked up from our last argument and your credit card has a twenty-two percent interest rate, so I can't let it lapse," he growled in a low, angry tone.

This line of conversation was uncomfortable for me. He had complained about my spending before, but never outright gave me reason to worry or made me feel we didn't have extra money lying around.

"Mitchell, you're making us sound poor," I said with a nervous laugh.

"We're getting there, Cece," he wheezed.

"You told me we're paying for the kids' college. If we're on track to make those payments, then how're we poor?" I asked.

"Because you rack up obscene credit card bills and buy dolls for $10,000. Dolls! Pieces of plastic with fake tits and hair. Stupid dolls are going to be the reason we can't make our mortgage payment," he said; in a voice far too loud for the venue, causing eyebrows to rise, and sending our server back the way he came.

"And you have thousands to put in college funds, but not to pay our mortgage payment?" I asked.

"I haven't put money in those kids' college funds for six months," he admitted.

"What? You said we were on target to pay for their tuition. We had a set amount each month you were contributing. Their education is so important to me, why didn't you say something?" I asked.

"I told you we were on track a year ago. And I've been trying to tell you we're not anymore ever since. I don't make the money your friends' husbands make. I'm not a surgeon or a partner in a law firm. I'm just a real estate agent who did really well when the market was good and now I'm struggling like everyone else. Cece, I haven't sold anything in a couple months. It's bad."

I didn't understand what he was telling me. I wasn't used to him being candid about failure and suddenly felt terrible, even though he was the one who was ruining our family with his affair, not me. I wouldn't let him guilt me this way.

"I won't buy anything else for a while," I said.

Our wine arrived, and the waiter asked to take our order. Mitchell usually ordered fish on this occasion, but he ordered lamb tonight instead.

"No fish tonight?" I asked, trying to change the subject.

"I had fish yesterday," he admitted, making me twitch.

"With your French fries?" I asked.

"Yep, fish and chips," he said as he choked on his words again, probably still trying to mentally compute our bills in his head, the lies flying out of his mouth so effortlessly now.

"You have to sell the doll, Cece," he said again.

"No."

"We can't afford it."

"Look, I won't shop for a while to make up for it, okay. Just take it out of our savings. Maeve always says her husband keeps a reserve savings for her, on the occasion she might overspend on a must-have, because he realizes the culture she's been brought into has imposed certain realities on her and he doesn't want to deprive her," I reasoned.

Mitchell clapped his hands together, making me jump and startling the couple next to us.

"Did the noise wake you up? Good! Cece, Monte is a plastic surgeon who makes millions of dollars a year. They could easily live in Alpine in one of those big daddy homes, but they choose to live in Montclair, because he's one smart son-of-a-bitch who will probably be retired in a few years. We don't have a reserve fund and our primary fund is draining fast. Because. Of. You. I've tried to go about this gently, but you're hurting us, and at this point, your doll just broke the damn bank."

"I realize we don't have their money, Mitchell. But I sacrifice. We're the only family who doesn't have a cleaning lady. Think of all the money I save us, cleaning our home myself."

"Your excuse is tired, Cece. And you love to clean and are too anal to let anyone else touch the house. Plus, you spend twice as much as everyone else on manicures and hand waxes to calm your fingers from all of your crazy scrubbing," he said.

"Mitchell, we all have our little secret wants. Things which are very private and personal and important to us, things we can't live without, which are worth more than the sum of money," I droned, looking up at him, waiting for him to get it.

"I don't know what you're talking about." He sighed, shaking his head.

Bastard.

Mitchell had the same look of dejection as the night in the car when we were driving home from the Bronx. He'd given up. We didn't speak to each other the rest of the meal. Not one more syllable was uttered for our longest silent night in the history of our dysfunctional marriage. The only sounds were the scraping of utensils on small white plates, neither one of us enjoying a single bite. He would pay dearly for his indiscretions. The credit card bill was just the beginning.

Chapter 5
Mommy Dearest

My visits with mother always comforted me, even though she couldn't understand a word I said. It was better that way. She was someone I could vent to, with a certain guarantee she wouldn't spew my secrets, a consoling sounding board that would never echo my sorrows. There in body, not in spirit, but it would be enough to get me through for now.

My mother had late stage Alzheimer's disease, and unfortunately didn't have a clue who I was anymore. I only went to visit her once a month to spare myself the heartache. But even as her mind left her, her obsessive compulsive disorder never did.

As I sat there, holding her dry, crackly hand, I couldn't help but think about the way things used to be before she got sick. By sick, I meant in the dementia sense; the OCD had always been there. It was my first fleeting thought of her compulsions; the impulses manipulated her life and everyone's around her.

I was six years old, playing with my sister and our easy-bake oven. My little brother had the flu. He would've been about one and a half at the time. His arrival into our family had been a surprise to my parents, who had only wanted two children. And they would grow to regret their mistake, better known as my handful-of-a-brother, Dominic.

My older sister, Natalie and I were home from school on summer break. My brother had vomited and my mother was in a tizzy about cleaning it out of the carpet before my father got home. My brother howled in discomfort on the living room floor. My mother had an obscene amount of plastic sheeting she used for all sorts of bizarre things. It was akin to the plastic wrap people used to cover their furniture. My brother was laying on a slab of it in nothing more than a white t-shirt and a diaper. He was shivering, feverish and desperately needed comfort. His eyes searched for someone to help him, his clammy legs shaking their chub on the plastic wrap as I watched from the kitchen.

"Mom, do you want me to help with Dominic? He looks like he's hurting," I said as I put my brownies in the pink oven.

"No, Cece, don't touch him! He has germs. The whole house could be swept with the epidemic. Your father has to go out of town tomorrow. He can't afford to get sick. We can't afford for him to get sick," she panicked.

My father was an airline pilot and made very good money for the times. However, my mother had always fretted over finances, making us feel like we were poor. Anytime we wanted anything, she would say we couldn't afford it, even though I knew we probably could. Finding a perfect place for new purchases put an extra stressor on her super-organized world. Everything had its designated location and everything was labeled. I think we were the first family of our time to own a label-maker.

My mother was frantic over Dominic's mess, but not as frantic as my poor brother who was writhing uncontrollably with no one to hold him. My sister seemed unaffected, stirring up our next concoction for the oven, destined even then to be a pastry chef. Natalie was two years older than me, but seemed oblivious to my mother's lunacy; or she only chose to ignore mother's fits as if it were not part of her world.

Natalie didn't have it. Dominic didn't have it either. I was the only one who got the bad gene. Lucky me.

My memory swept to her spraying Lysol all around my screaming brother. I remembered flinching as I witnessed little sprays of liquid spritzing Dominic's poor body as she decontaminated the area around him, treating her toddler like he had the plague. My mother scrubbed the carpet laboriously, yelling at my brother instead of offering any type of care. My sister continued to disregard the horrific scene, humming happily as she spooned out her next batch of goodies. I pinched her side and she whipped around with an angry face because I had disturbed her mixing. I pointed to Dominic and she shrugged her shoulders and turned away, not wanting to test my mother during one of her attacks. But, I couldn't concentrate on our bakery project as he wailed. I approached my mother, who by then was equipped with rubber gloves and a surgical mask. She held one of her yellow hands up, a look of warning pressed against her mask.

"Mom, I'm just going to pick him up and rock him and I promise I will hold my breath and wash my hands afterward. Please, Mom, he's so sad and hurting," I whined.

"Don't you *dare*. I don't need two kids with this disease. People die from the flu, Cece. Get back in the kitchen," she demanded.

I heard my brother yelp, "*Sissy, sissy.*" He couldn't say my name yet and when he tried to say *Cece*, *Sissy* came out instead, but either worked.

"And you girls better be cleaning up as you're going along. But that goes without saying," she said.

It did. She had trained us from a very young age to clean up every toy and crumb we dropped. Any failure on our part would launch her into hysterics. My sister and I had been her good listeners, but my brother had been a difficult child from the start.

It took hours of scrubbing before she was finally satisfied with the job she'd done. I teared up as I watched my brother cry himself to sleep on his makeshift mat, as I baked brownies in the next room. Mother never touched him, and only neared him when it was time to re-administer his liquid Tylenol through a syringe, keeping him in his quarantine near the spot on the carpet where he had vomited. As I washed my metal cake pan in the sink, our bewildered caretaker scoured her hands with Comet until they were raw. Her eyes were bloodshot with worry as she frantically meshed the white cleanser with her cracked, inflamed skin. I saw the blood begin to surface from the knuckle on her index finger.

"Mom, you're bleeding, stop it, you cleaned it all," I yelled.

"It's the influenza, Cece. I have it all over me. You shouldn't even be standing this close to me. You and your sister grab a mask if you want to stay down here. I can't handle three sick kids," she fretted.

The reddish water washed down the sink, but she kept scrubbing, unable to stop herself. Natalie didn't want to quit baking, so she grabbed a mask and ignored the commotion.

"Cece, grab a mask or get your butt upstairs. *Now*."

Mother's brown, mousy hair was pulled back in a hairnet she commonly wore when she cleaned. Her wild brown eyes bugged out from behind her mask as she worked to sanitize every fiber in the carpet. Acting as the attentive mother and housewife, she wore a dress the whole time. My parents were traditional and my father expected to come home to a presentable family and home. My mother worked overtime to paint his perfect picture.

I grabbed the mask and winced again as I looked at my half-clothed baby brother sleeping fitfully on his mat. I watched him twitch with an apparent chill.

"Mother, can I give him a blanket? He's shivering," I cried.

"And contaminate the blanket? Then, it will spread disease on everything in my washroom when I go to clean it and everyone will surely get sick. I can throw away the plastic. You have to use your head, Cece," she reasoned, tapping a raw finger to her temple.

At the time, it made perfect sense and I felt stupid for asking. Now, I look back and see how obscenely insane my mother really was. My sister made a comical wide-eyed gesture trying to give me an *I told you so* look as I re-approached her. Natalie was obviously more concerned with her cupcakes than my brother's well being or my mother's bloody hands. Then, I heard Dominic wake up again with a heave and a sputter.

"*Jesus Christ, not again*," my mother screamed.

Dominic threw up in the same exact spot my mother had cleaned for the last two hours. Teary streaks stained her mask. Mother pulled it away revealing two full streams down her thin face. She carefully placed the mask in a plastic baggie and threw it in the trash, making sure to Lysol the garbage can after her disposal. The steadfast germ-eradicator fastened another face cover and began again.

"Your father is going to be here in a half hour," she shrieked.

"Can I help you, Mom?" I asked.

"Cece, I swear to God, if you say one more word about coming over here, I will have your father take the belt to you when he gets home. Don't test me today," she hollered.

Her threat was enough to shut me up. My father had only whipped me once in his life. I was four years old and I had taken part of his prized coin collection and threw it down the heating register in our home. He loved his coins and I was only rebelling because my sister had gotten a piggy bank for Christmas and I had not. My father had some time off around the holidays and was cleaning his coin cases, which left the cherished medallions exposed and at my fingertips. I vaguely remembered thinking the slots in the floor looked like Natalie's four-inch rectangle opening in her piggy bank. I liked the sound they made as they *clang clang clanged* down the register. When my mother caught me metal-handed, she broke into sobs over how she was going to explain what I'd done to my father. She was actually worried for me and tried her best to compromise with him into not beating me because I was too young to know better, but she lost.

"Oh, she's old enough to know better, Anna. Don't worry, this will teach her a lesson not to disobey," he yelled as he came at me with the big leather belt.

Lash, lash, lash. Scream, scream, scream, and I left myself, retreating to the place children go when they're being beaten by their parents. I needed to be perfect. My parents required it. I could not make mistakes. I could not make a mess. And I always had to be on my best behavior for Daddy.

My father only did it once, but it changed things for me. The beating not only hurt like hell, but it altered my relationship with my father forever. I feared him. We all feared him, because he ruled by intimidation. Dominic would test him over time, and the terror imposed on him in his younger years would turn to blatant rebellion in the later ones.

I watched in horror again as my brother sat in a pile of throw-up. My mother dabbed at his poor body with a paper towel, keeping as far away as possible from him. He must have been so scared seeing her in the mask and rubber gloves, treating him like a leper.

After being gone for a week, Daddy would come home to an odd aroma of baked goods and cleaning supplies. What a scene he'd returned to—his two daughters wearing dresses and surgical masks; his toddler son curled up on the floor in pain on a polyethylene mat, and his nutso wife hovering over the carpet with her elbow-high, yellow, rubber gloves, scrubbing a stain which, had already been scoured away twenty minutes ago. My sister and I brightly offered him brownies and cupcakes to soften the scene.

"What in God's name?" he asked.

"Don't touch anything," Mother warned.

My father did a strange double take of us smiling behind our masks. He nodded, grabbing a brownie from my tray. I think I could vaguely see my sister frown because he did not pick her cupcake.

"What's wrong with him now? And why's he screaming? Can't you give him a pacifier or something?" my father asked.

We'd heard Dominic's cries for hours and hadn't deserted him yet but my father was already agitated and ready to bolt within minutes of hearing his incessant wails.

"He has the flu, Lenny. This is the second time he's thrown up. Go upstairs and stay away from here so you don't catch anything before your flight tomorrow," Mom said.

"Yes Ma'am. What's for dinner, I'm starved?" he asked as he threw his navy blue pilot's coat on the metal rack.

"I-I couldn't make anything. I've been dealing with this. There's a frozen pizza from Alberto's in the freezer if you want to toss it in the oven," my mother said.

My father gave her a disapproving look, as if to say, *So, you couldn't manage to throw in a frozen pizza for me.*

"I'm sorry, it's been chaotic here," she apologized.

"I can see that. Natalie, do you think you could handle throwing in a pizza for your old man? I know how much you like to bake," he said.

Dad still wanted to be served. He'd come home from work and the women's duties were to make sure he had a hot meal on the table and if his wife couldn't do it, he would move on to the next eldest female.

"Sure, Daddy," she said.

"Okay, sugar, well I'm going to go upstairs and use

the bathroom. You go put on dinner and I'll be down. Thanks, honey. And delicious brownies, Cece," he added to include me in what I now recognized as his male chauvinist monologue. Back then I felt pride in being singled out.

My father was well meaning, but too strict to be kind, and too stoic to be warm. He was raised as an army brat, with a short stint in the Air Force, before taking his flying commercial. There was no room for inappropriate behavior in his eyes. My brother survived the flu, but the memory is one that is burned in my mind forever. It's the ugly story that reminded me of her bugged out forty-year old eyes, and her thin pink lips warning me not to let it happen to me when she'd first begun to break. I couldn't hear her say it, but as I looked at her now, sitting in her wheelchair, I could feel the thought pass between us like an unspoken secret.

I took small comfort in the fact I only got a diluted version of the disease. Because when she put Dominic to bed the night he was sick, she didn't know I crawled into his bed and held him for hours until he fell asleep in my arms before I slipped back into my own bedroom. I would never, ever put my obsessions and compulsions before the welfare of my own children. And I would never let my husband hurt one of our kids. I would kill him first.

As my mother's mind slipped away, the only thing remaining, were her compulsions. She insisted on clean sheets every day. The nurses at her facility had to wear gloves when giving her a bath, and she would only eat and drink off glass plates and cups. We tipped the nurses extra to keep her happy at her assisted care facility. I left her that evening and went straight to bed.

After waking up in a sweat, I drifted back to sleep, my only thoughts—I did not want to end up like her.

****

My compulsions grew in the weeks following my fortieth birthday. My OCD was always something I could control, my overly organized life dumbed down to "neat freak" by my close family and friends. My husband knew I hung his shirts and ties in his gigantic walk-in closet sorted carefully by their color. What he did not know is how it pulled at my insides when he would make an outfit change and put a blue shirt back next to a gray one, instead of with the other shades of blue. I would put it back myself, and he never said a word, probably not noticing the switch.

We shared an online calendar, which helped him at first. However, as the kids grew up and more activities and social events arose, I had more colors and icons on the calendar than he could keep up with. We shared the calendar, but I was the only one who could really read it. I put everything on it. Mitchell once joked I'd left out bathroom breaks and wondered how I made it all day without allotting time for them.

Every morning, all of the dirty laundry in the house had to be washed, dried, ironed, and put away. I did not like to leave the house until this was complete. There were never any dirty dishes in the sink, and my family knew they always had to rinse their dishes and put them in the dishwasher or they would face my wrath. I required my hardwood floors to be impeccable. All shoes had to be taken off before entering my home, per the nice sign on my front porch. I remembered when one of Josie's friends teetered into our living room in her stiletto sandals, causing little nicks on my precious

Brazilian cherry floorboards. I politely asked her to remove her shoes, embarrassing Josie.

The next day, I bought a floor sander and smoothed down those divots and re-stained the floor. It was the only time my husband ever insinuated I might have a problem, but the truth was, I think he enjoyed having such an astute housekeeper.

My demons were speaking louder to me since I found out about Mitchell's infidelity. I had kept them under wraps for so many years, but they were banging on the door, fighting to get out. The more things spiraled out of control, the worse my fight for perfection became. I wanted to control everything else because I could not control him.

I needed my control back.

He'd pay for his poor behavior, but I hadn't decided on his punishment yet. Mitchell and Katelyn were no match for me. Destroying this little union would be like everything else on my to-do list.

Pick up the groceries—Check

Meet the girls for lunch—Check

Make Mitchell and Katelyn wish they'd never met—Check

And, if I could do everything from afar, like an omniscient puppet master, making them hate each other and fall apart without ever showing my face, all the better. Let them come to their own conclusions.

The idea had been born.

Unfortunately, my stress headaches were getting worse, making simple tasks more difficult. I'd actually found myself blacking out and coming to without knowing what had happened. I now carried a value-pack bottle of Advil in my purse and was convinced a brain tumor or budding aneurism brewed. I had to destroy Mitchell and Katelyn before it killed me. The very thought of dying, before I could get my revenge, made my vision blur into a single line. A distinct ringing started in my ear. I could not let them shame me into my grave. I could think of no worse way to leave this earth.

As I sat on the couch staring down at my polished floors, I waited nervously for my family to get home. The pounding started in my eardrums and worked its way up behind my eyes until the pain was so intense it blinded me. My thoughts of Katelyn and Mitchell were spinning out of control as the pain came on suddenly.

Perfect floors, freshly waxed
I bet Katelyn was freshly waxed
Laundry folded and put away
Katelyn picks up Mitchell's perfect, pressed laundry
Perfect family
Torn apart

My hot emotions were uncontrollable. As soon as the stress elevated and the blood pressure rose, the headaches seemed to follow. Stress-induced migraines. I had read about them on WebMd.com. This one was rather vicious and my last thought was I needed to lie down.

****

And England makes a play for Russia for the gold with a Triple Crown lutz in that program. What a show tonight...

I heard metal scraping on ice as I awoke on the couch in my living room to Josie blaring the televised Winter Olympic Games. The rest of my family was

70

sitting on various chairs as my husband sat at my feet on the edge of the black leather sofa, staring at me with unease. I had no idea how I'd gotten there. Josie scowled at me, but I could not figure out why. She probably decided she hated me today, like every other day since she'd turned twelve. *Hormones,* I told myself.

"You mumbled something about having a headache, honey," my husband said in an answer to my confused look.

"I did have a headache. I don't remember lying here."

"You've been having a lot of those lately. I think you should go see a doctor," Mitchell remarked.

Oh, how I wanted to cut his concerned tongue right out of his mouth.

He was the reason my mind was breaking.

"He said it was allergies," I lied.

I didn't even want to know the answer to why I was having headaches. More stress is all I needed with a terminal illness to obsess about on top of everything else. I already imagined the tumor growing larger every day, thinking about it constantly. If the tumor were a reality, it would take me over. The little demons would surely break open the door and there would be no closing it. And I would turn into *her* as I fretted over the diseased cells eating away at my brain. I wondered if this is what my mother felt like before she got sick. I tried not to think about it, because it only made me more paranoid.

"How are there allergens in the house? It's winter and you've been in cleaning overdrive lately," Mitchell questioned.

"That's for sure," Josie muttered, obviously

annoyed.

"I'm not sure. Mold, dust? You can develop allergies late in life," I answered, continuing to fabricate facts as I went along.

He was lying to me every day. I had no reason to tell him anything I didn't want to anymore.

"Okaaay," Mitchell answered.

"So are you watching ice skating, Josie?" I asked, changing the subject.

"Is that a rhetorical question?" my smart-ass daughter answered. She pointed to the television screen of a tiny woman spinning in a glittery costume.

"I'm surprised you're watching this, Cam," I said, diverting to my son, who always tried to at least pretend like he wanted to talk to me.

"The luge is next," he said.

"Can I see you in the kitchen, Cece?" Mitchell asked.

"You can see me right here."

My children rolled their eyes at my poor joke.

"Please," he repeated himself.

I got up wearily, feeling a little dizzy and walked over to our professional-grade kitchen island. I sat at one of the black, cushioned stools, which had taken me six months to find and pick out.

"What is it, Mitchell?"

It was nearly eight o'clock and he still had his suit on from this morning. He hadn't even taken the jacket off, which led me to believe he was actually working and not late because he was playing hot and heavy with his assistant. His forehead was creased in worry and his mouth was set in a grim line across his square jaw, popping out his one dimple I loved so much. She probably loved it too.

"We both know you don't have allergies," he said.

"They couldn't find anything wrong with me," I lied.

"Could the headaches be migraines?" Mitchell asked.

"They could be, but those can also be triggered by allergies too."

"Do you think you should go see a specialist, like a neurologist or something?"

"Who have you been talking to, where you learned the word *neurologist*?" I laughed.

"Monte," he answered.

"Please don't discuss my health with our friends. I don't need other people knowing my business, especially perfect Maeve and her perfect husband," I snapped.

"I'm just worried about you, honey. We've been married a long time, and I've never known you to pass out on the couch before eight o'clock without remembering how you got there. You're too put together for that and you just don't wind down that fast. Also, there was an empty bowl of ice cream in the sink," he stated, glancing sideways.

"Well, I didn't eat it," I snorted.

"The kids said they didn't eat it, Cece. If they didn't eat it, and I didn't eat it, and you didn't eat it, who did?" he asked.

"You know I wouldn't have left a bowl in the sink," I insisted.

"I know you wouldn't and I also know you aren't prone to eating bowls of ice cream in the middle of the day and passing out on the couch, so I'm asking you to go back to the doctor and see a specialist. I'm worried about you," he said.

"Mitchell, you and I both know you stopped worrying about me a long time ago." I said. He flinched at the force behind my words.

"What's your comment supposed to mean?" he asked.

"You know exactly what it means."

Then, I hopped off the stool and stormed upstairs before I gave myself away. I'd declared it another silent night.

Chapter 6
It's War

Even though I was still steamed over Mitchell's staged concern for my health the previous evening, I decided to fight. Fight for my family. Fight for my dignity. Fight for revenge.

Anita Botson, I was not. Mitchell and Katelyn could not, they would not, shame me like that.

So, like any woman scorned, I started researching my offender and his mistress. The plan was simple: Destroy their relationship at all costs, make Mitchell hurt the way he'd made me hurt, make Katelyn hurt worse than anybody should hurt. I was going to swat her away like a fly that had landed in the wrong place.

Squish. Bye, bye, Katelyn. It was time to decipher how big of a pest she was going to be, and if I could exterminate her from my life—forever.

I sat at his desk browsing through the online credit card bills, which he thought I didn't have access to. There were various charges from Brooklyn. I saw a recurring bill for two thousand five hundred dollars, which had been processed the last three months from K&G Realty, which was not Mitchell's company and not in his territory.

I was going into battle, guns blazing. It was essential I know everything about my opponents. I'd lived with the one for over a decade and thought I knew him pretty well, but there were things I still needed to learn. I knew nothing about her, but that would change. The stakes were high and she would lose, because she never saw me coming—neither one of them did.

There's so much personal data you can learn from someone's online social media profile. It was actually pretty scary. From Facebook, I learned Katelyn grew up in Toledo, Ohio and attended private school, where she was editor of her student newspaper and played clarinet in the band. She moved to New York City to attend college at Smith University and studied journalism.

She wore braces in her teens, as illustrated by one of her posted junior high photos. Her body didn't properly fill out until her senior year, as shown by another picture, still looking very much like a carrot-topped, string bean, before she'd dyed her hair a more suitable strawberry-blonde color in college. After viewing these old pictures (which I would have burned, deleted, and stricken from my memory), I discerned a few things about Katelyn McCallister. She was nothing more than a band geek in a business suit. She suffered from ugly duckling syndrome, still carrying her lack of confidence from her younger days, explaining her inability to accept my compliment at the Christmas party and her incompetence in maneuvering in women's footwear.

As she turned into a swan, I'm guessing the abashed young lady noticed the men's heads turn in her favor. In her early twenties her lean and voluptuous body took way, and while her red hair and freckled skin had always been a detriment to her beauty, she finally came to embrace it, finding the right color palette to make her look exquisite in just the right shade of green, as illustrated in a recently posted Christmas photo.

Those things were relatively factual and plucked right from the Internet, and the rest I deduced from my power of observation. My definition of Katelyn McCallister: a sheltered, small town girl with earnest values who moved to the big city to take the journalism world by storm, only to fall flat when the print world collapsed, crushing her dreams. She had bad timing. Determined to succeed, Katelyn ventured on to acquire her real estate license, drowning in debt, hoping the city wouldn't swallow her whole, knowing she couldn't call home for help, because daddy, a retired mechanic, didn't have the thousands she would need to dig her way out.

Unfortunately, once she made it into her new and supposedly promising field, *because real estate always held its value*—so they told her—the housing bubble burst, crushing her dreams, yet again. The story of her life was—bad timing. In one last effort to "make it" she interviewed for a position she knew she wasn't qualified for and that's when she met her knight-in-shining-armor, Mitchell Laramie, my underappreciated and overly successful husband, who found her innocent charm endearing and took her under his wing, only to fall for the wholesome Midwestern cherry bomb. I decided that was her story. And even if it wasn't, in my mind, that would be her story.

As for him. The missing piece of the puzzle lies in an undisclosed property in Brooklyn that was costing us approximately two thousand five hundred dollars a month. Two thousand five hundred dollars he claimed we didn't have to pay off our credit card and two thousand five hundred dollars not being deposited into our children's college funds. I had a feeling my secret weapon for my private war was hidden in this piece of real estate.

Bottom line was: He should've been more careful. All of the attention I paid to our home and our children and our lives to make sure everything was perfect. He should have known better.

It wasn't hard to get the address for my husband's mystery property from the Dumb Dumb at K&G Realty. I could hear the bubble-gum chewing, bleached-blonde, big-haired nitwit through the phone. All I had to say was, "Excuse me, I'm Mitchell Laramie's assistant and I was calling to verify rent on a property. Do you have any listed under K&G in his name? I want to make sure they match our records. There's been a discrepancy at the bank."

There was no social security number or other form of identification needed. Just a *crack, pop* of her gum, the hard taps on a keyboard and *voila*—the address. If Facebook was scary, an idiot receptionist in a world who didn't care anymore was damn near petrifying.

My drive to Brooklyn gave me a thrill. I felt like a detective disguised in my oversized shades, my hair pulled back in a concealing scarf, with my seat back a little farther than normal, pimping in my Mercedes Benz sedan. Mitchell and I had matching Mercedes in true dream house couple fashion. Mine was white and Mitchell's was black, and they each had the same gorgeous creamy, tan interior of my choosing.

My glee of my voyage deflated when I hit the city traffic. I hadn't driven into the city by myself in years. I'd always taken the train or Mitchell drove us everywhere, and I'd forgotten how unnerving it could be. The ride from Midtown to Brooklyn was awful and I really didn't want to get my car dinged up, because that would prompt questions from Mitchell, whom I needed to keep in the dark as long as possible.

Attack the opponent when they are not looking.

I made it there in a little over an hour. I parked in front of the brownstone in Park Slope, staring in awe at its beauty. I had only been to Brooklyn a handful of times in college, so I did a little recon on Mitchell's hidden treasure. Park Slope was a highly sought after neighborhood in Brooklyn, popular for the young professional looking to start a family. Of course, I scoffed at Brooklyn, the place where parents chose to raise their children when they couldn't tear themselves away from the city. But something about this place made me feel jealous before I even stepped inside.

The city was a great place to live in my twenties, but I wouldn't want to raise my children among the riff raff, no green space, people-packed-upon-people atmosphere. My children needed room to breathe, a big backyard to run the bases, play on the swings, and nice, clean streets to ride their bicycles like I had growing up in my Connecticut suburb. I watched a mommy push her stroller down the sidewalk, nervously smiling at me, as I'd been parked there staring at the building next to hers for far too long. Part of me wanted to know all about it and the other half wanted to bolt in the opposite direction.

The beautiful old building had all the ornate fixings of a lux brownstone. A chunky cement-color filled the bottom half where the large wooden doors were housed, with two picture windows rimmed in dark metal on either side. Matching, black metallic sconces graced the doorway. North of the door, red brick expanded the rest of the way to the tippy-top of the two-story building. A smooth cement set of steps led up to the front stoop, which was surrounded in dark metal fencing to match the windows and sconces. The neighborhood had wide, sweeping sidewalks made for taking long, romantic walks.

My visions of lovely strolls were broken by a pop of red bursting out of the door and leaning over to hastily stretch in her exercise gear. I swiftly ducked down behind my steering wheel, but nosed up enough to see her nonchalantly hide the key to the entrance of her home in a special slot under the doormat. She was dressed in black spandex pants and a matching zip-up long-sleeved top, trying to conceal her action with a lunge-squat-move, but when she bent down, I caught the glint of silver slip into the special place under the mat. Why would anyone be so stupid? Any passerby could've been watching her. She was *that* stupid because she was the naïve, sheltered girl from Toledo, Ohio who I'd pinned her to be. Something nagged at me that she was comfortable enough with this location to change into her workout clothes.

I knew I had limited time to investigate before she got back from her run. My plan had changed from spying to breaking and entering. I smiled to myself as I carefully got out of my car and crossed the street, letting myself into the brownstone with the hidden key, carefully placing it back under the mat, and locking the door behind me. My heart thumped in my chest as I stood in the doorway frozen, filled with wild anticipation. I started to get dizzy as I moved through the foyer and realized I needed to breathe.

Breathe Cecelia.

I didn't know how much time I had. In the event she was as out of shape as I was, she would be going for a very short run, in which case, I needed to move fast. The inspection of the bedroom off the foyer would be first. I didn't know what I expected, but it wasn't this.

"You've got to be kidding me," I whispered to myself.

I saw my husband when I walked into her room, or was it their room? His picture was everywhere. It looked like a year's worth of photographs of them all over the city, and I suddenly felt sick as it dawned on me they'd been together a lot longer than I'd thought.

Steadying myself in the frame of the bedroom door, my arms shook like jelly as I fought to stay upright and conscious, clamping my lips together so tightly I thought I might suffocate. The shock was painful as I tried to take in the floating images in the room, my eyes beginning to cross. I removed one trembling hand and smacked my own face into focus.

Concentrate Cecelia.

Katelyn was obviously big into pictures, but there was something disturbingly juvenile about her decor. I wrinkled my nose at all of the couple's photos in their cutesy little frames with taglines and gaudy fixtures attached to them. It looked like a college kid was living there, or maybe a recent graduate, but certainly not a grown woman. So tacky, all the jammed frames in the tiny space, threatening to take over the room. As someone fanatical about home decoration, I wanted to scream—*white space—let it breathe!*

The picture of the two of them in Central Park

twisted my stomach, making me hold my breath again, until I had to force myself to take a gulp of air. It was one of those fast pictures, real in the moment, where you had to ask a stranger to take it. Or worse yet, the kind where you were so darn cute someone offered to take it for you.

In one of them, Katelyn's hair glinted a fabulous auburn-red next to the autumn leaves with the sun behind her. Mitchell's cheek pressed up against hers in a huge smile. He had seemed to grab her so quickly for the photo, a long strand of her mop clung to his neck from the wind, the rest flapping behind her like a curly cape. They looked so happy.

My gut wrenched hard, right there. It wasn't just an affair; he really did love her. That fact was going to make my job harder. Suddenly, her pest level had graduated from an annoying fly to a nest of hornets.

The reality check forced me to grab onto the dresser to balance myself as the heat emanated from my ears to my temple. This was really happening. I had known it was, but I hadn't had the proof until now, and the truth hit me like a fiery blast across the face. Mitchell was in love with another woman. It wasn't just a fling, and my heart was officially broken. My desire for vengeance was the only thing keeping me upright as I struggled to find my footing on the cream Berber carpet—so fresh, soft, and new, just like her.

One other picture on the dresser nearly broke me. I fought my reflex to turn away as I examined it, recognizing Tony, the owner of the restaurant from the Bronx. So, Katelyn had been the one to show him that place. I'd wondered how he'd ended up there. Her selflessness probably brought him to his knees after dealing with me for so many years. It was Thanksgiving Saturday as evidenced by the orange and red decorations and, well, the big fucking turkey in the background. The bastard could have been spending time with his children on the long weekend, but instead he was gallivanting around town with Miss I-Take-Pictures-To-Celebrate-Everything, and oh, I like to spend my holidays giving to the needy too. *Just perfect.*

My online research showed she had somewhere close to nine hundred photos on her Facebook page, as if she needed to post them to validate her life. She'd been smart enough not to post any of Mitchell, although, I'm sure being the photo whore she was, it was killing her inside.

Gut Wrench #2. She definitely lived here. All of her clothes were hanging neatly in the closet, and unfortunately a few of his shirts were in there too. Seeing his clothes hanging next to hers was about as bad as it got. I stopped breathing again, my chest burning, my eyes watering. This was really happening to me. I took a deep breath and kept going.

The bathroom was next. Her medicine cabinet housed a diaphragm as a means of birth control. I found this odd. Who used those anymore? It was so 1980, and I didn't even know they still made them. And then I saw all of the medication in the cabinet was in liquid form. She had liquid Tylenol, a bottle of liquid Amoxicillin; the same pink stuff my kids were given when they had ear infections. She even had a tiny bottle of liquid Vicodin, which I didn't even know existed. So, it looked like perfect Katelyn couldn't swallow pills. Really? You're how old and you can't swallow a pill? Another child-like characteristic. I bet she couldn't give a proper blowjob either. If she didn't like pills in her mouth, how could she handle anything else?

She also had a list of grocery items that were made with nuts and various nut oils posted in the cabinet on a little sticky note next to an epinephrine pen. Could she make this any easier for me? This was almost a waste of my super-sleuth abilities. So, not only could she not swallow pills, Katelyn was also allergic to nuts. There was so much I could do with the information I'd just found in her medicine cabinet. It perked me up a little bit from the beating I just took in the bedroom.

Tick tock, I needed to move.

A whimper of an animal brought me back to the task at hand. I walked toward the sound to discover Dexter, a black and brown terrier of some sort, penned up in the other bedroom. He snarled at me as I entered the bedroom/office, but there wasn't a whole lot he could do from his cage.

"Your mommy's been a bad, bad bitch," I told him.

Dexter barked at me maliciously as if he knew what I'd said. I wanted to kick the cage, but as much as I hated dogs, animal cruelty was not in my blood.

There were work papers spread all over her desk. I thumbed through them quickly, but they were mainly Mitchell's listings in Manhattan, his main territory. And then, my second hidden weapon revealed itself. I picked up a real estate receipt from East Hampton, NY, purchased by Ms. Katelyn McCallister.

The Hamptons?

I knew she couldn't afford a place in East Hampton on her assistant wages. I read the receipt carefully noting she had rented a cottage every weekend from June—August, peak season. East Hampton was nearly three hours away from where we lived and if she was planning on seeing Mitchell, I didn't see how this fit into the equation with all of his fatherly obligations. The clock on my phone caught my attention as I snapped a photo of the address on the receipt. I had to get out of there. It had been forty-five minutes already.

As I was about to make my way out of the office, I heard the door unlock and creak open, and the huffing of a naïve little twit.

Oh shit*!*

I almost wanted her to find me. It would scare the bejesus out of her and I knew she didn't have the will to fight. But I had to stick to my plan. Keeping my end goal in sight, I scurried into the bedroom closet instead. I wasn't about to let them find me out. Not until I got the ammo I needed to win.

The mutt started barking relentlessly, trying to tell his owner there was an intruder in the house. Guarding her was his job, and I supposed the little fucker was going to be my end. I should have kicked the cage, put him in his place.

"Dexter, my goodness! I know you don't have to piddle, I just let you out before I ran," she said.

Piddle—ugh. Of course she called it that. Dexter howled ferociously, banging at the metal cage, smashing his little face into the grated holes.

"Geez, boy, okay, okay," she said.

The old floorboards groaned as she moved closer making me squeeze my breath tighter with each step she took forward. As Katelyn neared the cage, each padded footstep quickened my heart, an accelerating drum. It was game over if Dexter got out. Like any good dog, he would immediately go to the closet door and start scratching madly until she opened it. I thought maybe I could knock her out when she opened the door without her seeing me. I rested up against the back of the closet, fire extinguisher clutched in hand, which I'd had to move to make room for myself. Pushing my way into the cramped spot, I now held the extinguisher fiercely above my head for use as my exit weapon.

I pictured myself bashing in her skull with the weapon. I saw a delightful array of little pieces of skull mixed with red hair and blood. She would never see me coming. The hornet's nest would be extinguished quick and easy.

Katelyn came back into the apartment seconds before I was about to leave. I couldn't get over this woman's bad timing. It would be the death of her, literally, if she took a few steps closer. I felt the pitter patter of her feet grow even closer as she came within inches of the cage. I propped the extinguisher up further over my head, ready to deliver the deathblow. When her fingers hit the jangle on the cage's metal clasp, the vibration of her phone seemed to stop her cold.

"Hold on, Dexter. It's Daddy. I can't let you out right now. You just calm down. You just piddled."

"Hi baby," she said.

"Yes, I really want you to come tonight. My girlfriends are in from out of town and I would really like them to meet you. They've heard all about you, but they think I'm making you up because I can't post you on my Facebook page," she whined.

"I am not obsessed, it's a cultural thing. And a respectable woman shouldn't have to hide her man. It makes us look bad."

"I know, soon enough you will be mine and we

won't have to hide anymore."

"Okay, see you tonight. I'm so excited for you to finally meet them."

"Hey, Summer's on the other line. Can I call you back? All right, see you tonight. Love you too!"

Love you too. Double, triple, gut wrench times ten.

"Hi girl. I went for a quick run. You're in town already! I thought your flight didn't get in until three. Crap. What airline again? Okay, I'll be right there, hang tight," she said.

Katelyn hung up and Dexter started to yelp again because he had something very important to tell her if she would only open his cage.

"I can't let you out right now buddy. It's going to have to wait until I pick up Summer. Sorry, Dex," she said.

Moments after I heard a car pull away, I exited the brownstone and made my way to my vehicle. Katelyn was long gone. Eager to have her best friend meet her love. *Ugh.*

I sighed as I slid behind my wheel, sweating, shaking, and heart-broken. The more I learned, the worse it got. I really wanted to hightail it to The Hamptons and finish my real estate quandaries for the day, but my headache had turned into a raging migraine.

These episodes were definitely stress-induced.

I knew I should've left immediately because Katelyn would be back within the hour, but my vision was blurry, and I really needed to shield my eyes from the afternoon light. Dexter's closet was dark and the migraine had subsided for a few minutes in there, but it hit me with the full force of daylight as I emerged onto the street.

As I squinted into my steering wheel, I saw floaters everywhere. It was as if little fairies were flitting around, their sparkly wings dotting my peripheral view with pixie dust. For a moment, I thought I saw a woman with sunglasses and long blonde hair leaning against my car. I was ducked down and perhaps she didn't see me. It didn't matter, I couldn't tell her to get her ass off my Mercedes, because I was paralyzed in place as my ears kept ringing and the pain continued to throb relentlessly.

I would only shut my eyes for a minute...

Chapter 7
Liar Liar

My cell phone vibrated on my lap, waking me up from my street slumber. My eyes flickered open to sunlight streaming through the windshield. *Where am I?*

I poked my head out my driver side window and found myself still parked in front of Katelyn's apartment. An hour had elapsed. I blinked my eyes and rubbed the bridge of my nose, trying to gather myself. I was really going to need to see a doctor soon. I feared I might blackout while driving next time. But I wanted to complete my mission first. If I knew I was dying, I would never be able to take her down. I would lose focus. I assumed Twiddle Dee didn't see me on her way back to her apartment, if she was even there yet. It was time to continue with my journey.

The missed call on my cell phone was from my mother's nursing home. After checking my messages, it was time to cut my mission short for the day. My mother had gone into seizures, which were unrelated to her dementia, and they were requesting my presence at the hospital. I phoned my sister and brother, but neither one picked up and I was forced to leave the bad news on their voicemails. As I made my way to the hospital, I prayed for my mother. Her mind had escaped her, leaving a disturbed shell of a woman, and even though I had already grieved the initial loss of her, I still wasn't ready to let her go. I don't think you're ever really ready to lose a parent, no matter how bad their disposition.

I needed to conjure up some serious emotions, because I would not let Katelyn win tonight. The scenario was a little worse than I'd thought and it was time to get dirty. I called my husband and he surprisingly picked up on the first ring.

"Cece, I'm glad you called. I wanted to let you know I have a big client coming in for the weekend. I'm going to have to work a lot tonight and tomorrow," he said.

"You can't work tonight, Mitchell," I bawled, real streaming, heartfelt cries.

I pictured my mother reading me books when I was a little girl to drive some authentic sadness into my voice. She may have been crazy, but she was a damn good storyteller, reading me three books every night until I was in junior high. And I loved it.

"What's wrong, Cece?" he asked.

"It's my mother, she's sick. She's in the hospital. She's having seizures and it looks really bad. You're going to have to pick up Camdyn from his soccer practice and take Josie to her sleepover at Collette's," I said.

"They're going to have to get rides, Cece. This client is for a multi-million dollar deal," Mitchell lied.

Oh, he was playing even dirtier. His family needed him, my mother was sick and he was bailing to be with her. Time to turn it up a notch. She would not win.

"I don't care if it's a billion dollars, Mitchell! You need to be there for your family."

"I know you don't care, Cece. Believe me I know you don't care. But this deal will help me pay off the damn doll that's still on our high-interest credit card."

BastardBastardBastard.

"Mitchell, how can you be talking about money and clients and credit cards when your wife's mother is in the hospital?"

Match. Point.

"Cece, I feel bad about your mother, but she's been sick a long time and I'm sure she would want me to do this for our family to help get her daughter out of debt."

"Mitchell, she's dying, okay. The nurses pretty much told me, I didn't want to say the words over the phone. She's on her death bed and I need you," I cried.

Game.

"Oh, wow," *Long pause.* "I'm sorry, I didn't realize it was that bad. Okay, okay. I'm sorry. What time are all the kids' events tonight? I will come to the hospital right after I drop them off. Unless you want them to see her first."

"No, no, they don't need to see this. They aren't even close to her," I whimpered.

"It's okay, Cece. It's not your fault. She got sick before they got a chance to know her. I'll just tell them she's in the hospital. I'll be there as soon as I can."

"Okay. I love you, Mitchell," I squeaked. It was just as hard for me to say the words as it was for him to hear them. The spewed lies made my throat burn with acid.

"Love you, too. See you soon," he muttered reluctantly.

It had been an eternity since either one of us uttered the L-word.

The back of my neck prickled at how good the words sounded coming off his tongue. I wished I hadn't liked it. The confliction made my stomach sink at how much I truly hated him for ruining our marriage.

****

Well, Karma sure is a bitch. She's a nasty, little troll that sneaks up and bites you in the ass when you're not looking. I received one disturbing voicemail from my mother's nursing home asking me to get to the hospital because she had a seizure. But when I arrived, she was in cardiac arrest. They had her stabilized for a moment and she asked to see me. I was floored and a bit scared. She hadn't said my name in seven years, and now she was asking to see me?

Had she known all the times I was there—or more importantly, all the times I wasn't?

Walking into her room felt surreal, with monitors beeping, and doctors hovering over her with freshly used defibrillator paddles, not ready to pack up and leave as the symbols on the machines blared insufficient numbers. I knew they weren't supposed to let me in there, but she asked for me, and they probably knew it would be her last chance to talk to me.

As our eyes locked, I was the one who stopped breathing. It really was her. She was the mother who taught me how to braid my hair, tie my shoes, bake a cake; the mother staring back at me was not the woman lost in a blind mental storm whom I'd been visiting for the last seven years. My body lurched back, as I teetered on clumsy feet. I hadn't looked into those lucid brown eyes in almost a decade. She was a sad sight with her brown, mousy hair turned gray, sweaty and clinging to her face, mouth hanging open, parched lips, sunken cheeks and a desperate plea dancing on her lips.

"Mother?"

"Cece, is that you?"

"Yes, it's me, Mother,"

"Don't let her," she croaked.

"Don't let who, Mom?"

"Don't let her turn you into me," she whispered.

"Who, Mom?" I asked, my voice becoming shaky.

"She'll come when you're not looking, Cece. I can see her in you. Be careful you don't turn into me," she sputtered.

Those were her last words.

The monitors screamed one last straight line. A nurse ushered me out of the room as men with masks and blue scrubs fought to save her with tubes and needles. But I knew she was really gone this time.

When Mitchell showed up I didn't have to fake my tears. My shock and dire need for him was all too real. He found me crumpled over in a green, plastic chair, a mess of tears and guilt, but I would only give him the tears version. I wouldn't let him know I felt somehow responsible for her death because I'd damned her to her grave before I knew she was really dying. That cuckoo could stay in its clock.

"Oh God, Cece. Is she gone?"

"Yes," I gasped.

"Oh, I'm so sorry. I know it's what you said over the phone, but I was hoping it was you being overly dramatic," he said.

My husband showed up that night. He wrapped his arms around me and lent me his shoulder as I cried for my mother.

"Did you get to see her before she went?" he asked.

I was in full hiccuping sobs as I remembered the moment—one I would never forget.

"S-she talked to me."

"What do you mean?" he asked.

"She asked for me, Mitchell. She had a weird point of clarity right at the end. She asked for me by name," I cried.

"Oh my God," he whispered, "What did she say?"

"She told me not to turn into her," I cried.

Mitchell's eyes flung open, brow furrowed, mouth pressed together, seemingly unsure of what to say to make it better. He held me then like he loved me. It was a substantial, all-encompassing, arms-tight-around-my-whole-body hug. He let me press my head against his chest and bury it there.

Mitchell still loved me. I could feel it in his embrace. It was the authenticity of emotion conjured over a decade of spending your life with somebody. But the truth was, I wasn't sure if I loved him anymore. His arms felt familiar and comforting, but my love for him had been replaced by something black and cold ever since I'd left the brownstone in Brooklyn. And the monster, the one who'd roared me to sleep on my steering wheel; he'd been saying some bad, bad things that were beginning to scare me.

"Little pieces of skull mixed with red hair and blood."

"You should've taken care of the pest problem right then and there," the voice whispered.

It wasn't that I necessarily wanted *him* back, but I wanted my old life back, and to get it, she had to go. My social life had revolved around *our* friends. I wasn't sure they'd still be my friends in the same capacity if they weren't *our* friends, and losing the connection was another reason to fight. I'd lost him, and I took partial responsibility for the loss, but she was the main problem. She needed to go.

"She was probably just babbling, honey," Mitchell said.

"No, you don't understand. She looked right at me, with her eyes, not the empty ones, her real eyes. She asked for me by name. She hasn't known my name in years. I'm worried maybe she knew I was really there on my visits and I should've gone more often. Oh God, what if she was trapped in there and I only went to see her once a month?"

"Honey, the doctors said she slipped away a long time ago," he comforted, shushing me like a child.

"Then why did she remember me all of a sudden? What if the doctors were wrong?" I asked.

"You did what you could, more than your sister did, and sure as hell more than your brother. And you can't change it now. Honey, I'm sure you comforted her enough."

"And I've been having these headaches, Mitchell, maybe she came back one last time to warn me I'm going nuts like her," I said.

"You're not going nuts, Cece. Take it easy. She simply passed. Now take a deep breath and try to think about what you're saying. She's been sick for so long and you shouldn't take what she said to heart."

Mitchell said all the right words. Everything I needed to hear. He had such a knack for verbal pacification and saying the appropriate thing at the right time, a skill he'd used at work to allot us a very nice lifestyle. I appreciated the ingenuity of it all, his words like soft music to my ears. He was such a rock back in the day, when he was my real, unshared husband.

"Okay, okay. I know it was just some hard last words to hear, yeah know? Especially with how I've been feeling lately," I sniffed.

"You need to go see a specialist. Monte gave me the number for the neurologist he recommended."

A new battle plan entered my grief-stricken head. There was no rhyme or reason to my brilliance, and I was angry with myself for thinking of anything other than the loss of my mother. However, the right piece of information for my projects sometimes materialized out of thin air, and I had to take its organic creation as it came.

"Okay, I'll go," I said definitively, "I need you right now, Mitchell. I know we've had our differences lately and every marriage goes through its ups and downs, but I need you to be present right now. I'm going to have to deal with the funeral arrangements, and will need you to be around for the kids. Also, I want you there when I see the specialist. If it's something bad, I don't want to find out alone," I whimpered.

"Okay, okay honey," he answered; squeezing my head into his chest forcing me to smell the same spicy cologne he'd always worn. The familiarity of his arms. The feeling of his nose pressed against my cheek. It was so very soothing and revolting at the same time. The monster roared loudly again in disapproval. My feelings were a mesh of hurt and vengeance. Mitchell was the enemy, but I needed him right now.

"Do you think you can be there for me?" I asked.

"Of course," he answered.

"Thanks for being here tonight."

"Where else would I be?"

My lip twitched. I knew exactly where he'd be and had to look away and bite the flicker on my mouth. As I followed my husband home from the hospital, I tried not to think about my mother's haunting last words. I couldn't help but fear maybe she was right. My mind would go like hers. This unraveling as imminent as a freight train howling through a railroad crossing. I couldn't stop it, and as it got closer, it got louder and more intense.

Distraction was my only weapon against it. Refocusing on my mission gave me purpose. My thoughts trailed to Katelyn and my victory for the evening. How embarrassing for her. I could see it play out in my mind like a bad network movie. All of her Twiddle Dee twats piling into her swanky townhouse, getting gussied up for their big night out in New York City. She would probably try on a few cheap dresses or maybe the more expensive ones Mitchell bought her, while describing how wonderful her older, yet extremely good-looking boyfriend was.

"Oh, I can't wait for you to meet Mitchell," she'd gush.

Then she'd show them her obnoxious collection of pictures to prove he existed, not revealing why she hadn't posted any of them on her very public Facebook page. Or maybe she would lie and say something like, *"Mitchell isn't a fan of having his picture posted on social media,"* or *"Mitchell doesn't feel we should post our private moments on the Internet."*

I could see her lying to cover up the awful truth. She was too pure and innocent to admit she was a home wrecker. But when he made the call to tell her he wasn't coming, that's the moving picture I wished I could've seen. What would she tell them then?

"My boyfriend's mother-in-law died. Oh, whoops, I guess I forgot to tell you he was married, but he won't be for long, because he's leaving her for me."

I'd give anything to see her big, freckled grin disintegrate, as she had to tell her closest friends Mr. Wonderful had to cancel on her. She'd been so excited earlier. He would be cancelling on her a lot more lately. I would make sure of it.

****

The following day when I told my children Grandma passed, they each gave me a hug, probably more for my comfort than theirs. I was saddened they never got to hear the animation in her voice when she told Hansel and Gretel or had the pleasure of tasting her homemade spaghetti and meatballs. But I was also thankful they were spared the pain of losing someone they loved. I hadn't taken a good look at either of them for so long, wrapped up in my own drama.

Camdyn appeared alarmingly aloof, a faraway look barely visible under his longish bowl of hair, hanging too shaggy over his somber, young face; somber from playing too many violent video games. Camdyn had threatened to quit soccer if we didn't let him continue his maximum two hours of gaming per day. He continued playing and chatting with friends he'd never meet, so we could ensure he would continue to socialize in a tangible setting with real people. We acknowledged his behavior as shy and backwards, but as long as his grades were good and he was happy, we tried not to overreact.

When I hugged Josie, her ribs protruded from her long, slender back, her eyes grayish and unhealthy. Josie's dance had become more competitive as she jumped into the older ranks. I knew she had been under increased pressure and tried to be supportive, but she didn't look well. Her black dress, which had fit her a few months ago, bagged around her shoulders and hips. She was wasting away and I had been too busy to notice.

My beautiful daughter, a perfect combination of the two of us: rich, brown, long hair and eyes to match, now all sunken cheekbones, jutting collarbones, and knobby ballerina knees. As we waited for relatives and friends to pile in, I grabbed her hand, but she quickly pulled it away.

"Josie, honey, we are going to see the dietician. Maeve's husband recommended him."

I'd had enough. There was no more giving Josie choices, or catering to Josie's harmful behavior. My mother had just passed, and my husband was having an affair, but there was no excuse for missing the biggest tragedy of all in my household—my daughter starving herself.

But how is that possible? I watched her down two chicken kabobs last evening.

"I don't need to see a dietician, Mom. You said you understood. I'm competing for the lead role in Sleeping Beauty," she protested.

"Well Sleeping Beauty was just tired, she wasn't emaciated, and you're thin enough, too thin. You don't look well, honey."

Josie rolled her eyes at my lame joke, but her easy demeanor changed quickly to spite.

"You're the one who told me I needed to measure my food better if I ever wanted to get the lead."

"Josie, I would never say something like that. Your father and I have been trying to get you to stop putting your food in measuring cups, it's not right for a young girl like you to be so conscientious," I whispered.

"Mom, you did tell me that. You had the nerve to say it right after you polished off a bowl of ice cream and left it in the sink last week," Josie revealed.

I felt the gut wrench and the tears pile beneath my eyelids. My daughter looked right through me, turning her head away, wounded and hateful.

"Josie, I haven't been feeling well lately. I haven't been myself. I've been having headaches and I don't remember saying that or leaving the dish in the sink," I admitted.

"Sure Mom. How convenient you don't remember it now," she said, obviously not believing me.

The first group of people walked through the door of the funeral home, forcing me to pull it together. A doctor's appointment would be the first thing on my agenda this week. Hurting myself was fine. Hurting my daughter was not. My girlfriends all gave me tight squeezes, offering condolences. I pulled Maeve aside as she passed through.

"How are you, dear? I am so very, very sorry," she said in her elegant voice.

"I'm not well, Maeve. I've been having awful headaches and Mitchell said Monte has a friend I can go see."

"Oh yes. I didn't know if I was supposed to be privy to such information. You don't worry yourself. I'll ask Monte to call him personally and we'll get you checked out right away, love. My mother used to have migraines. Dreadful," she whispered.

"Thank you, Maeve," I said, kissing her cheek.

"You're so very welcome. Anything I can do to help. I have Xanax in my purse if you're in need," she joked, winking at me, although she was probably serious.

My siblings and I greeted all of our guests and played the part, but none of us cried. We had a strange relationship with our parents. Dominic hadn't even shown up to bury our father when he passed away of a heart attack a few years ago. Dad and my brother mixed like oil and water. Dominic was rebellious, testing my father's patience on far too many occasions. My brother was a wild child, a bad seed, and there was nothing my father could have done to change him, but lord, had he tried—with the constant lash of his thick, leather belt. Dominic had escaped too many times into the dark place children go when they're beaten, never to come back again. He hated my father, enlisting in the army the day he graduated from high school.

My brother was either coming down from a cocaine high at the funeral or fighting his next fix as he stood there, agitated, blinking too many times, shifting his weight and rubbing his eyes and nose. I decided he was fighting a fix, trying to stay sober for her funeral. Between his drug problems and his war scars from Desert Storm, Dominic was a mess. He'd been a mess before he got deployed and he was an even bigger disaster when he returned.

And Natalie remained overly unaffected as usual, staring off into space, doting over her two daughters, making sure they were processing death properly. She was a good person, just lost in her own world most of the time. Natalie was a pastry chef who worked part-time for a special events coordinator. My sister had the personality of an artist. She was a dreamlike, whimsical adult; acting as freewheeling as the colorful swirls she created on her delicious goodies.

Our mother's death affected each of us in different ways thanks to our unconventional and dysfunctional upbringing. My sister ignored problems, my brother self-medicated, and I succumbed to them. We all had our coping mechanisms for how we survived our crazy family, and we respected each other's vices.

Despite his issues with addiction, Dominic had a special bond with Camdyn. For some reason, my son would talk to Dominic, where he shied away from most other people. Maybe it was because Camdyn was his only nephew, but they'd connected early on, before Dominic was so messed up.

"If you like Call of Duty: World of War, you should play Call of Duty: Modern Warfare. So much more realistic. It's badass," I overheard Dominic tell Camdyn.

That may have been the other common bond—their love of military video games. I know they played each other online from time to time, but Dom was usually working when Camdyn used his allotted two hours a day after school.

"I haven't tried Modern Warfare yet, haven't beaten World of War to start a new one," Camdyn said.

"It trumps it, man. You should quit and step up to the big game," Dominic challenged.

"Hey, are you still selling and trading guns on the side?" Camdyn asked.

"Nah, too risky, paperwork, can't ship 'em so you have to personally deal with screwballs. But I will tell you what's hot right now—hand grenades. Collector items. And you can ship them for cheap," Dominic said.

I didn't understand their fascination with weaponry. Just like they didn't get mine with dolls, I guessed. I was just happy my son was interested in something other than video games and talking to someone real. I'd gone days without having a real conversation with him and told myself he'd always been a quiet kid, but it was starting to worry me.

The viewing ended on Monday and the burial was on Tuesday. All I could think of when I looked at my mother's body were her final words, *Be careful, you don't turn into me.* I replayed them in my mind in the guttural way they came out of her mouth, over and over again.

I tried to focus once again on my big win instead, so I wouldn't lose my composure in front of my family and friends. I'd taken Mitchell away from her all weekend, the one weekend she wanted him there the most. And he'd held me and told me he loved me.

The biggest win of all was when I told Mitchell I needed him physically and he complied. We were making love by Tuesday evening. And not simply sex, the real thing: tender kisses down my neck, arms wrapped around my body, Mitchell moaning my name, falling into each other kind of making love which hadn't occurred in years.

He might've thought we'd made love, but for me it was only a revenge fuck. God, it was excruciating. The annoying breathy sound he makes when he orgasms. I pretended he was someone else. Like the dirty-hot owner of the coffee shop who'd had a crush on me for years. The important thing was, the next time Mitchell saw Katelyn, she would see the guilt in his eyes, and she would know what he'd done. I was counting on it.

Chapter 8
Cottage By The Sea

Life resumed on Wednesday. I actually couldn't wait for Katelyn to see Mitchell again so she could taste me on his lips. She would know as soon as she kissed him something was wrong. Every mistress should recognize the remorseful kiss of a cheater. It might be enough to end things right there. Either way she would be hurt. I'd blown a piece of her away. She would start to think she was the foolish other woman and he would never really leave his wife.

I enjoyed the three-hour drive to The Hamptons. It was long, but peaceful. The landscape changed dramatically as I drove toward the uber-rich, south fork of the pseudo-island.

It was the end of February in New York and some areas were still covered in snow. For the most part, the beachy, green-spaced, historical scenery mixed with the new money gorgeousness of the distinguished community lived up to its reputation. I had never been to The Hamptons before. Being a Jersey girl, my friends and our husbands didn't venture up this way. We vacationed at the Jersey Shore, in the nicer area— not the fist-pumping, Guido-ridden, boardwalk area. The Shore was close and convenient to where we lived and there was a lot for our kids to do—in the fist-pumping, Guido-ridden, boardwalk area. But the kids loved it and never got into too much trouble.

We all had *shore houses*.

The Montclair neighborhoods chatter every summer would go something like, "So what shore house are you renting/buying/selling this year?"

It was always a shore house though. And yeah, we went other places too, but as far as the New York area went—it was The Jersey Shore when you referred to going to the beach in my house.

But this was different.

It didn't get more elite than East Hampton. *Bucolic Bitches!* Houses resembling castles, spread vastly among the different harbors, meant for hosting parties fit for the stars. Sure, you had your lower rent areas, but even those were a little too high-class, with rentals easily jumping into the tens of thousands of dollars a week. I'd rather go to Europe if I were going to drop that much coin.

My question was: What was Katelyn doing with a rental property here?

I was looking for a "cottage" in East Hampton, as it was described on Katelyn's receipt. I watched in awe as the water pushed away from the dismal gray clouds in large, rolling waves, the beaches getting grander and more beautiful as I drove further east. My navigation system led me down a private driveway to a small, gray, barn-like cottage situated across the street from the water. It was small and quaint with tons of landscaping and a fenced in backyard with a pool. There was still a flyer in an info tube on the outside of the house that read: *Rent to Own.* I grabbed the flyer and read the description:

Nestled among tall hedges for optimal privacy yet

located in the center of East Hampton Village. Just a short walk to Main Beach, The Palm, Guild Hall and Polo Ralph Lauren, this East Hampton treasure is the vacation spot of your dreams.

Special Note: The owners will not be finishing the pool house and may offer the property at a reduced price for those looking to buy

(Prices Range from $999—$1999 per night during peak season June—August)

"Excuse me, Ma'am."

"Oh!" I gasped.

The late-forties, blonde woman in a sharp business suit appeared out of nowhere. She had eager blue eyes and a beautiful, but fake smile, the words— *Saleswoman*, practically tattooed on her forehead.

"Didn't mean to startle you. I'm Karen Rice, the agent for this cottage. I was just stopping by to check on a few things for my open house tonight. This property's already rented out for the season every weekend, unless you were interested in weekdays, in which we do have some availability. But the owner is looking to ultimately sell it," she said, nodding to my flyer.

"Oh darn. I was really interested in renting it for the weekends this summer. Do you know if the renter was planning on being here every weekend and if they might be interested in subletting it to me for a few weekends this summer?" I asked.

"Oh, I don't think so. There was another, um, let's see...couple," she paused awkwardly, "I believe they were already planning on swapping weekends with them. I showed the property to all four of them together. I believe the one couple had kids, because they were talking about how much they'd love the beach. I don't recall showing it to you though. How did you hear about it? It's a great find for the price, reduced because of the construction," she explained.

What other couple? Our friends? Certainly not our friends. But none of the infants she hung out with could afford this—so who? And the kids? Not my kids. She wasn't taking them away from me.

"I fell in love with it online and drove all the way from Manhattan on a whim to check it out," I answered despondently. My heart was burning with thoughts of my children running on the beach with Mitchell and Katelyn.

"I'm so sorry. It's been sold for a couple of months. It's too bad you didn't notice that. It should've been posted on the website."

"It's all right. Do you think you could show me the inside and then maybe I can get a jump on it for next year?"

"Sure, and it's still available for purchase today, although I have to tell you the young couple did express interest in eventually purchasing it. But, if you were to make me an offer today, I would have to honor your offer," she said, steely teeth gleaming.

"Let me check it out first before we get ahead of ourselves," I remarked.

Karen nodded with her obnoxious smile, not missing a beat as she whipped out her keys. She let me through the front door and I was introduced to the little cottage by the sea. The interior was comprised of pieces of gray, thick cut stone lining the walls, meeting the home's sloping ceilings made of wooden, earthy slats. An old-fashioned, brassy chandelier hung over the center of the barn wood dining room table, which was long and sat six. There were eight, long rectangles for windows spanning the length of the cottage, letting plenty of light into the enchanted space. The fireplace was all stone, a large piece of matching barn wood for the mantel. Rows and rows of darkly stained bookcases lined the walls, next to the vast wine rack. The owner must have been an avid reader. And drinker.

The rest of the house was country-cottage style with white bead board, white kitchen cabinets, and pedestal tubs in both master bathrooms. There were two masters on the tiny second floor, the only bedrooms in the house. The outside of the home boasted a small pool and Jacuzzi area with a detached, unfinished pool house. The unfinished structure had yellow construction tape all around it, but I asked to see inside anyway.

Everything in the pool house was done except for the finishing touches. The drywall was up, but the walls unpainted. The cabinets were all fastened with no knobs. The water worked, but had no faucets. It made me sad someone had deserted their project so close to completion. The pool house, if that's what you wanted to call it, was a teeny-tiny space, one sitting room and a closet, probably for storage.

"The investor pulled out before finishing it and listed the place, but it was near completion," she explained, "so what do you think?"

"It's lovely, although I'm not in the position to buy today."

"Well, you haven't even asked the price. It's listed for six hundred thousand dollars. It's a real steal for being practically beach front," Ms. Rice said.

"It's a good deal, but I can't make purchases

without my husband," I said, using one of Mitchell's favorite buyer smokescreens.

"Well, let me know when he can come by. I have other properties for rent if you have time today."

"I actually don't. But thank you, Ms. Rice. You've been very helpful."

****

The drive back from East Hampton wasn't as cathartic as the drive there. Now, I had learned Mitchell and Katelyn had a place in Brooklyn *and* a summer home in The Hamptons. He was really planning on leaving me and doing a total one-eighty with his life. What about his children? He loved them too much to abandon them. I couldn't figure out how he was going to make all this work and keep me in the dark at the same time. Did he think I wouldn't figure it out? I had to move fast to dissolve this pest problem before he started disappearing with her to their cozy cottage on the weekends.

I had an idea. I stopped at the coffee shop down the corner from where we lived. It was a favorite meeting place for the girls and me, but I wasn't there to see them this time.

The owner, Sam, had flirted with me since the very first day he opened *The Coffee Bean* five years ago. It was an innocent exchange, but one I enjoyed. He would see me coming and get my skinny latte ready before I entered the door. Sam also had the daily horoscopes posted every day at the counter where you picked up your drink. He would place one chocolate covered espresso bean on my lid every time, because he knew I liked them, and then read my horoscope upon pickup. Some days if I were dressed up he would tell me I was lovely or ask me when I was leaving my husband for him. It was all in good fun, but I loved that he didn't do it with any of the other gals—only me.

Mitchell hated Sam, labeling him a granola eating, pothead, Liberal. Sam drove an old Subaru with stickers like *Oil War, Tree Hugger,* and *Free Thinker* plastered on the bumper. MSNBC was always on the television at his shop and if you uttered the words Fox News, you'd be tossed out on your ass. Odd atmosphere to have news on while you drank your coffee, but that was Sam. He opened up his shop in the wrong part of town for his politically charged antics, but it didn't seem to hurt business much.

I found Sam strangely endearing. I loved how his long, thick brown hair flapped around on his head when he got really excited, and how his wild brown eyes were always animated like a stoned muppet. I needed a dose of Sam today, even if it was pretend flirting. A hot drink after my long drive wouldn't hurt either.

"Pisces: You need to deal with someone who is definitely not as they appear to be. That doesn't mean you're getting cheated or hoaxed, but it could mean you are the savior when the mask comes off," Sam read, as he handed me my latte.

"Hi Sam. Wow, that's a good one," I commented.

"Hi pretty lady. Who's cheating you? Hopefully, not your hard-working husband. When would he get the time?" he asked.

I had to smirk at the irony of both my horoscope and his question.

"That's yet to be seen," I offered.

"Deepest sympathies, Cece. I was very sorry to hear about your mother."

111

"Thank you. It was a surprise."

"It always is," Sam shot back.

Not really, I thought. Some people know they're going to die. It was such a "Sam" comment and he said it in a way that made you believe him. I picked up an application.

"So, I read your sign on the door. You hiring?" I asked.

"Josie's not old enough to work yet, is she? What is she, thirteen now?" Sam asked.

"That's right, she's officially a teenager, yikes. But I was actually the one wondering if you might need some part time help. I could only do a few days a week until three o'clock, because of the kids and never on weekends because of all their events," I explained.

Sam dropped the blender he was cleaning into the sink making a horrible clatter.

"You serious?"

"Yeah, I mean I've never been a barista, but I'm a quick learner," I said, leaning over the counter, watching him fumble around.

"Not that I don't absolutely love you, because you know I do," he winked, "but what in the world do you need a part time job for?"

"I racked up some debt. Debt that is causing my marriage some undue stress. If I make an effort to pay some of it back, it will get Mitchell off my back," I said honestly.

"Jesus, Cece," he said laughing.

I loved when Sam laughed. He threw his whole head back and let out a full belly roar when he thought something was really funny.

"Don't laugh at me."

"I'm not, honey. Maybe I am, I'm sorry. How much debt do you have to repay? Not trying to be nosy, just assessing the damages," he said.

"Ten thousand dollars," I said.

I didn't intend to tell Sam all of these details, but he was like the town bartender. He had a way of getting information out of you and I never minded telling him my business, because I knew he wouldn't judge me.

"You ladies and your wants and needs. That's why I'm not married. Be here tomorrow at nine a.m., Toots," he said, laughing again.

"Really?"

"Yeah, we'll start you out a couple of days a week. I'll even help you keep a tally of all your pay stubs until you hit ten thousand dollars. If you're spending it all and not saving enough, then we will have to reassess your goals," he joked, waving his finger at me.

"Okay, Sam. Thanks!"

"This is going to be fuu-uun," he said, as he snapped his towel at me.

"Nice, my first job in twelve years. See you tomorrow," I said.

The next part of my plan involved a trip to the grocery store. Mother used to say Natalie was Cinnamon. And Dominic was Spice. And I was Everything Nice. Not this time.

I would make Mitchell's favorite dinner, not because I aimed to please, but because I aimed to lure him away from Katelyn with man's second biggest weakness—food. Number one had already been a wild success. My goal was to create a fissure, plant a seed of doubt, unravel their romance before it took flight. Or at least throw a wrench in his flight plan before they started disappearing with my children to their little beach hideout. The thought of those two taking my kids faraway made my stomach sizzle like the onions and garlic in my stockpot.

Tonight I would prepare spaghetti and meatballs, using my mother's sauce recipe in honor of her stellar cooking. I hadn't made Mitchell's favorite meal in a couple of years because of my daughter's issue with carbs. I decided after seeing her at my mother's funeral, she *really* needed the carbs, and she wasn't allowed to leave the table until she ate something with gluten in it. I didn't care if it was a single fucking noodle.

****

Josie's lip curled up at the sight of the feast I laid out for my family. Spaghetti and meatballs, a large garden salad, thick, crusty, Italian bread, and an apple crumble cake for dessert.

"What's this?" Josie asked.

"We're eating one of Grandma's signature dishes in her honor. It's also your father's favorite. He's been working so much lately and you've shrunk down to nothing. We could all use a nice meal. And you're not allowed to use your damn measuring cups tonight," I demanded.

Camdyn's face lit up. He obviously liked pasta, but I wouldn't know, because he never talked to me.

"How was your day, Camdyn?" I asked.

"Fine."

"Did you do well on your math test?"

"I got a B. Is Dad coming home right after work today?" he asked, looking eager to dig into the meal.

"Yes, in a few minutes," I answered.

"Can I play my game until he gets here?" Camdyn

asked.

"I suppose," I replied.

I didn't know for a fact Mitchell was coming straight home, but I had an inkling his day hadn't gone so smoothly. He arrived fifteen minutes later. He threw his keys across the counter, in a huff, tossing around the mail, not looking up to greet anybody. I smiled. Katelyn had figured out he'd slept with me and she was pissed, so Mitchell had run right back home where he belonged. He suddenly noticed the delicious aroma and turned to glance at his family, all seated, waiting for him to join them.

"Did you make pasta?" he asked.

"I did. I wanted to make it in honor of my mother. And I know you like it too, so…"

"Yum, nice," he said.

I remembered my mother always telling me the way to a man's heart was through his stomach. Mitchell was totally looking for a fight when he came through the door. I could tell by the way he was rifling through the bills he was looking for something to squawk about. But I hadn't purchased anything in a while. And then came the overwhelming waft of delectable food and he suddenly changed his tune.

Everyone dug in, even Josie. She only ate a small portion of pasta and meatballs, and loaded up on salad, but it was more pasta and red meat than she had eaten in a year. My husband was so pleased he had seconds. He sat back at the table appearing bloated and satisfied.

Bam. Mission complete.

"Dinner was good, Mom," Camdyn said.

"Thanks, honey. I'm glad you liked it," I beamed.

I couldn't have been happier in that moment,

relishing in the feeling of total family balance, if only temporarily. Camdyn rinsed off his sauce-splatted plate in the sink, threw it in the dishwasher and was off to pursue his video game. Josie gave me an approving half-smile and excused herself as well.

"Yeah, thank you, it was great," Mitchell said.

"You're very welcome."

"You seem to be in good spirits today. I know how hard this week's been for you," Mitchell commented.

"Yes, it was. And it made me rethink a lot of things. It made me want to be a better person, and a better wife. I'm sorry for my overspending, Mitchell. I haven't bought anything since the doll."

Mitchell flinched. It was the apology that got him. I never apologized for buying anything before.

"Well, that's good, I suppose. Can't change who you are though, Cece."

"Sure you can. I wasn't always this way."

"It's only been a few days. Just wait until some big sale comes up and you go shopping with the girls or when you pass a store window and see the *perfect* pair of shoes you can't live without," Mitchell said with a gasp.

"Mitchell, I want you to take me seriously. I really want to be better. It's why I got a job."

"You got a what?" he asked, dropping his silverware in the sink, making us both jump.

"I got a job. Down at *The Coffee Bean* a couple days a week, and no nights or weekends. But I intend to pay back the ten thousand dollars. I don't want you to have to work so hard to pay off my debt," I proclaimed proudly.

"You're going to work for that hippie nutjob?" he

asked.

"Sam's harmless," I answered.

"Clueless is more like it."

"He's a legend in his own mind," I joked.

My husband laughed, his half-smile popping out his dimple. I had made him laugh and missed what it sounded like—a small, clipped cackle. We sat at the kitchen table and talked a little while, something we hadn't done in months. He was fighting with her and laughing and talking to me again.

All I needed to do was plant the seed of doubt enough to make him believe in us again. It was like creating an optical illusion, two images flipped in a two-way mirror, ghost of Christmas past and ghost of Christmas present, and if I could confuse him in my little funhouse to choose my distorted image over hers, I'd succeed. I was turning him. I could feel it.

When we climbed into bed at night I scooted up behind him, rubbing his shoulders, kissing his neck, pulling him to me.

"Not tonight, babe. I'm tired. Rough day at work," he said.

"Something happen?" I asked, trying to take renewed interest in his career.

"I've had this new partner since the beginning of the year and he's driving me nuts. They're splitting up my territory and listings a little bit. Seems when one salesperson makes too much in one geographic area, they like to do this to get more bang for their buck. Sucks. And, he's a little too flamboyant for my taste," he griped.

"You'll figure it out," I said.

My fingers found their way to the drawstrings on

his pajama pants, but were quickly swatted away.

"Cece, not happening tonight. You're acting very strangely lately," Mitchell protested.

"Okay. I just miss you," I said.

"Well, you'll be tired too, once you start working. You'll see," he said.

Chapter 9
Coffee, Marijuana and Stimulants

Katelyn's birthday was Friday, March sixth.

I knew this because her Facebook page told me so. Her post Thursday morning read *Taking the whole day off tomorrow to spend my birthday with someone special☺* . And yes, there was a real smiley face on the child's page. If Mitchell were to cancel on her two very special occasions in a row, what might she do then? Would she tell him to screw off and go be with his wife? I sure hoped so.

I phoned Maeve the moment I read her post.

"Maeve, is there any way you can ask Monte to call the neurologist and ask him to see me as an emergency tomorrow? Something's really wrong. I blacked out last night for the first time after a migraine. It was scary," I lied with a fake, shaky voice.

"Oh dear, I'm going to call Monte for you right now and see what we can do. I know Dr. Gibbs is hard to see on short notice, but Monte and he are good friends and hopefully he'll squeeze you in," she said.

"You're a doll," I said, "I really hope he can and this isn't anything too serious."

"Me too, love. Okay, I'll ring you as soon as I get an answer. Let me get Monte on the phone before he goes into surgery."

"Okay, Maeve. Thank you so much."

"Don't thank me yet. Call you in a bit."

My second day at *The Coffee Bean* was surprisingly enjoyable, after a first not-so-fun day of shadowing Mr. Personality. Being a barista was pleasant work, and I put as much care into making the perfect latte as I put into everything else I did in my life. I knew what it was like to get a poorly made beverage; where the barista didn't add enough of one thing, overkilled on another, or simply didn't take the time to properly mix or steam the drink, leaving the consistency insufficient. It might be drinkable, but you knew when it hit your lips something was off. I made sure each and every one of my drinks was made with special care—*Cecelia-stamped.*

My job also kept my mind off my marriage. However, even though a healthy dose of Sam every once in a while was a good thing, the everyday, high-energy, politically-charged Sam was a bit overwhelming.

"No, man. You think gas prices are high now. You wait until this summer. You'll be trading in your big SUV out there for a compact car like the rest of us. Oil War, my friend. That's all we're doing over there," he argued with a customer.

The frustrated three-piece suited man took his drink, shook his head and left.

"Sam, you don't have me on the schedule tomorrow, do you? I have a doctor's appointment," I said.

"No, tomorrow's Friday. You said, no weekends. I was going to use you a couple of days during the week to help with my regular morning rush. I want to see how much you can really handle. Rusty old lady," he said.

"Who you calling old?" I asked.

"You know I think you're one sexy momma."

"I still got it," I joked back, making my shoulders dance.

"Nice moves," he said, "Are you sick or something, why the doctor's appointment?"

"I've been having headaches."

"Well, why didn't you say so? I have the perfect cure for headaches. My treatment is herbal and I can give you a free sample," he said.

"Sam, I'm a mother. I can't smoke weed."

"Tell your kids it's for your headaches. It really works for them. If I get a bugger of a headache, I say screw Advil, fuck Tylenol. I take a couple hits and I'm cured. I'm not talking about smoking a whole joint, just a few puffs and the headache is gone immediately. I don't have to wait thirty minutes for it to kick in, killing my productivity at work, and my liver along with it, like some other shit. It's the best-kept secret. People won't try it because it's taboo and the government has their own reasons for not legalizing it. It has to do with their own dollars, if you haven't guessed," he said.

My snicker of a laugh said it all. And Sam got mad when you didn't take him seriously.

"Cece. There are doctors in California who swear by using medical Marijuana for headaches. There are studies on it."

"Oh yeah? You have any of those studies handy?"

"No, but I can get them. I've read them all. The THC in the marijuana does something to the part of your brain which controls pain. It's all I remember."

"And these are published studies?"

"Yes, they are published and reputable studies," he said all haughty, holding his chin up high.

"Well, you show me those studies and I might think about it if these doctors can't help. How about that?" I reasoned.

"Go natural, Cece. Try the green approach first. You don't need their products, they'll only make you think you do," he insisted, pointing to his head.

Sam didn't quit when he had a point to make. Somehow, he made it sound as if I was choosing not be eco-friendly by not smoking pot.

"Sam. I'm trying to get back on my husband's good side and smoking marijuana is not going to help my cause. I promise if the doctors can't figure it out or if their medications don't work, you'll be the first person I'll call," I assured.

"Suit yourself. Spend all your money on overpriced drugs. It's going to take you longer to get to ten thousand dollars than I thought. Fund the government; go on, like everyone else. Got a problem, pop a pill, and complain about the price. Waah," he went on.

My phone rang to break up the going nowhere, circle of shit conversation which often transpired with Sam, starting with our flawed government and ending with our flawed government.

"Hello, Maeve."

"Hi dear, I was able to get you an appointment with Dr. Gibbs tomorrow at eleven a.m. He's in Clifton off Allwood St. in the big medical building. Do you know where it is?"

"Yes, I know exactly where it is."

"Super. Now I guess he does MRIs in the same building, and he said it could take a while, so plan on being there a long time, should he order one. Do you have anyone going with you? I don't want you to be alone for the tests."

"Mitchell's going with me."

"As he should. Marvelous. Okay, well I'm glad I could help. I have to run, I'm late for hot yoga," she said.

"Thanks so much, Maeve!"

"Anything for you, dear."

Perfect. What would be the best way to approach Mitchell? I couldn't demand he come with me. No, it had to be willing, because she was really going to lose her mind over this one. Katelyn had tolerated him sleeping with me and if she was like any other hot-blooded woman, she was one second away from leaving his two-timing ass if he so much as made one more sidestep in the wrong direction. Especially if that sidestep was in my direction. He would have to choose me over her. It had to be his choice. And then she would leave him. And he would feel the hurt of being left too.

I texted Mitchell. Then he couldn't argue with me. The one-way communication of a text message was a beautiful thing.

—*Honey, I don't want you to be scared, but I blacked out after dropping the kids off at school today. I woke up at The Coffee Bean. I don't know how I got here. The doctor was able to squeeze me in tomorrow at 11. He's in Clifton. Please take the day off. Love you and thank you for being there for me when I need you.*—

No room for him to wiggle out of that one, and by adding the kids into the mix he couldn't say no. He wouldn't let them be endangered. Our spoiled children wouldn't ride the bus and Mitchell sure as hell didn't have time to drop them off in the morning.

He didn't respond right away. Perhaps he needed more time to stew.

Julie and Callie walked into the shop around ten o'clock. None of my friends knew I'd taken a part-time job. Callie bopped up to order her skinny latte first and didn't see me ducked behind the machine. I snickered to myself thinking my surprise reveal would be funny. After Julie ordered, I popped my head above the espresso machine.

"Hi girls!"

My greeting was not well received. Callie nearly dropped her drink, bobbling it and cupping her left hand under her right.

"Oh shit," she said.

Julie's lip curled up as if she just smelled something foul. Instead of surprised and abashed greetings from my friends, utter shock and disgust was what I received.

"Callie, did you spill your drink? I'm sorry I scared you. Do you want me to make you another one?" I asked.

I wanted to make sure her drink was just right. I saw some of the foamy goodness had spilled out, making my OCD tick.

"No, no it's fine. Nice apron. Why are you wearing it?" she asked, shocked.

Julie still stood there, the bad-smelling look still affixed to her petite, round face.

"I took a part-time job. Just getting a little bored, and out of home projects to do, and I wanted to contribute a little to the household. You know, since I've made a very large purchase recently," I said, raising my eyebrows.

"Holy shit, he's making you pay back the doll," Julie gasped.

"No, he's not making me. I wanted to. I wanted to get a job," I insisted.

"Why?" Callie asked.

"Haven't you ever thought about it, since your kids are grown up and don't need you as much. Don't you ever get bored?" I asked.

"No, not really. Not enough to make coffee," Callie responded.

"What's wrong with making coffee, Little-Miss-I-married-a-terrorist-and-am-living-off-his-fraudulent-money," Sam chimed in.

"He's Turkish, Sam. How many fucking times do I have to tell you he's Turkish, and not a terrorist," Callie said.

"They're in on it too, Callie. Have you ever looked at how they treat their women? Very possessive. Watch out, Mr. Slumlord will toss you out on the street too if you don't pay the piper and give him what he wants," Sam rambled.

"Sam, you're such an asshole," Callie said.

"You love me though, or else you wouldn't keep coming back," he argued.

"You're lucky there's not another coffee shop closer to where I live," Callie seethed.

"No loyalty. I'm just looking out for yeah," Sam insisted.

Ahmet was Callie's super-hot, kind of shady, multi-businessed husband. He owned laundromats, car washes, and a series of rental properties in seedy areas all over the city. Ahmet was a fine specimen of a man; tall, broody-dark with black hair and bedroom eyes. I could see why Callie fell for him, and as long as she had his money to spend, she didn't question where it came from.

"Of all the places to work," Callie said sharply.

"They were hiring and I like coffee," I defended.

Julie held her unpleasant stance, not saying a word since she called me out on having to pay for the doll.

"Okay, well, we're going shopping. Have a good time working. Looks fun," Callie teased.

"Thanks ladies, have a good day," I said.

I watched them walk out, noses in the air, lattes to lips, wondering why they were so irked about my new part-time position.

"If you think those bitches are your friends, then I feel sorry for you," Sam said.

"They were very bitchy, even for them," I agreed.

"They think they're too good to make a cup of coffee. They treated you like you were a second-class citizen. And why lie about why you took the job? If it's to pay something back, own it. Shouldn't have to hide who you are from anyone."

"I don't mind working. I didn't lie."

"But you wouldn't be working if it weren't for a doll? Can you explain that one, because I'm confused," he asked.

"I'm a doll collector."

"But you didn't spend ten thousand dollars on a baby doll?" Sam asked.

I looked down, cleaning the espresso machine, ignoring Sam.

"You did spend that much on a baby doll," he said, drawing in a deep breath.

I looked up to see Sam's googley eyes, cheeks puffed, face turning red, holding in laughter, until he popped like a crazed cartoon character, laughing at me for five minutes straight, composing himself and then losing it again, in between saying, "I'm sorry, I'm sorry," with tears forming in the corner of his eyes.

"I'll have you know this year's fashion show revolved around collector dolls and was so overbooked people didn't have seats and were turned away. There are tons of people exactly like me. It's more common than you think," I said, defending myself.

"Excuse me, did you just say doll show?" he asked.

The same cheek-puffing, laughter erupted and he had to excuse himself as another rush of men in business suits entered the shop. Sam ran out the back door, leaving me to fend for myself. Luckily, men in business suits were what I know.

When he returned his eyes were glossy, but he had settled down.

"Are you high?" I asked.

"I had to do something to calm down," he said, with a placid giggle now.

"So my hobby is so bizarre, you had to drug yourself? Really Sam?" I asked.

"No, I wanted to smoke. But you gave me a good reason," he responded.

"Oh, grow up," I said.

"Really, Cece? You're the one who collects little girls' dolls and you're telling me to grow up?" he laughed again.

"Touché, my friend. Touché."

Chapter 10
Don't Test Me

Mitchell took a half-vacation day for my doctor's appointment. I knew he actually took time off for her birthday, but he would tell me it was for my appointment. Mitchell let me know he had to go into work afterward. We argued briefly over his pressing "business" meeting, but it was short-lived when I brought the safety of our children into the picture. I fixed him eggs benedict for breakfast, another one of his favorites. He wolfed it down with delight, and instantly became a little more pleasant. *The way to a man's heart...* My mother's words were still helping me through a troubled time.

"I actually like working at the coffee shop and I've earned a whole one hundred and twenty eight dollars toward my debt, after taxes about seventy-seven dollars. Only nine thousand nine hundred and twenty-three dollars left to go," I said cheerfully.

"You actually figured those numbers out. That's so sad."

"I'm going to pay you back every penny. I might even keep my job afterwards, because I enjoy it. And I'm one badass barista."

"I have no doubt about your coffee-making capabilities. But what about the other hundreds of thousands of dollars you've racked up over the years, what about them?" he asked.

"I thought I would start here."

"So you're starting near the end."

"Why, are we dying soon?" I asked. "What's ending?"

"I don't know what you're trying to prove, Cece."

"I'm trying here, Mitchell. Can't you appreciate what I'm trying to do? For you and us and our family," I said.

"Why now?" Mitchell asked.

"My mother's passing made me realize I want to be a better person, okay?"

"Sure, and I appreciate it. It's—you're not yourself, is all."

"I can't win with you. I spend your money, you yell. I try to earn money and you complain."

"It's all great, Cece. But you are who you are, is all I'm saying. Let's go see what the doctor says, okay?"

"All right, let's go," I said.

****

The crowded waiting room was way too hot. It was the beginning of March, the first warm day in a while, and the thermostat was still preset to seventy degrees. Mitchell wore his dress shirt and tie, hoping to get back into the city and work after my appointment—back to her. I neglected to tell him about the possibility of an MRI, *Oops*. Fifteen minutes into waiting, Mitchell was yanking at his collar, beads of sweat building up on his forehead. I asked the receptionist to turn down the heat, but she said the whole building was set to one temperature and she didn't have control over it.

We didn't get called into the exam room until eleven thirty a.m. Mitchell kept looking at his watch, shaking his foot and checking his phone. He blamed his irritability on the heat, but every minute I forced him to sit there, was another minute I kept him away from her. She had to be livid, hopefully mad enough to walk away for good this time.

The doctor finally showed up at eleven forty-five a.m., apologizing for his lateness, explaining he'd had a difficult case. Dr. Gibbs looked over my chart briefly, asking me a couple of questions over his bushy gray eyebrows. He was concerned mostly with the blackouts, saying they weren't so common with migraines, and recommended I undergo a MRI.

"Great, hopefully we can get it done next week. The sooner the better." Mitchell piped so enthusiastically I thought he might bust something. He had one thing on his mind and it was speeding this appointment along so he could meet his girlfriend.

He would choke on his last words. I grinned knowing what the doctor would say next.

"Well, Mr. Laramie, you'll be happy to know we own and operate a high-tech testing facility right in this building. If we're really concerned about a patient, we provide same-day services. The technician will be back after lunch and will be able to scan Cecelia today. Because she passed out shortly after driving, we need to get this done promptly. And it's probably not a good idea for her to operate a vehicle until we figure out what's going on," he recommended.

"Thank you so much, Dr. Gibbs," I said.

"So, after lunch, meaning one o'clock?" Mitchell asked, annoyed.

"Yes, Veronica, the tech, will be waiting for you downstairs in our testing facility," Dr. Gibbs answered.

"And how long will the test take?" Mitchell asked anxiously.

"Plan on an hour and a half," Dr. Gibbs said.

"An hour and a half?" Mitchell yelled softly, but enough to show alarm.

"Is this a problem, Mr. Laramie? The sooner the better, is what you said and I agree," Dr. Gibbs said confusedly.

"No, no problem," he muttered.

"Okay, well I will read the results with you after your test. Good luck and relax," Dr. Gibbs directed, eyeing over Mitchell with torqued lips.

****

I suggested we grab lunch for our hour hiatus until the test.

"This is taking a lot longer than I thought it would," he said as we were seated at the grubby diner near the office complex.

"I asked you to take a whole vacation day. Besides, how often do we get to spend the day together?" I asked.

"Why in the hell are you so chipper?" he asked.

"Why in the hell are you so angry?" I asked.

"I had a client I wanted to meet up with and it's hot as balls in that building. I don't want to go back."

"Mitchell, I could be dying. I might find out I'm dying in two more hours. Do you want me to be there all alone? I'm sorry, but your priorities are all screwed up. Me and the kids should come first, not work."

"If you might be dying, why aren't you obsessing over it, like you normally would when something is out of place? You seem almost happy about it," he accused.

"I'm trying to be more positive. Make me

131

paranoid, why don't you."

"Well, if I can't meet my client I'm going to step outside and let them know, if that's okay?" Mitchell asked.

"Sure. Shall I order you the Reuben?" I asked.

"Please," he grumbled.

Mitchell was gone a long time, probably fifteen minutes. By the time he came back the food was being served. He was still red-faced from the long exposure to the heat in the office or was it from the lashing he'd just received from her over the phone? The top two buttons of his collar were undone, exposing his white t-shirt, which was soaked through, his tie shoved God knows where. He fidgeted, massaging his hand over an imaginary knot in the back of his neck, refusing to make eye contact with me as he took his seat in the red vinyl booth. I let him boil inside, watching his teeth gnash into his Reuben sandwich, not even tasting the food. We didn't speak the whole meal. She had really let him have it. Maybe he would be the one to walk away after he realized all women were needy, nagged, and placed constraints on a man's life.

Veronica was waiting for us when we returned. She gave me a blue hospital gown to change into when I got there. I felt my chest tighten and held my breath as I took the gown. I hadn't mentally prepared for the fact I might receive some very bad news regarding my health. My mind had been preoccupied. Mitchell was fiddling on his phone when I let the air back out, nearly passing out.

"Cece, what in the hell," he barked as he caught me.

"Sorry, a little nervous," I whispered.

"You were holding your breath again," Mitchell accused.

"Yes," I sighed.

"She holds her breath when she's nervous," he explained to the tech.

"Do you want me to get Dr. Gibbs?" Veronica asked.

"No, no, it's my nerves. I really want to get the test," I explained.

"Okay, you can relax. It's an easy test and it doesn't hurt, just a bit long," she said.

I watched Mitchell wince at the word, *long.* It was painful. I was standing there in a hospital gown waiting to get a life altering test and all he could think about was *her.* Veronica gave me earplugs and explained the noises the machine made were very loud, like a jackhammer. A large cylindrical machine waited for me as I lay down on the table. Veronica explained a scanner would go above my head, and she gave me a call button I could click in case I became uncomfortable during the test. An eye mask and a pillow were provided to ensure I wouldn't have to use the button. Mitchell helped me onto the table and held my hand, probably to play the good husband role in front of the tech. His hand was clammy and limp. He looked down at me staring at him for support.

"Breathe Cecelia, breathe."

I let out another colossal gulp of air. Holding my breath had always been my defense mechanism to fear and sometimes I didn't even realize I was doing it until my lungs started to burn or my vision blurred.

"Cecelia, do you want to wait until you're calmed down to go into the machine. I don't want you passing out in there," Veronica said.

"No, please. I'm fine. I'll be fine," I insisted.

"Are you sure?" she asked.

"I'm sure," I responded.

"Okay, now relax. If you have any discomfort at all and need to be removed, just hit the button and we can have you out in five seconds," Veronica assured.

"Okay," I said taking another deep breath.

Everyone walked out of the room leaving me lying on the cold table in the darkness. Then, I was slowly sliding into a donut-like machine with an opening smaller than a tanning bed. Good thing claustrophobia wasn't on my short list of mental problems; although, the OCD was in full effect now.

Brain Tumor. Aneurism, Infected Abscess, Hydrocephalus, Spinal Cord Injury, Stroke, Brain Cancer.

The realities I had been pushing off for so many weeks were pouring through the mental floodgates now, threatening to overcome me. These were all of the fears I had displaced with thoughts of how to ruin them. My heartbeat quickened, *thump, thump,* as the table slid into the foreign tube. It looked awfully tight in the little hole, like the sides might be inches from my skin. I wondered if the cushioned parts of the machine suctioned around your body once you were inside, like the device they put around your arm to take your blood pressure.

Thump, thump, thump. I felt the headache starting at my temple and knew I had to stop it or I would not make it through the test. I'd gotten better at warding off the headaches lately by focusing intensely on something else to distract me. My eyes honed in on the machine pulling me into its force field on a gradual, beckoning, conveyor belt. I imagined it might be a space transport system, teleporting me into a different life where my husband and children loved me, and my friends weren't snotty bitches.

The donut on the front reminded me of an image I'd seen recently. What was it? Oh yes, it was Katelyn's diaphragm. The round birth control dome she must be using so she could have unprotected sex with my husband. This spurred a new line of thinking. My heartbeat lightened back to normal, my headache subsiding, as I began to contrive my backup plan. I needed an alternate game plan if this one failed. Every good General had a Plan B. The MRI machine gave me an idea.

I could:

    A. Poke holes in her diaphragm now since I
       knew how to break into her apartment.

Oh, how an unwanted pregnancy could break up a good love affair. Mitchell liked her because she was uncomplicated, young, and vibrant. All of the things unsustainable over any long haul in a relationship. Every shiny ornament faded over time. Everyone grew old. No relationship was free of difficulties. Hopefully, he was figuring out no relationship was perfect.

The *whack whack whack* of the machine broke my delicious planning for a moment. It was really loud. Veronica told me it would be, but it sounded like I had my head pressed up against a wall with someone hammering on the other side. The earplugs made it sound as if I were underwater. I didn't like the feeling of the submerged, banging wall. I fought to refocus on the task at hand. Plan A was wrought with unpleasant consequences for my whole family. My children would have a stepsibling and there was a chance Mitchell could run off to be with his new family. I had to think of some other options.

I could:

      B. Plant nuts in her food, steal her Epi pen and let her meet her bitter anaphylactic end.

Murder seemed extreme. However, I did want to completely get rid of her, so I didn't want to rule it out. I realized because her apartment was in his name, a murder would likely implicate him in the crime, leading us to bankruptcy. The finger might also get pointed back to me and I certainly couldn't go to prison.

Or there was always:

      C. Blackmail

I didn't have a good angle for this one yet. She was so squeaky clean I couldn't find anything on her, but everybody had something to hide.

I spent a lot of time in the tube hatching out each plan and what I could do to end their affair. Nothing seemed to stick the way I would like. None of the options had the genius of every other project I'd taken on. I would figure it out. But I also had to remind myself this was Plan B. Hopefully, I didn't need a Plan B.

It really wasn't fair to them. They were pawns in my game. I could manipulate them to turn left when they wanted to pivot right. I liked the control and the pain I could inflict on them from afar. Maybe I would make them both suffer until one of them gave up; my own little mental torture chamber of fun.

Mitchell didn't want to admit it, but I knew he liked the new me. The one who was making an effort to work and pay back my debt, something I never would've done in the past. The one who cooked his favorite meals and suddenly took interest in his career and his happiness.

The test took the whole eighty minutes. I snapped out of it, nervous, and wondering if it had taken so long because they had found something wrong. Veronica let me know the doctor would be in shortly and to go ahead and get dressed. As soon as I saw Mitchell, I knew he had spoken to Katelyn again. He looked pale and stone-faced. Had she broken up with him because he said he couldn't make it again?

"Well, it wasn't so bad," I said.

"Good, I'm glad," he said curtly.

Once back inside the exam room, I took his clammy, corpse-like hand, feeling his lack of support in his sad grip. His eyes were set blankly on the door. He was biting his lower lip.

"Is something wrong? You look like the one waiting for the bad news," I said.

"No, worried about you, is all."

Worried about me or worried about her?

We were moments away from finding out if I were dying and all he could think about was her. Mitchell was so distracted, squirming around, sweating under his collar, checking his watch and his phone every few minutes. Good ole Dr. Gibbs was taking his time and it was now close to three p.m. If we got out of there that minute, there was no way he could make it into the city, have any kind of quality time with her, and be back for Josie's ballet performance by six o'clock. Josie had gotten the lead role in Sleeping Beauty. Mitchell had planned a daytime birthday rendezvous with the scarlet harlot so he wouldn't miss his daughter's evening performance.

It was three thirty p.m. before Dr. Gibbs made his rounds.

"Well, I have good news Mrs. Laramie. There was no tumor or otherwise alarming results found," he announced.

"Oh, thank God," I whispered.

I let out a big sigh, feeling the pinpricks on my scalp wash away. Mitchell sat there nodding, lips pressed together.

"The bad news is, we don't know why you're passing out. Veronica mentioned you hold your breath when you're nervous. Do you?" Dr. Gibbs asked.

"Sometimes, I do," I answered.

"Have you been under a lot of stress lately?" he asked.

"Well, yes," I responded.

"Can you talk to me about why you do this?" Dr. Gibbs asked.

"My mother passed away recently and her last words to me were hard to hear. Mitchell and I have been fighting over money and a few days ago I started a new part-time job to make up for the money troubles. My kids also are having some issues which are causing me stress as well," I rambled.

Wow. I didn't even realize all of my problems until I spit them out for the doctor. It felt good to get it out. Not to mention the biggest stressor of all—the affair.

"Cece, are you always aware you're holding your breath when you're doing it? I know the question sounds a little silly, but try to think about it," Dr. Gibbs said.

"Downstairs, I had to tell her to breathe, doctor," Mitchell added.

"I guess, sometimes I'm not aware I'm doing it," I admitted.

"Here's my guess. And believe it or not it's not the first I've heard of this. You're having stressed-induced migraines. When you become stressed you hold your breath, sometimes unknowingly, until you make yourself pass out," he said.

"That's crazy," I insisted.

"It makes sense, you almost passed out downstairs," Mitchell argued.

"This is what I'm going to recommend. I'm going to prescribe you migraine medication, a standard triptan. Take it as needed to start. If you find you're having them every day, we'll talk again to discuss a daily regimen," said Dr. Gibbs.

"Sounds good," I said.

"And be more aware of your breathing. When you're having migraines, make a conscious effort to breathe," he said.

"I'm definitely going to pay more attention," I promised.

I was so happy I wasn't dying, if he'd told me I needed to stand on my head twice a day for thirty minutes and sing the national anthem, I would've been ecstatic.

"Now Mitchell, you're going to need to provide a little more of a stress-free environment for Cecelia. Try to keep the fighting to a minimum and for the first week on the meds I would like you to do the majority of the driving. This means all of the grocery shopping, shuttling the kids, only until we can rule out anything else. Just because the MRI didn't pick up anything doesn't mean there isn't something neurologically awry," he said. This was working out way better than I could have anticipated. A doctor-ordered prescription for more time with the family could only spell disaster for anything he had planned with Katelyn in the near future.

"Okay," Mitchell agreed.

Dr. Gibbs did not like Mitchell. He kept twisting his lips at his reactions to his responses. He could tell they weren't genuine. Mitchell looked angry when we got back in the car.

"Well, I'm so happy it was nothing serious. We have time to go to the Thai restaurant and pick up the steamed chicken and vegetables Josie likes. You know she gets nervous and how she won't eat anything if it's not something light. I'll call, what do you want?" I asked.

"Whatever, I don't care," he answered.

I rang the restaurant, placed the order and when I got off the phone Mitchell was biting his lip and clenching his jaw again, like in the diner.

"Something wrong? We just got very good news."

"Are you fucking kidding me, Cece?"

"What?" I asked flabbergasted.

"I sat in a steaming hot doctor's office all damn day, for hours, to find out you've been passing out because you hold your breath! Are you fucking serious?"

Are you fucking serious, Mitchell? You're taking out your frustrations of missing your mistress's birthday on me?

"Now, the migraines are real and he still isn't sure

140

why I'm passing out," I defended.

"He told you why you're passing out. Because you're making yourself pass out," Mitchell said through gritted teeth.

"Well, at least we ruled out anything serious, you should be happy," I said sadly.

"I'm happy as a fucking lark," he griped.

"Did you miss the part where Dr. Gibbs said you needed to provide a stress-free environment for me?"

"Did you miss the part where you work at a coffee shop and we have a very high mortgage to pay and if I don't sell any apartments we don't have a house anymore?"

"You're impossible. Just drive. I don't want to fight before Josie's show, she already gets nervous enough."

"She's the one who needs to see a doctor, not you."

"She refuses to go to the nutritionist."

"How about a psychiatrist? She's obsessed with dancing. Obsessed with being thin. You know she has *it* too, right?"

"Don't say something so stupid."

"She does. She has it too. It's time to realize it."

"Drive, just drive. I'm done talking to you."

It was silent time again. For the rest of the evening—silence.

Chapter 11
My Foiled Plan

One minute I was in a cylindrical tunnel being transported into a fantasyland where I could practically see my old life snapping back together in clean, certain lines, only to be brought back to a harsh reality where my husband was leaving me, shattering my vision, the shards of my carefully drawn out plan coming back to shred me.

She cracked, he cracked, and I really fucking cracked. Disclaimer: Pay attention to this part—I *really* fucking cracked.

All of my research and careful planning backfired. Katelyn didn't leave Mitchell after he missed her birthday date. She gave him an ultimatum instead. It was me or her. Guess which one he chose?

I wouldn't go through the—*Woe is me, how could he do this to me?* I was too old to start over and too proud to go through a public divorce. But I never got the chance to wallow in my self-pity, because he didn't want me back. Most men fought for their families, but he seemed almost relieved to put it out in the open, eager to start over with Little Miss Thing, in all of her ten-years-younger glory. What I was hoping for was a mid-life crisis. What I got was a true love affair.

The lawyer's office was dank and smelled of wetness and mold. It reminded me of the smell of damp laundry left in the washer in the dead of August. An odor my OCD had forced me to experience a few times when I couldn't complete my chores before running the kids to their various summer activities. Of course, the whole time I was driving to their events I would obsess over the uncompleted task, until I could get home, rerun the machine, and be at peace for the morning.

There would be no peace this morning. Mitchell had denied my pleas for marriage counseling. He didn't care when I fake-cried and begged him to give us another chance. He wasn't buying my sob story this time. I even tried to use the kids as a last defense, but that didn't work either. He was done with me. Done with us.

The kids didn't even seem overly affected by our announcement of divorce or the least bit surprised when we told them. They'd seen us fighting for years. Josie looked almost relieved when we told her, and Camdyn just shrugged us off and ran into his room to play video games. I let him play all night long, as Mitchell retreated to the couch for his last night's rest in our home. I laid alone, crying hysterically into my pillow, while animated gunfire pounded through my wall from the next room over. We were a house full of muffled cries and gunshots.

Mitchell packed up everything and left the next morning to officially relocate to his new place in Brooklyn. And he expected me to be okay with it. I was baffled. It felt like such a sneak attack.

"So Cecelia will get the house, and Mitchell will continue to front the expenses for the mortgage. Sign here to agree," the lawyer said.

I stared at the papers in a daze. I'd taken my

migraine medicine in the morning, but it didn't stop the hot pinpricks in my hairline or the monster's unsubtle growls.

"Stop holding your breath and please sign," Mitchell commanded.

I exhaled as I signed the paper, looking at him with disdain. I had lost.

"And by signing this paper, Cecelia gets the white Mercedes, all of the furniture in the home, and other furnishings around the property…" I had stopped listening; watching the slick lawyer's mouth move, but nothing was audible to me.

"Sign here please," I barely heard him say maybe three times before I signed the next paper.

"You've agreed to joint custody with Mitchell. He will receive custody of the children every other weekend," the lawyer said.

"It hardly sounds like *joint custody* to me. It sounds like you're a part-time, weekend dad, shirking all of your parental responsibilities so you can be with your mistress," I said.

"This is the only way it could work. The kids have school. I can't shuttle them from Brooklyn to Montclair every morning," Mitchell reasoned.

"Then why the hell did you buy a place in Brooklyn?" I screamed.

"So I can be close to work and still afford to pay for two mortgages," he said.

"Bullshit. It only benefits you. Don't try to make it sound like it benefits anyone else. It's so you can live the life of a free man with your little twit of a mistress," I argued.

"Her name is Kate, and she's not my mistress,

she's my girlfriend. Get used to it," Mitchell said.

"Oh, fuck you. Her name is Katelyn. You can't even say her real name because it sounds so juvenile, you gave her a grown-up name instead."

"So, we're not signing this paper then on the joint custody? We can do it a different day. These terms sometimes take some, uh, discussions of compromise, which will force you to communicate further," the lawyer said.

"Oh, screw it. He doesn't want to be a father anymore? I'll sign to that. Desert your family, for a dumb, young girl," I insulted.

"Quit talking about her like that. She's going to be in our children's lives for a long time, and you need to be civil for them."

"No, I don't. I don't have to do anything, Mitchell. I can make this transition as hard for you as I'd like. And here's a newsflash for you—she will have expectations for you to meet too. It's not like life is going to be so much better with her, like you think."

"Oh, I think it will be. I'll be able to leave a dish in the sink, my socks on the floor. Hell, I might even be able to put a blue shirt next to a black one in my own closet without getting my head bitten off. I won't have to worry about every little thing I do and say and how it will affect my obsessive-compulsive, bat-shit-crazy wife."

"Well, sorry for keeping a tidy house. Have fun living with the home wrecker who lets you be a complete slob."

I slammed my pen down without signing, sitting with crossed arms, focusing intently across the table at my cheating husband.

"I'm done for today. We can finish this some other time," Mitchell said as he threw his pen across the table and bolted out the door.

"Go on, run away, you're so good at it!" I yelled at his back.

I was a really sore loser. I waited until I was sure he was gone to exit the building. I jolted around the corner of the second floor building, rubbing my temples. Roaring. The monster was roaring in my ear now.

Pest problem.

Little pieces of skull mixed with red hair and blood.

As I was waiting for the elevator, I felt a tap on my shoulder.

"Excuse me," the woman said.

"Oh," I said, as I jumped, much like the reaction I had the first time I'd met her. She seemed to emerge out of nowhere. "Are you following me?" I asked the mysterious blonde woman from Mitchell's holiday party.

"Yes and no," she hissed lowly, hiding behind sunglasses and a head wrap.

"You were at Mitchell's place in Brooklyn, weren't you?" I gasped, remembering her leaning against my car in her sunglasses and the same green scarf she wore now. Everything was such a blur that afternoon, but I remembered those small details now. I backed away from her, nervous of my femme stalker.

"My name is Dinah Petrovic. It seems we have something in common. May I take you to lunch?" she asked in the same thick accent.

"I'm sorry. Do I know you from somewhere other than the party?" I asked, creeping further away from

146

her.

"No, but I know your husband very well," she said.

I looked at her in bewilderment. He couldn't have another mistress. Where would he get the time or the fortitude for that?

"And how do you know my husband, or soon to be ex-husband?" I asked.

"It's a long story. But I know a way for you to make your husband pay for what he's done to you. Lunch?" she asked again. The outside of the divorce attorney's office was the perfect place to hook me with this kind of question. I was intrigued.

"Sure," I said.

"By the way. The brownstone. Next time, use the window in the kitchen. It's always open."

"But how do you…"

"Follow me," she said, cutting me off.

Dinah ironically picked the same crappy diner Mitchell and I had lunched at the previous week. I grimaced at the red vinyl booths and the same elderly woman who had taken my order before my test.

"This place okay?" she asked, sensing my disapproval.

"Yeah, Mitchell and I ate here recently," I said.

"Really? I had coffee here while I was waiting for you to get out of your appointment and noticed Edna was hard of hearing. I didn't want our conversation to be overheard," she said, the "r" in *overheard*, stressed by her accent, making it sound like overherrred.

She was right about the hard of hearing part. I remembered when Mitchell had stepped out for his phone call and I tried to order him a Reuben sandwich. Edna had said, "The Cuban Sandwich?" And I had to repeat my order speaking two octaves louder.

"Where is your accent from if you don't mind me asking?"

"I'm Russian," she said.

Dinah was a beautiful woman, but her overly plump lips, stretched round face, and entirely unwrinkled complexion were the markings of too much plastic surgery. She looked almost too perfect and the definition of the word—fake. I marveled at her high cheekbones, and guessed they came authentically with the package. She was probably my age, but looked much younger.

Dinah was going for the incognito look with her long, bright, blonde hair pulled up in a green kerchief, similar to the getup I had on when I broke into Katelyn's apartment. She took off her sunglasses and overcoat to reveal striking, glass blue eyes and perky, augmented breasts. None of the women in my group of friends looked like her, but she seemed strangely familiar to me.

Edna came over and I ordered a chicken salad and ice water.

"And for you?" I asked Dinah.

"Nothing," she said.

Edna stared at me all twitchy again, the picture of senility with a scratchpad.

"Nothing for her," I said as the old woman continued to bobble her pen with shaky hands.

"Oh. Okay, dear," Edna said with wide eyes.

"I thought you said we were eating lunch?" I asked.

"I'm not much of an eater these days," she answered.

Judging from her wiry, long frame, I had no doubt she was telling the truth. It was still irksome she had invited me to lunch and yet refrained from ordering anything.

"I have a sweet tooth, but I'm watching my figure," she elaborated, drawing out the "r" in *figure* and patting at her ribcage. "Besides, I couldn't ask you to pay for me."

I couldn't imagine the unsmiling foreigner liking anything close to *sweet*.

"Excuse me?" I asked, in regard to paying for her.

"He's cut me off. You'll see. It will happen to you too, along with your well-to-do friends who weren't your friends before you had money," she remarked.

"I'm sorry, how do you know me? And how do you know my husband?"

"Let me ask you a question, first. Did your husband ever mention he had a new partner?" Dinah asked.

"Briefly, yes."

"His new partner is my husband, Nikolay Petrovic," Dinah offered.

"Okay, sounds familiar now when you say the name." It was starting to make sense. Dinah knew I was Mitchell's wife at the Christmas party, because her husband was assigned to become his partner come the New Year. He'd probably pointed us out to Dinah at the party.

"And they are a, what do you call it, buddy, budisky," she said.

"Buddy, buddy. Like good friends? It's odd because he wasn't too thrilled about splitting his listings and his territory with someone else. Splitting territories means splitting money, and Mitchell's not a fan of sharing his money with someone else, believe me," I howled.

"Well, the reason why I'm here is so we don't have to split our husband's hard earned money with anyone else," she said, arching her eyebrow. Her forehead didn't wrinkle a bit. It was like she was made of clay.

"Huh?" I asked.

My food arrived, and Dinah gestured for me to eat. I dug into my salad, while Dinah went on. She was going too slow for me. She was the type of person who needed a long build-up before she could get to the story, like she was aiming for a dramatic telling. Or she was just foreign and it was her way of explaining things. Either way, she was making me anxious.

"Mitchell didn't like my Nikolay, until he realized my very charming and talented husband could bring in a whole different set of clientele and make them both loads of money on properties, which had not sold in months."

"Okay," I said impatiently.

"You have somewhere you need to be?" she snapped.

"No," I answered, suddenly scared of the intense woman.

"You see, your husband and my husband have something in common. They have both decided to leave us for younger women. Nikolay's mistress is ze' owner of a catering company they used for one of their open houses. Her name is Lucy. Some little brown-haired girl with what do you call it, space in front teeth," Dinah said with disgust.

"Gapped teeth. I'm sorry," I said.

"Don't be sorry yet. I haven't signed all of the

divorce papers. Once you sign those things, it's over."

"And what do you plan to do?" I asked.

"You mean what do we plan to do?" Dinah said, raising her barely-there eyebrows at me.

"Excuse me?"

"Cecelia, what drives your husband? What would you have to take away to ruin him and make these little tramps lose interest?" she asked.

"Tell me what you're trying to say," I said finally.

"Money, Cecelia. Their life's work. All of the pride is wrapped up in their big sales," Dinah explained.

"Okay, and you think we can take their self-importance away from them?"

"With this, we can," she said as she pulled out her cell phone.

Dinah showed me an application on her smartphone with a little plastic device sitting next to it.

"And what is it?"

"It's a Supra Key application. I can get into any of their listings with this," she said.

"I'm still not understanding. What is it you want us to do, Dinah?"

"We sabotage their professional lives. He is rich hero to his mistress. You lose the money, put financial stress on the dream life he's promised, he loses the girl. He becomes loser. Nobody wants to be with a loser. If there's no girl, there's no reason for a divorce. If there's no reason for divorce, we don't have to split their money," Dinah claimed.

"But, then I'd still be stuck with him?" I pondered.

"For a little while, but then you won't have to split your kids with her either," Dinah said with disgust.

Images flashed of Josie and Camdyn frolicking on

the beach with Mitchell and Katelyn. I thought I might be sick.

"My kids. I almost signed a custody paper today saying I'd share them, and to think…" I quivered.

"Well, then looks like I got to you in time. Whatever you do, do not sign a custody agreement."

"But, I have to for the divorce."

"Shh, you need to sit back and listen," she demanded.

Who was this strange Russian woman shhshing me?

"Go on," I said.

The thought of giving up the kids, even for a weekend, had been the hardest part of this entire ordeal. I'd never thought he'd actually leave me for her, so it didn't niggle at me too badly, but when I found out I had lost, it'd done something very bad to my soul. If he was going to shame me and take them away, I wished him dead. I really did. They were everything to me. She was not fit to raise my kids. She was a child herself.

"For me it's about destroying him, keeping his money and getting my friends back," Dinah revealed.

"It looks like we do have a lot of things in common. And, you're right. Mitchell would be lost without his career. A broken man. He thrives on success." My wheels were turning.

"Of course, he does. Imagine what failure would do to a man like him?"

"Yes," I licked my lips at the thought of Mitchell and failure. How unattractive it might make him look to Katelyn. "Thank God, I still have my friends," I gushed.

Dinah smirked at me and raised her eyebrows as if

she didn't believe me.

"What do we do next?" I asked, sucked into Dinah's wicked little fantasy. It was nice to have someone to conspire with for a change.

"I have ideas. But I will let you think about it. I will meet you here a week from today, next Thursday, same time? I'm not giving you my cell phone or email. I don't want us to be placed together if ze' shit hits the fannie," she said.

"You mean, the shit hits the fan," I said.

"Right. Whatever. Well, I will be here next week. If you show up, I'll assume you're in," she stated.

Chapter 12
Back to Work

"So, I decided you should definitely fuck me to get back at him. It's only right, Cece. An eye for an eye. A penis for a vagina," Sam said.

"Please don't sexually harass me at work. I have enough stress." I sighed.

"You know I'm kidding."

"No you're not."

"You're right, I'm not," he said laughing, "But I will let you come to your own conclusion."

"You're going to be waiting a long time."

"I'm very patient. I once waited two days in the rain for tickets to a Phish concert. It was so worth it. I'll wait. You'll come to me when you're ready," he said, snapping his towel at my butt.

"Sam," I tried to yell, but ended up giggling instead. He looked very much the dirty hippie part today, with his long, unwashed hair tucked behind his ear and tie-dyed t-shirt peeking out beneath his green apron. As I pivoted around the baked goods to avoid a towel flogging, I caught an intoxicating waft of patchouli and blueberry scones. Sam's five o'clock shadow and budding goatee combined with his a-little-too-slick brown hair gave him the hot grunge appeal of someone who might be fun to sleep with once, but never twice.

"Oh and hey, I wanted to tell you I found a blow-up doll we can throw into the mix and have a little fun with, what do you think?" he asked, raising his eyebrows with a suggestive little smile on his face.

"Sam. You're sick," I yelled.

"It's a joke. I'm trying to cheer you up. You're so bummed. He was a bum. Really, never liked the guy," Sam said.

"Really? Couldn't tell."

"Hey, the girls were here over the weekend, sat outside. I was surprised not to see you."

"You're kidding? What day?" I asked.

"Saturday."

"Well, I wonder why they didn't call me."

"Because they're bitches," he responded.

"Sam, they're my friends," I said.

"Yeah, they find out their girlfriend's husband is cheating on her and they don't invite you out for coffee. Huh, great friends," he argued.

Thoughts of Bootsy dragging her feet to the mailbox returned, her pajama pants getting caught on the undersides of her shoes as she slugged along. I let Sam's words ruminate like the scents of mocha and vanilla all around me. It was happening. I'd been shamed.

****

After work I drove to Maeve's house. As she opened the door, her beautiful face puckered as if she were expecting a delivery of roses and got handed a pile of poo instead.

"Hi Maeve, can I come inside?" I asked solemnly.

"Oh Dear, this isn't a good time. I was just putting supper on," she said.

155

"Cooking anything good?" I asked.

"I'm afraid I've only bought enough salmon for the five of us."

"Oh no, I wasn't inviting myself, simply asking what you were having," I said awkwardly.

"Salmon," she said again.

"Right, I heard you the first time."

"Yes, well, perhaps we can catch up another time?"

"Perhaps," I said, as I made way down her elaborate, paver stone driveway.

I stopped at Robin's next. Chaos met me at the front door. At least three of her five children were screaming. She held one of her wailing baby girls as her toddler boy clung to her leg. Robin's friendly face twisted into a disapproving scowl.

"A little crazy here," she yelled over her brood.

"Who is it?" I heard Marcus bellow.

"It's Cece," she yelled back, "Can you please give Ava her pink eye medication before they all get it!" she screamed.

Robin turned her head to see if he heard her.

"That's not Ava, that's Aubrey!" Robin screamed.

"Dammit," I heard him mutter.

"What is it, Cece?" she asked.

"I came from *The Coffee Bean* and Sam had mentioned all of you girls were there on Saturday and I wondered why no one called me," I said.

"Oh, well," she said, sighing. "Look, we're all busy and you have your personal things you need to deal with and we didn't want to impose," she claimed.

"Impose? Well, don't you think a woman going through a divorce might need a coffee chat more than ever?" I asked, red-faced.

"Look, I hate to cut you short, but we're trying to get packed up so we can leave for a long weekend and go to Marcus's parents for my nephew's Bar Mitzvah. As you can see our exit strategy is not going well. We'll chat soon, okay? I'm sorry for everything going on right now," she said.

"Okay. Didn't mean to bother you. Good luck getting on the road," I said.

My scalp felt hot as I got back into the car. I popped some medication before the migraine could get me, but the pills didn't seem to be working lately. I wouldn't try to venture over to Julie or Callie's house. I couldn't take any more rejection. My worst fears were coming true.

****

I woke up in Manhattan at midnight, blinking my eyes three times to make sure I wasn't dreaming. Nope, clock said four minutes after twelve and I was definitely in Manhattan. It would go on record as my longest blackout ever. I saw the parking tickets piled under my windshield wipers. I grabbed the damp pieces of paper totaling around five-hundred dollars.

Shit, I would have to work a lot more shifts at The Coffee Bean to pay those back. Oh shit, the kids!

I looked at my cell phone and there were twenty missed messages. Five from my children, ten from Mitchell, a few from my sister, a couple from Maeve, and one from Sam. I called Mitchell first, knowing he would be livid. He picked up on the first ring.

"Cece, what the hell. Where are you?"

"I blacked out again. I woke up in Manhattan. I'm sorry, on my way back now," I said.

I heard Josie in the background ask if I was all

157

right.

"You're at the house?" I asked.

"Of course, who'd yeah think was going to take care of the children while you were taking your nap or whatever other harebrained scheme you're trying to lure me back," he accused.

"Mitchell, this wasn't intentional. Do you really think I would endanger our children?"

"Who knows how far you would go at this point, Cece."

"Get over yourself. I'll be there in a few minutes."

"Great, I would like to get a few hours of sleep before I have to get up for work tomorrow," Mitchell griped.

"You mean you aren't staying? Who's going to drive them to school? You know they will pitch a fit if they have to ride the bus," I said.

"Nooo bus," I heard Josie wail.

"They'll survive. I see what you're trying to do here, Cece. No, I'm not going to stay the night, you conniving, relentless woman," he snapped.

"Nooo bus," Josie screamed.

"Don't talk about me like that in front of them. I'll be home soon," I said, my thoughts a foggy jumble.

Mitchell was in his car the moment he saw me pulling in. He didn't offer to exchange a single word with me and refused to roll down his window when I tapped on it. He sped out of the driveway. He was convinced I was plotting to get him back, but I wasn't. The cat was out of the bag. The only thing worse than someone's knowledge of infidelity in a marriage was the reaction they had when you took the cheater back.

"Oh, she must not have been able to afford living

on her own without him. Poor girl had to take him back."

"It was for the kids I'm sure, but how can she sleep next to him at night?"

"I wonder if he'll just turn around and do it again."

These were the catty words spoken by my friends in regard to Ginnifer McIntyre. The smiling-even-in-the-rain-after-just-leaving-the-salon little blonde who'd had to bail her husband out of TSA-jail after he'd fallen ass-out of the airplane bathroom while trying to join the mile-high club—with someone other than her.

Ginnifer with a large smiling "G" had stuck by her husband citing God and their kids and every other excuse people used to mend their picket fences. The McIntyres still fluxed in and out of our social circle, but she'd been shamed for sure. And so had he; white ass hanging out of a plane, trying to screw in the most detestable and unclean place on earth. Or above earth, rather. Thrusting in and out while other people's shit dust swarmed all around them—disgusting. I'd rather fuck on a park bench.

The idea of taking Mitchell back at this point made my stomach twist. He was out of my life, yet the demon who had taken permanent residence in my mind hadn't stopped roaring for revenge, making my thoughts harder and harder to reign in. I wasn't sure if Dinah's little plan to destroy their business would be enough to appease my vengeance.

Annihilation and dirty linens.

Muddy boots and empty ice cream bowls.

Sometimes the thoughts were totally unrelated and I'd find myself sitting somewhere just mumbling them out loud. It was my broken mind coping, but the mechanism it used was frightening and uncontrollable.

The other day I'd wondered what it might have smelled like after I'd smashed Katelyn's skull in with a fire extinguisher. The spy novels I'd read always characterized blood as having a metallic taste to it. Would the smell of Katelyn's blood be like a tarnished, sweaty penny? For some reason I couldn't get the missed opportunity out of my head. How different would things have been if I'd connected the metal fire extinguisher to her head when I'd had the chance?

I didn't want there to be a need to inflict pain on them. He was the father of my children. And she was probably a nice girl, though a stupid, simple one. However, if stupid and simple were a means for death, half the population would be wiped clean. But, the dark, cold, grimy part of my subconscious begged for something more; its claws getting sharper and hungrier with each passing day, screaming for affliction. If I could give it what it wanted, I knew it would stop and leave me in peace.

Annihilation and dirty linens.

The satisfying proposition of killing them in their bed made me smile. To end them where they began. The thoughts ran their course on their own, and of course, it concerned me, but I'd assumed it must've been the coping mechanism for lots of wronged women.

Maybe, I'd ask Bootsy to lunch and commiserate. "So Anita, did you ever wonder what the mistress's blood might've smelled like after your husband cheated on you?"

Asking such a definitive question might not be the

best way to broach a new friendship. And I didn't have to resort to socializing with Anita yet. My friends just needed time to digest the news and realize they still loved me, for me, and not for the circle completing us. I had to be worth more to them than the sum of the events we'd spent together.

This migraine business was serious though. This last blackout had been the longest. It had been a very stressful day and I hoped the following ones would be better. Lately, I felt there were more times I was blacked out than awake. There was no time to return to the doctor. Besides, I had a new plan to hatch and a partner to carry it out with this time. For my new battle plan, I would man up and join forces.

Chapter 13
Hand Grenades

"So who is she?" Natalie asked.

"Who, Strawberry Twatcake? Mitchell is leaving me for his ten years younger assistant. How cliché is that?" I asked.

"Very. And I know you like to give her these little nicknames, Cece, but let's start with her real name, which is?" my sister asked.

"You mean, Little Red Riding My Husband's Manhood," I said.

Dominic let out a rip of a laugh.

"Oh, for God's sake. What's her name, so I know who I'm trash-talking?" Natalie asked again.

"Just call her The Freckled Firesnatch, and we'll all know who you're talking about," I insisted.

My sister pursed her lips, shook her head and waited, while Dominic snorted in amusement.

"It's Katelyn McCallister," I said.

"Katelyn?" my sister asked.

"Yeah, you know her or something?" I asked nervously.

"No, it's her name. Addison has a little girl in her class named Caitlyn," Natalie said.

"I know, right? Even her name is immature. No one from our generation has that name. He calls her Kate to make her sound more grown up, but she looks like a baby. It's sick, really," I said.

"Well, did he give you a reason why?" Natalie asked.

"Different pussy," my brother answered.

My sister and I both turned up our noses, not understanding how we were related to the uncouth, crude, grown man before us. You would never know Dominic was raised in a strict household where both parents expected nothing but the best, because he was the worst.

He was a colicky infant. He broke every bone in his body as a child, acting as his own stuntman; jumping from roofs, climbing trees, sneaking out of his bedroom as early as age seven. Not to mention the trouble in school—the detentions, suspensions, and finally expulsion. My parents placed Dominic in a private school his senior year so he could earn his high school diploma. And then there was the neighbor's cat that went missing one summer. We never did find out what happened to it, but Dominic always hated that cat.

My brother could find trouble at the bottom of a garbage can if he dug far enough. He was drawn to it. Dominic was also drawn to violence. He was expelled from high school for breaking a kid's nose in a very bloody school fight. The assaulted boy was foolish enough to steal Dominic's new stereo system out of his car. Back in the day, my brother's stereo system was his prized possession, but the only music the kid could hear after Dom was done with him was the whistling of air through his broken nose when he tried to breathe. You didn't mess with Dom's Motley Crue.

Full Metal Jacket was his favorite movie and *shoot em up* video games were always a favorite. Before there was *Call of Duty* there was *Mortal Kombat* and before it there was *Contra*. Dom had a special place in his heart for things that went boom. It was no surprise when he enrolled in the army straight out of high school. And for once, my father was actually pleased with him, thinking it would give him some discipline. Our father and grandfather had been veterans, so it seemed fitting. After years of being bent over my father's knee and lashed more times with his leather belt than any of us cared to remember, Dom had decided to do something to make his old man proud.

Until he was honorably discharged a few years later for things he refused to talk about. Or as my father put it, *dishonorably discharged.* He'd worked a number of security guard positions since then, trading weapons and military collectibles for money as often as he went through fast women with daddy issues.

"Dom, Gross. I think there's more to it than sex," I said.

He threw up his hands in defense, all fidgety, surely coming down from a high. He took both hands, placing them behind his buzz cut, and cocked a knowing smile at me.

"Really, Dom, they were married for fifteen years. Something you would know nothing about. There's a lot more to it than you know," Natalie defended, whipping her dark brown hair side to side in disapproval.

"Less than you pretty ladies think," he insisted.

"Oh Dom, you know nothing about marriage and even less about women," I argued.

"And you two knuckleheads know nothing about men. Listen, when your husbands are free of you, they *are* thinking about sex with other women. And, I hate to tell you this, but about fifty percent of the time when they are with you, they are also thinking about sex with other women," he proclaimed.

"You're full of shit," Natalie protested.

"Really, do some research on how many times a day a man thinks about sex. I know you both think I'm a dummy, but I'm actually really fucking smart. I've made some bad decisions in my life, but I'm not stupid. I read, ladies. I watch the news, ladies. A study from a little known source you may have heard of, called CNN, reported men think about sex nineteen times a day. Now, I want you to ask yourself and think about this based on your current sex lives. Do you really think they're fantasizing about you all nineteen times, every single day?

"Exactly."

"Which leads me to my first point, which is—different pussy. If you throw a juicy, red, steak in front of a tiger who's been eating old meat for the last ten years, and you give him the choice between the juicy steak and the old meat, which do you think he's going to choose?"

"Are you saying we're old meat?" Natalie asked.

"Yeah, you broads are old meat. Sorry, love yeah, but you're no spring chickens."

"You're such an asshole," I said.

"And I hate when women need to know why. Oh why me, why did he do this, why why why? Who the fuck cares. He did it. Why do you always need a motive? And the answer most of the time is simply because he could, but they'll never say that. Opportunity knocked and he opened the door and said, fuck yes, I'm sick of this wrinkled, old—" he started.

"Okay, okay. We get it Dom," Natalie said.

"But, I'm sorry, Cece. I was really happy for you. You girls are my heart. And now, I'm really pissed," he raged.

Dominic's coked-up, wide dark eyes looked lethal all of a sudden. I didn't know what happened to him during his deployment in Desert Storm. All I knew, was he was *Mischievous Dom* when he left and *Frightening Dom* when he came back.

"It's okay, Dom. Some of it's probably my fault for spending too much money and not appreciating him enough. What's the quote about appreciating men, *Treat your good man right, or a real woman will*," I conceded.

"Oh, bullshit Cece. You're an awesome mother and a good wife. Don't let the son-of-a bitch put this back on you or make you feel guilty." Dom raged.

"He's right Cece. He's the jerk here, not you. Don't beat yourself up," Natalie said.

"He's got you all mind-fucked into believing this was your fault. All cheaters do the same thing. Don't fall into the trap. Women love to abuse themselves. Fucking love it. Listen, you're a product of your own environment. He bought the house in that neighborhood with those people. You were going along with what everybody else was doing."

All of what he said was true. Maybe my brother wasn't a homicidal cokehead after all.

"True," Natalie chimed in.

"I'm going to kill the bastard. I didn't know he tried to turn it around on you, probably trying to turn your kids too," Dom said.

"Take it easy, Dom," I said.

"Cece, he needs to pay. I can do it quick and easy, bang, pow, motherfucker." Dom screamed. The proposition was tempting, but how would his death really benefit me? His life insurance policy, I supposed, but it wasn't exactly the route I wanted to go yet. Leaving my children fatherless was an abominable concept. And knowing the bastard, he'd probably taken my name off the policy already.

Dom wasn't looking at us anymore. He was blinking too fast, his eyes floating all around, tongue pressed to the side of his cheek. For the fist time ever I thought I identified with the bloodlust curdling on his lips.

"Dom. Dom. Snap out of it. He's the father of my children, I can't have him killed," I said.

We drew unwanted attention from the patrons at the little café in the more working class Connecticut suburb we grew up in.

"Oh shit," I said, as I put my hand over my face.

"Well, listen here. I could rough him up a little bit so he knows his place," Dom whispered.

"There will be no roughing up. No one is getting hurt," I whispered back.

"Have it your way," he said, rubbing his nose and watering eyes, then taking his whole palm and massaging the front of his face.

Natalie shook her head.

"Let's get these papers signed, so we can collect our pittance from mother's estate and be on our way," I said.

"Yous don't enjoy my company?" Dom asked with a hearty laugh.

"Once a year is okay, twice is pushing it," Natalie joked.

"Not trying to be short. I've just had my fill of lawyers' offices this year," I complained.

They both gave me a sympathetic frown. We signed the paperwork and I thought of how different my life might have turned out if Mitchell and I would have settled in this neighborhood like my sister had. I'd have a whole different set of friends and might still be married. Our neighborhoods were less than an hour away from each other, but I might as well have lived in a different country. I couldn't live there, though. I didn't want to be haunted by the ghosts who chased me from my childhood; didn't want to be reminded of the glass bubble of my past.

Dom lived somewhere in the city. He was always moving around for various reasons, usually related to a job change because he screwed up the last one. I never knew how he always got gigs or who would hire him, especially positions involving protecting others and carrying a firearm, but he always managed to find employment.

"Well, this should pay last month's overdue rent and this month's. I think I will take the rest of the month off," Dom said, laughing.

"Why, are you late on rent? Out of work again?" Natalie asked.

"No, but I met a stripper who changed my life, until she took all my money," he said, laughing again.

"You're going to have to grow up sometime, Dom," I said.

"Says who? Look what good it did you," he said.

"So you're employed?" Natalie asked again.

"At the moment, yes. But my real money has been in hand grenades lately. I can ship those fuckers and not worry about it. Couldn't do the same with guns. Grenades don't reap as much money as guns, but I don't have to meet with the screwballs in person, and there's a real market for them. I can get like two to three hundred dollars a pop, and more if they still have the pin in them."

"You can't ship live grenades." I yelled.

Again, the tables around us were leering with alarm.

"Shit," I whispered again.

Natalie and Dominic found it comical, pointing at me, doing a little crazy swirl with their fingers around their temples.

"Stop it, you two."

"Sure I can. They don't know what's in those boxes and they make it through their screeners, never had a problem," Dom said.

"Dom, what if one would go off? Wouldn't you feel bad if you killed all those people?" I asked.

"I package them real good, Cece. Lots of padding and paper," he said matter-of-factly.

"Dom, these aren't picture frames, they're grenades," I explained.

"I know what they are. Ex-Army," he whispered, mocking me, and pointing at him.

"Well, can you tell me in advance if you're going to be shipping any to my zip code, so I can get out in time," Natalie joked.

"Certainly. And, I don't get live ones very often, so chill. Cece, your son seems to be real into them. Actually, he's interested in my entire inventory. You might have a fourth line military brat on your hands," Dom said.

"Whatever keeps him engaged in the real world is good, I guess," I reasoned.

"All right. Papers signed. Meeting's adjourned. It's been so lovely speaking to you gorgeous women. And Cece, let me know if you change your mind about, yeah know," Dom said, shooting his eyebrows in my direction.

"Oh Dom, stay out of trouble, will ya," I said, as we all got up to leave. Dom threw some money on the table for a tip. A penny rolled out of his wallet, spun around and landed heads up on the twenty-dollar bill. I took a whiff of air and thought it smelled like blood.

****

Sam asked me to come in Saturday night. He said he wasn't feeling well, but didn't trust any of his other part-timers to handle the money and close up shop. I wanted to tell him I was far sicker than he was and the last person he should trust with money, but I said okay, praying a blackout wouldn't occur again tonight. I'd spent most of Friday in a fog, fading in and out, finding myself curled up naked in my bathrobe in my bed at midnight, not knowing how I got there. Most of the day was a complete blur too. I checked the dishwasher before I went to bed to make sure the kids had been fed. They had, but the dishes were still dirty in the machine. Like my laundry, I always ran them and put them away before I went to bed. I needed to go back to see Dr. Gibbs.

It was a slow night at *The Coffee Bean* until Julie and Callie entered in a rush. They wore far too serious expressions to be meandering in for a latte.

"Hi ladies," I said.

Neither one of them had cared to call when they heard about my divorce, so I wasn't overly concerned about whatever was bothering them.

"Two skim lattes, please. Cece, did you hear about Robin?" Julie asked.

"What about her?" I asked.

"Her house was broken into," Callie whispered.

I dropped the cup on my hand, scalding myself. *Shit.*

"What? Is everyone okay?" I asked.

"They were out of town for something," Julie said.

"Oh yeah, her nephew's Bar Mitzah. She told me they were going to Marcus's parents' house. Do you know where he's from?"

"Long Island. A neighbor reported the door being left hanging wide open and knew they were out of town. Robin rushed home to find five hundred thousand dollars in jewels missing. Some of the things were her mother's. She's very upset. They didn't make it into the safe. Apparently the jewelry in there is worth close to a million. They tried though. There were crowbar marks all along the safe, but they couldn't break in," Julie said, tears in her eyes.

"*Holy shit.*" I whisper-screamed.

"Yeah, I didn't even know she was leaving. I called this morning to see if she wanted to go shopping with us and she told me," Callie said.

Oh, another girl's outing I wasn't invited to. Thanks for the support, bitches.

"Well, that's awful. I have a question, though. Why in the hell would a burglar leave the front door open?" I asked.

"Maybe he got spooked? It was odd. They don't know. And the security cameras were disarmed, which is scary. So they have no video. The cameras were operated from Marcus's office," she said.

"Oh yeah, in that box which controlled the whole house," I said, remembering the enormous canopy of wires and asking Robin what it was, fearing one of her tribe might get tangled in it.

"The police don't know how they found it," Julie said.

"Thieves are smart, they were probably casing the joint for months," Callie added.

"Casing it from the inside?" Julie asked all snarky.

"Whatever," Callie said, brushing off her big sister.

"Does she need anything? Are they okay?" I asked.

"She's really upset. There were a lot of family heirlooms, which can't be replaced, but other than that she said she's fine. I will keep you posted. We wanted to let you know," Julie said.

"And sorry about Mitchell," Callie added.

"Thanks. It is what it is," I said as flippantly as she had said her peace.

They obviously didn't care or they would have called.

"So where is Half-Baked anyway? Out back dancing with Mary Jane?" Julie asked.

"He called off sick, left me to man the station," I said.

"Ugh, well I hope your shift goes fast," Julie grimaced.

"Thanks, and please let me know if they catch the guy."

"Will do," Julie said as they left.

Chapter 14
Off With Their Heads

Little ladies strewn all over my ivory castle in a mess of nude flesh. Blondes and brunettes beheaded, beautiful dresses ripped to shreds, scattered body parts like a war village hate crime. Their preserved bodies ripped out of their boxes, limbs torn off. Perfectly curled hair ripped from crystal tiaras. Years of collecting—gone. My private museum smashed to pieces. They didn't take all of them, only the ones worth the most money. And yes, the number one Minsk doll was among the stolen. There were a few left in their boxes, but the majority were disembodied, their cases damaged to the point of worthlessness. My heart squeezed in my chest. How could someone do this? Why would someone do this to me?

I fell to the floor in my bathrobe sobbing.

"No, No, No." I shouted.

Josie was staying overnight at her friend's house this weekend. She had been spending a lot of time away from home lately. I heard Camdyn fling open the door, but I couldn't look at him. I couldn't take my eyes off the devastation.

"Mom, what is this?" asked Camdyn.

"Were you home all night?" I asked through tears.

"Yes."

"Well, how did this happen?" I asked.

"I don't know. I've been playing video games. I had the volume up full blast," Camdyn said.

"I came home from work at nine-thirty, had a pounding headache, took a shower and went to bed, Camdyn. How did this happen?"

"Mom, I don't know," he said honestly.

"How long have you been in your room playing?"

"Since after dinner," he said.

"You've been playing video games for six hours straight?"

"Yeah, you were at work, so I figured why not."

"Who did this?"

"Mom, we need to call the police," he said, "He could still be here."

"Who?" I asked.

"Mom, someone came into our house and did this."

"How?" I asked.

Camdyn called the police while I sat in a stupefied heap on the floor and allowed my twelve-year old take control of the situation.

"Get dressed Mom, they're coming over," he said.

I went into my room and threw on some clothes. For some reason after showering I had been going to bed naked in my bathrobe. It was a new habit among many others I had recently developed. When the police arrived, they found a point of forced entry through our patio where someone had jimmied open the door. There were gouge-like scrapes around the lock, like someone had worked at it awhile before it gave way.

I suddenly remembered the part of Julie's story where someone had tried to pry Robin's safe open with a crowbar and offered that information to the police. They were well aware of Robin's case and were perplexed by this one.

Two male officers came to the house and didn't try to hide their amusement at the fact I was calling in regard to stolen dolls. They were smug, young cops in their late twenties. Officer Marlow had an austere build, top heavy, with short, brown buzzed hair like my brother. He wore a permanent smirk and didn't try to hide his sideways glances of bafflement to his partner. Officer Guiterez was a kinder, small Latino fellow with a soothing voice.

"So you're saying someone broke into your house while your son was playing video games and you were sleeping to steal baby dolls?" Officer Marlow asked.

"They're not baby dolls. They're collector dolls. Beautiful, expensive, collector dolls," I answered.

"Sorry, collector dolls. And no one heard anything?" he asked.

"I heard some banging around in there, but I thought it was mom, home from work. She cleans a lot and I thought she was doing what she usually does," Camdyn said.

"You're saying these dolls were collectibles, worth some money?" Officer Guiterez asked.

"Yes, I'd been collecting them since I was a child. It's a real loss for me," I said, breaking into sobs.

Officer Marlow held one eyebrow arched in disbelief. I wanted to smack the arrogance off his face. I thought of my last social tragedy at Maeve's party and realized these officers probably saw far worse devastation than this, so I held my tongue. Officer Guiterez was more sympathetic, but I could tell they would both have a good laugh about this one after they left.

"I'm sorry about your lost items, ma'am. It's always hard when it's something you can't replace like a family heirloom or a keepsake," Officer Guiterez offered.

"Thanks, so what can you do to catch who did this? I think it's related to Robin's break-in. They were only a couple of days apart and we don't get home invasions around here. It has to be the same guy," I insisted.

"Mrs. Laramie, how much would you estimate the total dollar amount of the missing dolls?" Officer Marlow asked.

"Oh, wow. Probably, at least $30,000, maybe more."

"It doesn't add up Mrs. Laramie," Officer Marlow said.

"Excuse me?" I asked.

"The Bernstein's had half a million in jewels taken. If this thief was interested in a big type of score, why would he want to go to your house for this much smaller amount?"

"Drug addicts will do anything for money," I responded.

"Drug addicts could live off the Bernstein's jewelry collection for years. And, jewels are easier to trade for money than dolls, which would have to most likely be posted online to sell. Something I suggest you be on the lookout for in the coming months. The typical mentality of a drug addict is more living day to day and they aren't usually much for saving up for the future, so I don't see how your theory is plausible. If they were after money, a jewelry heist should have been enough and the dolls would be small potatoes to them," he explained.

I thought of Dominic. This was true. He lived day to day, like when he said, *"I don't need to work the rest of the month now,"* after we received mom's small inheritance.

"What about the crowbar?" I asked.

"Lots of thieves use crowbars, and by the sorry state of your door they could've used anything really," Officer Marlow argued.

"Well, then who do you think did this?" I asked, frustrated.

"I'm thinking this is a personal attack and it's someone who knows this would really hurt you," Officer Marlow said.

"Why?" I asked.

"A couple of reasons. I know you aren't able to process this right now because you're upset, but how many roughneck thieves do you think have any clue as to the value of one rare doll over another?" he asked.

"Not too many," I answered.

"I would venture none. So, then, how would they know which ones were worth a lot of money and which ones to leave?" he asked.

"They could have done online research? I also had them arranged in my glass case according to their appraised value. My highest priced dolls were on the top shelf and those were all taken. They probably could've figured it out," I reasoned.

"Possibly, but unlikely. I still think this has to be personal. The person who did this was sending you a very clear message by not only stealing your prized possessions, but also vandalizing some in a rather heinous manner. To me, this is someone trying to threaten you. I would advise you to take caution for a little while until we figure out who did this. You might see our cruiser a lot in the coming months doing drive-byes as well, to check in on you. Do you have a security system in the house, Mrs. Laramie?" Officer Marlow asked.

"No," I said.

"I would probably get one," he said.

"Ma'am, is there anyone you know who would wish you harm right now, preferably female, since this doesn't feel like it has male written all over it to me," Officer Guiterez said.

"Now what makes you think it wasn't a man?" I asked, getting even antsier.

"Assaulting the dolls feels like a female vengeance thing to me, but my gut feeling is totally based on a hunch, not anything else," Officer Guiterez said.

"Well, my husband and I are going through a divorce, and he has a mistress, but she and I really haven't been in contact and there hasn't been any type of exchange between us," I said.

"I'd like to question her. Do you have her address?" Officer Guiterez asked.

"Sure," I said as I gave it to him.

They swept the room for fingerprints, but came up empty. Officer Marlow determined they must have used gloves, as the only fingerprints on the dolls were my own. They questioned Katelyn the next day. She had an alibi; although it was that she was with Mitchell all night, which made me leery. At the same time, I couldn't imagine the innocent twit having the nerve to do something like this, especially while I was home.

I phoned the girls, but no one picked up. I left voicemails for all of them letting them know the

Montclair burglar had victimized me, as well. I expected a phone call back from each and every one of them, but no one called. I'd lost my husband, my friends, and my dolls all in one week. There was nothing left for me to lose. Dinah was right. And right then, slouched over in the doorway of my broken room, in the aftermath of my obliterated house of dolls, was the moment I decided I would join her.

****

The mysterious Russian woman was there at noon on Thursday, waiting for me in the red vinyl booth with her blonde hair pulled back in the same green scarf and oversized black sunglasses. Edna approached the table and looked at us like she had never seen us before, blank stare fixed straight ahead with her stick pen pressed to her ancient guest checks.

Dinah's European fashion trends were already rubbing off on me. Female friendships often had a sharing effect, as I'd find statement pieces of theirs I'd like and mimic accordingly. I'd purchased my own collection of thick-fibered, decorative scarves, which hung like a beckoning rainbow in my side of the closet, assorted by bold color in ROY-G-BIV order. I was hoping she'd notice my bright Kelly green one today, similar to hers, but this hard lady wouldn't comment on such a trivial matter.

"Chicken salad and iced water. Chocolate cake for her," I said, pointing to my new friend. Dinah snarled at me. It was supposed to be a gesture of goodwill since I'd decided to join her vigilante cause, and because she'd told me she was broke. I guess she didn't see it that way.

Edna walked away, her face twitching a little as

she sized me up over her shoulder. Or twitching, because it's what elderly people do sometimes.

"So, I take it you're here because you've decided to take control of your future," she said. (Future came out like—*Fuchere.*) She unwrapped the scarf from her head and slammed it on the table.

"I've come here because I hate the bastard for taking everything away from me and because I have nothing left to lose," I announced, throwing my hands up in defeat, and following her lead by ineffectively thumping my own head wrap down on the table. Dinah wrinkled her nose in disapproval at my pathetic attempt to imitate her.

"So your friends have turned, have they?"

"Um yeah, they did. I didn't think they would, but it did happen with them. Like with Bootsy." I sighed.

"Who's Boots?"

"Never mind. It's one of my old friends. I can't believe the other girls turned on me."

"You don't fit anymore. It's an inconvenience to have you around now."

"That's a horrible thing to say."

"It's true. You were part of a group, like a club. Say you're part of a bicycle club, but you decide you don't want to bike anymore? The thing which bound you to the group of people is now gone and they no longer feel obligated to associate with you. Your common bond is broken, and now, as they try to find a place for you as a walker, while everyone else is biking, you're just an inconvenience. You slow everyone else down," she explained.

"But I want to bike. He took my bicycle away," I whined.

"And now you have to get it back. But in the meantime, the only people who are going to be your friends are the other walkers," she said, pointing to herself. "And, unfortunately, your kids suffer as they can't bike with the other bikers' children either."

It saddened me.

Dinah was totally right.

It wasn't unusual for Camdyn to be anti-social, but Josie hadn't gotten a single phone call from any of her neighborhood friends since we'd announced our divorce. She was suffering so much already. She didn't need us to perpetuate her problems by making her an outcast.

I'd made several appointments for her to see a dietician, but we never made it there. She gave me every excuse in the book.

"I'm exhausted from dance, you're going to have to reschedule."

"There's nothing wrong with me. I ate a full dinner. This is child abuse."

"I just got my period. I have cramps. I can't."

And when she ran out of excuses, she'd physically refuse to get into the car. I was at my wit's end. Katelyn wasn't equipped to handle my daughter.

"Right. I think I'm starting to get it."

"Well, I need you to catch up a little quicker, because our first plan of attack is today."

"You have a plan already?" I asked, surprised.

"Of course, I have a plan. Do you think I'm a fucking idiot?" she said, (idiot coming out like *id-eee-it*).

Edna came back with our order and set it down in the middle of the table. I shoved the cake over to

Dinah's side of the table and told Edna, "Thanks."

"Okay, dear," she responded with large, aging eyes, shaking her head back and forth.

"Why do we come here again? They have a shitty chicken salad and she's nuts," I whispered.

"Because she can't hear our plans," Dinah reminded me.

"Right, which are?" I asked.

"Kill their business," Dinah said, stabbing her cake with a fork. "Cut off their balls," she continued, cupping her hands.

"What did you have in mind?" I asked, wide-eyed.

Dinah plopped down a printed out page of property listings in Manhattan, which had the sell prices displayed next to each one.

"Mitchell had money troubles before Nikolay came along. Did he tell you?" Dinah asked.

"Not in those words. He said he hadn't sold anything in a while."

"Ha. Yes," Dinah enthused. "He had his best year followed by the beginning of a year with nearly no sales at all."

"Well, we had savings though. What about those?" I questioned.

"He would have had savings. If his wife had not spent all his money." Dinah grinned widely.

"I see," I said, clearing my throat.

"Don't worry, guilty here too," Dinah admitted.

I picked up the listings, tiring of Dinah's story-telling already. There were four addresses on the list: one in the West Village, one in Soho and two in Tribeca. The ones in Tribeca were two units side by side in a new building.

"There has to be more than this," I said.

"Yes, but those are the big kills and also the ones he shares with Nikolay, so it's mutually beneficial. We take out these targets and their year is sunk. He can always pick up new listings, but he's going to need to be really productive this spring if he's to pay three mortgages with no safety net. And when the shits hits the fans, who do you think he's going to kick out? His family or his mistress?" she asked.

"It's shit hits the fan," I said.

"What?" she yelled.

"The American phrase, it's shit, not 'shits' hits the fan. Not trying to be condescending, simply helping with your English, which is very good, may I add. So, how do you plan to sabotage these sales, exactly?"

Her glacially blue eyes told me never to make fun of how she talked again, and I would not. This woman was scary.

"I've been doing my research, extensive research. I've been inside each of these units and have creative ideas, but you have to just trust me. And you can't tell anybody about me. It won't be hard because you don't have any friends, but no family, not anyone, okay?"

"Thanks for reminding me I have no friends and okay, I trust you. I'm interested in what you're saying, although I'm not sure how biting the hand feeding me is going to benefit me in the long run."

"What about biting hands?" she asked bewildered.

"It's an American expression. Why am I ruining the business of the man who is paying my mortgage? Doesn't that hurt my family?" I asked.

"It's temporary. There's always new properties, new clients, but he's vulnerable and overextended right now, so we have to move," she said in a hushed whisper.

The property in the West Village was listed for seven million dollars. Mitchell had only sold a few properties of sizeable dollars in the past, and it could definitely make his year. My finger traced the six zeroes in wonderment.

"Yes, that's the one we'll start with. There is a prospective buyer flying in from L.A. who has looked at the property several times. Our husbands believe this final look today will seal the deal. However, his wife hasn't seen the property yet. The husband is flying in today to take a final walk-through and spend the weekend in the city. His wife is flying in on Monday to approve and sign the papers. Our timing has to be impeccable with the Supra key. It sends electronic reports back when someone has entered the building.

"They probably don't look at this with too much scrutiny as long as reports are sent around the time they were actually in the building. Which is why, we need to enter right before or right after they're in there with my Supra app so they don't suspect anything. He's showing the apartment at three o'clock today. We'll wait for them to leave to plant the goods and then by the time his wife enters the building, it will be a done deal," she said excitedly, wrapping her bleached locks back up in her scarf, signaling the end of our meeting.

"What will?" I asked, doing the same with my hair.

"You will see. You will have to trust me," Dinah said with her conniving grin.

She got up to leave and for some reason the only thing I could focus on was the sharp object she'd shoved so vehemently down the center of the cake. The fork stuck straight up in the air, dead center. Her aim was impeccable.

Chapter 15
Something's Fishy

We were like Thelma and Louise driving into the city to raise hell, if Louise were a cunning Russian woman, and Thelma were a scared, petulant housewife that is. My bold-hued scarf was coifed around my hair, my sunglasses shielding my fear. I had lost my friends, my husband, and my dolls, but there was one thing I did have left to lose—my freedom.

I loved the West Village, the home of the uppity-ups and some of the most beautiful, old real estate in the city. We pulled up near the tall, brick complex on our target list. Dinah instructed me to park in the alley where we would be hidden from the outside world. She had a cooler of an undisclosed nature in the backseat. I followed this eccentric woman's lead, listening to everything she told me because I wanted to believe it was true.

Dinah had such a sense of purpose when she spoke and everything seemed to be cautiously planned out. Carefully crafted lists backed by solid planning; I was already in love with my new friend.

We waited patiently in the alleyway for my husband and his client to approach the 1840's Greek revival building, mystery cooler in hand. The gut wrench had me doubled over at the thought of being seen. Dinah told me to pull it together, so I straightened up and took a deep breath. Right on cue, Mitchell and a tall, slender man in dark jeans and a gray sport coat entered the building.

I used to love my husband in that sell-mode, all amped up, blood racing through his testosterone-fueled body, anticipating "The Big Sale." He loved this shit. He lived for it. And I was going to royally fuck up his day. Even though, I wasn't sure how yet.

He would lose this listing. He would lose confidence in himself. He would become depressed, and then she would lose confidence in him. The monster clawed its ugly arm up my belly and out my mouth, extending its claws out to reach him. A black smile spread silently beneath my surface as we waited for them to exit the building. At the same time, I was nervous as hell of getting caught breaking and entering, and screwing with Mitchell's business. I'd spent a lifetime watching him build it.

They didn't stay very long and left the row house, laughing and back-slapping the way men do before they're going to make a business deal. I heard a muffled something about Monday and closing things up and then they were gone and we were on the slate front porch. Before I could say *go* we were stepping on the wide-planked pumpkin pine floors of the gorgeous property.

Dinah said we had to move quickly so if Mitchell saw the Supra report he would just assume it was him who had entered the building. I was skeptical Dinah's phone app would work, but it was too easy. She swiped her smart phone along the box, it clicked and *Presto*— the keys inside the box were now inside her hands, and then we were inside the seven million dollar listing.

"We don't have much time, do as I say," Dinah whispered, even though we were the only ones there.

When she opened her cooler she had two bags of one-pound mussels. Yep, the slimy little sea creatures I loved to indulge in over a good marinara sauce when visiting Little Italy.

"Are we cooking Moules Mariniere?" I asked.

"What do you think of these lamps?" she asked, ignoring my joke and handing me a screwdriver.

"I love tiffany lamps," I answered, annoyed by her need to give a prequel in our rushed state.

"Great. There are eight of them spread throughout the living room and bedrooms. Unscrew the bottoms and place a mussel entwined in the wires of each one, try not to mess-up the actual wiring. They will fit. I got the smaller ones," she said.

"I will handle the fireplace, the inside of the shower rods and the utility panel in the kitchen. Now move and make it neat and tidy and don't break anything. There are Clorox wipes in my purse in case you get messy," Dinah informed.

Oh, how I loved my crazy Russian accomplice. I could definitely handle *neat* and *tidy* and I was awed by the brilliance of her plan. I had to admire a woman who traveled with her own Clorox wipes.

My task was completed in fifteen minutes flat. I should've felt accomplished. However, sabotaging the listing my husband had worked so hard to procure left me jaded. I hated him, but he did work hard, and he was still providing for our family.

Mitchell and Nikolay would show the property to the missus on Monday and be horrified, but Dinah didn't seem the least bit fazed by messing with her husband's business. She pressed her overfilled lips together and shook her head at my doubtfulness.

"They won't have another buyer in there for ages. This was a big one. They'd worked for three months just to get an interested party and the interested party almost turned into a sale," she said grinning.

Her words did little to comfort me. Sinking back into the driver seat, I tried to channel Mitchell's reaction to his sabotaged listing.

Devastated. Disappointed. Wronged.

Those emotions had been echoing throughout my entire body for months, and it was time Mitchell got a taste of his own medicine. His confidence would be shattered, his livelihood compromised. Katelyn's livelihood compromised, too.

Perhaps, he'd promised Katelyn a piece of jewelry chocked full of diamonds if they'd closed the deal. Surely, Katelyn would be too simple and stupid to recognize the designer of the jewelry Mitchell had probably boasted about, but he'd make her pine over it anyway so she'd feel super-special when she received it. And now he'd have to renege on his celebratory present and she'd become angry for not getting something she'd never really wanted in the first place.

It's exactly what Mitchell Laramie did to women. He sold them on fantasies he'd self-created and then turned around and crushed their dreams. He'd probably make Katelyn feel guilty for it somehow too, her being his assistant and all.

I dropped Dinah off at the diner. She exited my car and slammed the door without saying another word. Hot and flustered emotions emanated all over my body from my day on the prowl causing me to shake my hair out of its kerchief and shove it in the passenger side glove box. I noted in the car how Dinah sat with perfect, rigid posture, seemingly in a state of discomfort. When I touched her side of the seat, the leather was cool to touch—icy just like her.

****

Mitchell arrived at my house Monday evening to speak with the security company personally on how he would like the system installed. I was curious how his West Village appointment went today, but I could tell from his sourpuss expression when he entered the house the business deal was dead.

"They're here already," I said, surprised.

The dark expression he wore was all too familiar. Wrinkled brow, half-smile, popping out the smirky dimple, anger etched in his eyes. Time to pick a fight. His business deal fell through and he was there to oversee the installation of our security system and use me as a punching bag. The kids greeted him with warm hugs. They missed him and I don't think they really blamed him for leaving me.

"Hi kiddos. I want everyone to be careful until they catch this guy. The security system should help and hopefully they got what they came for and won't be back," Mitchell said.

"I don't get who would want mom's dolls and how did they even know she had them. She kept those things under lock and key," Josie said.

"Those are the same questions I had. I was going to speak to your mother about that very subject. Why don't you put the groceries away, while we talk," Mitchell suggested.

I had just gotten home from the store. Plastic

grocery bags toppled over one another on the counter. The security company had gotten there earlier than expected and I had to abandon them for a moment.

"What do I smell?" Mitchell asked, as Josie unpacked a white paper parcel.

"I'm cooking orange roughy in marmalade sauce tonight, you must smell the fish," I said, a smile playing on my lips.

"Ugh," he said.

"What, you don't like orange roughy anymore?" I asked.

"I've had enough fish for one day," he mumbled.

"What?" I asked, laughing.

"Never mind," he said.

"How are things going?" I asked.

"I'm not here to chitchat. I need to know if this doll thing was your stunt or real. I need to know because I'm worried about my kids. If it was something you orchestrated to get me back here or to draw my attention, then please tell me. I won't be mad. It's hard enough being away from them, but to have me think someone was actually in this house digging around while Camdyn was in the next room," he started, having to take a break, getting a little emotional.

"You can't be serious asking me that question?" I said in disbelief.

"Cece, you can tell me. I understand this is hard on you. But it's not fair to have me think they're in danger when they're not. It's not fair and it's cruel. I've never been cruel to you. I would never do something like this."

"Mitchell, you know how much I loved those dolls."

"I know. It's the way you've been acting, I don't know what to think anymore."

His arrogance made my cheeks hot with embarrassment. The bastard thought I still wanted him back. He'd actually thought I'd maim my own dolls in an attempt to get his attention. Like a little girl who'd left bruises on her arms and legs and told the teacher her daddy did it.

Annihilation and dirty linens.

If he only knew what I really thought of him. It was moments like these I wished I could pull a Bootsy and take him for everything he had, but then he'd never really hurt the way I had. Only his pocket would. And she'd never get what she deserved either for ripping our family apart. Worse yet, she'd have access to my children every other weekend. The cooler, younger stepmom, who didn't know a damn thing about raising a child, stepping in to befriend them and upend me. I couldn't lose my children to her.

"Mitchell, I want you to go upstairs and look at the room," I demanded.

"No, I hate your stupid room. I hated it when I lived here and I hate it even more now."

"Mitchell, please go look at what they did. You will know it wasn't me when you see it. I haven't been able to go in there and clean up the mess yet, it's too much for me."

"I'm not going up there," he refused, shaking his head.

"Mitchell, did you hear what I said? I haven't even been able to clean up the mess yet."

The words sank in as I watched his shitty grin turn into shock. I hadn't left a mess behind since the day he met me. He turned without looking at me again and lumbered up the stairs. He came back shortly after, brushed by me in the kitchen, grabbed a roll of trash bags and the broom and headed back upstairs. I followed him this time and stood in the doorway as he put dismembered doll parts in large plastic bags. My husband showed up again that night. Exactly like when my mother passed away. He showed up to help me, and it made me feel like he cared—if only for a moment.

He picked up the remnants of a brunette with her gorgeous burgundy gown shredded to edgy satin pieces with scissors or perhaps a very sharp knife. Clumps of hair lie next to her tattered costume, along with her beauty pageant sash, which was now wrung around her torn off head.

"I remember this one. I got you Miss New York," Mitchell said.

"Yes you did," I sighed sadly.

He frowned as he placed her in the garbage bag.

"Do you think they can maybe be salvaged?" I asked, hesitant to let him throw away the remains.

"I'm going to put all the damaged dolls in here and then some day when you're able, you can go through them. I'm going to sweep up the glass and put it in this bag and take it out. I'm sorry this happened. It's a shame."

"So you believe me now?" I asked.

"Yeah, I believe you. I just wish you were lying, because now I'm really worried about the kids."

Chapter 16
Shitty Day

Daylight streamed through my bedroom blinds, the shimmer reminding me of the stainless steel espresso machine at work. Work. *The Coffee Bean.* How had I gotten home after my terrible migraine last night? Surely, I didn't drive. On second thought, I think I did drive. My mind was a little fuzzy, like the tiny dust angels slowly floating past my window.

Bang. Bang. Bang.

My door rattled and children screamed. As I came out of my weird little daydream, the kids were pounding on my locked bedroom door. They were going to be late for school if I didn't snap to it. I threw on a dirty sweat suit and charged out the door. Like an alien life form, I emerged from my bedroom—W*hat have you done with my real mother,* their eyes read. I hadn't left the house without a shower and makeup since their inception into the world.

"Well, come on, I'm not feeling so hot," I defended.

They climbed into the car reluctantly, not speaking.

"Well, now don't be so surprised. Haven't you ever had a day where you didn't feel like getting ready?" I asked.

"Everybody does, but you don't. Remember when you had bronchitis and you made me put your eyeliner on for the contractor coming to work on the house? You were coughing so hard you couldn't hold your hands still long enough to line your eyes, but you still wanted to look good, so you made me do it. I was only nine, but you told me to stay in the lines like a coloring book," Josie recalled.

"Why, don't you have a memory like an elephant," I chirped.

"And to not even shower with your OCD, well, I feel like I need to call someone to take you to the hospital," Josie went on.

"Josie, relax. I'm going through a divorce. If I want to sit around in my damn pajamas and not shower for a week, then it's my prerogative, okay?" I snapped.

"Fine, sorry, you're just out of the norm," she said.

"Is anything normal right now? It's time we all throw out the old normal and accept the now, which is shitty. It's shitty and it's what your father wanted, not me," I said.

No one said another word. I dropped them off, ducking the other parents, hoping nobody would see my unconcealed, grimy face and fat pants.

****

After a much needed shower, I met Dinah at lunchtime to see what new crimes she had for us to commit today. She looked pleased, her giant lips pressed together in a slight smile. She took her sunglasses off today, as if she was ready to face the light.

"Everything okay?" I asked.

"Better than okay. The deal in the West Village sunk or should I say stunk," she said, a full smile spreading slowly across her face.

"Great, so the buyers walked?"

"Oh yeah. The smell was horrific and they couldn't find the source. Mitchell and Nikolay offered to have it fumigated, thinking a rodent or some other animal had snuck in and died, but the buyers walked."

"Great news."

She pulled her listings back up—our hit list. I admired her prioritizing them according to their showing dates.

"We're getting lucky. Mitchell and Nikolay are both showing the property in Soho today to an art trader. Next week, we'll have to meet on Friday instead of Thursday to finish up our work."

"I've been trading my Thursdays for Fridays at *The Coffee Bean*. Seems all the youngsters have been calling off Friday nights leaving Sam shorthanded. I'll have to ask Sam or see if my brother can run Camdyn to soccer Friday," I said.

"Do you think I give a fuck about your minimum wage job or your kid's soccer practice? You're coming next Friday." Dinah said sharply.

"I can ask my brother, Dominic, but he's ex-army, keeps a lot of guns and dangerous stuff in his apartment. He also has a drug dependency issue, so we don't like having him drive our…"

"Again, I. Do. Not. Care. Toughen your children up now so they don't end up as spineless as you are," she scolded.

"Okay, shouldn't be a problem," I mumbled.

"And it's going to need to be at night, so get someone to watch them," Dinah said.

"Mitchell and the whore have Josie and Camdyn for the first time next weekend. So I'll meet you after I see them off. It will be a difficult day for me, so this will give me something to keep my mind off it."

"Glad I can provide entertainment for you."

"You went from pleasant to *not* in about ten seconds," I said.

"Now you know why my husband started fucking someone else," Dinah remarked dryly.

It was time to quit prodding the bear. She was scowling so hard at me I thought her giant upper lip might pop.

"So, what's the plan for today?" I asked carefully.

"You'll see. I will need you to take one hundred dollars out of your bank," she instructed.

"Why?"

"Because we will need it and I'm cut off. Did he cut you off yet?"

"No, I have kids. I don't see him cutting them off."

"I do. Take the cash out while you can, trust me."

I paid the bill and we climbed into my car to head into the city. We pulled through the ATM and I took out the money without finding out its purpose.

"We have to make a stop first," Dinah said.

"Where?" I asked.

Dinah placed an address into my GPS leading us to 59th street. She told me to pull over near Central Park. I wondered what sea creatures we were picking up today. I saw a bum approach our car and faced forward pretending I didn't see him as he talked to the vehicle. Dinah rolled down the window.

"What're you doing?" I asked.

She put her hands up and silenced me with her eyes. Those light blue things were like lasers when they were pissed. I shut up.

"Hi Murph, are you still okay with our plan?" Dinah asked.

"Still payin' me a hundred bucks to do it?" he asked through rotting teeth.

"Yes, of course," she said.

"Oh yeah, I'm loaded up and ready to go," he said, smiling, baring more missing teeth among his darker ones.

"No guns. Are you talking about loaded guns? I will not have guns in my car." I yelled.

"No guns, keep your voice down," Dinah hushed.

"Nope, got a few bucks this afternoon to get me some Mexican from the street vendor. Had extra refined beans," Murph said letting out a big belch.

"Dinah, this man is not getting into my car," I protested.

"Oh, he's getting in your car. I know him, he's harmless and he's pivotal to our plan," she stated firmly.

Murph was a dirty vagrant clothed in an old army jacket, ripped khakis and tattered boots. He smelled of urine and whiskey and I guessed either heroin or crystal meth was his drug of choice from the looks of his teeth. He wore a full brown beard caked with his last two meals. I held my nose as Murph entered my backseat, rubbing his dirt-stained fingers all over my leather interior in wonder, turning it from cream to brown. My OCD ticked and I held my breath to block out the stench and calm my nerves. I thought about pulling over and kicking them both out onto the curb, but I kept driving.

I would definitely make Dinah scrub my car with her Clorox wipes when this was all over. I sure hoped the bitch brought them this time. I pushed on the gas, anxious for this to be over, speeding past all of the trendy shops lining the streets of Soho.

"Slow down, Cece. You don't want to draw attention to us. Remember Mitchell and Nikolay will both be there today." she yelled.

"If you didn't want to draw attention to us, you shouldn't have picked up a bum. There's a bum in my back seat, Dinah," I panicked.

"Hey, I can hear you," Murph complained, half-belching.

"You will thank me later," she said, half-smiling.

"I doubt it," I said.

We had to pull into a parking lot this time, which was going to make it very difficult to exit inconspicuously with Murph. We bought Murph a coffee to keep him happy while we waited and hid around the corner near Broadway and Broome. People poured in and out of chic nearby stores like Top Shop, blanketing us from the targeted white-washed, brick building in the bustling, hipster section of Manhattan. We thought Murph would draw attention, as this wasn't a typical area for vagrants, but all of the New Yorkers were numb to his existence and too busy shopping to notice.

I heard Mitchell's sales pitchy voice come barreling around the opposite corner. It was the *Well, I have something for you today* voice he used when he was really trying to impress. We both took a peek at our exes. We were well hidden in the corridor and they had their backs to us. I finally got to see the infamous Nikolay. He was a good-looking man from what I could tell; well over six feet tall, dark longish hair falling to his very high cheek bones in the same round face structure as his Russian wife. He had a sweet smile; too sweet to be Dinah's husband. He looked like a "nice" guy, the kind you'd trust to housesit your dog or even your kid. He had pink, cherub lips, trusting brown eyes and the all too sweet smile. His gray suit looked expensive, as did his leather shoes, reeking of success and money.

Mitchell wore his black suit and red tie. He often referred to it as his power suit. He needed to close this deal. His eyes were popping out of his head, his smile strangely wide, his laugh overly haughty. Oh yes, he needed this sale. The buyer wore the look of an artist, dressed in all black, thick-rimmed glasses, spiked blonde hair.

"Are you sure they aren't closing today, it looks like it to me?" I whispered.

"This man has an art show tonight and does not have time to close this evening. He'll tell them to draw up the paperwork and then he'll sign upon inspection on Monday, only ze' inspector will find something that doesn't pass," Dinah hissed.

"What will they find? How do you know all this? And how can you be sure?" I asked.

"You vill see," she said.

I was getting really tired of the *trust mes* and the *you vill sees*. I would have a chat with Dinah and explain this if we were going to be partners I would need to be in the loop. They left the building and Mitchell looked very pleased as he shook the man's hand.

"See ya in the office on Monday," Mitchell said.

"See ya then, gotta run," the buyer said.

All three of us entered the building shortly after. I had always loved Soho for the boutique shopping, but mostly because it was young and fresh. The West Village had a very elegant, yet stuffy feel, whereas Soho had a very hip, urban vibe. If I could have afforded to live there in my twenties, I would have. But I wouldn't have fit in. I wasn't cool enough. My imagination pictured the hipsters living in Soho hanging out in little coffee shops featuring open poetry readings, kids wearing lots of black, quoting Nietzsche, and talking about the newest Indie band playing in the city. I wasn't enough of a cool cat. I was always more of a scaredy cat. Especially, right about now.

We snuck Murph into the four million dollar pad with an open layout and industrial-style paneling, complete with twelve-foot ceilings and sleek, light-colored hardwood floors. Beautiful artwork hung on the walls next to the abundance of over-sized windows.

"This place is gorgeous. What're you going to do to it?" I asked fearfully.

Dinah's lips pinched together in mischief as she said, "I suggest you turn around. You're not going to want to see this."

"Where at?" Murph asked.

"Right there in the middle of the room," Dinah said.

"Here?" he asked, pointing to the center of the large studio apartment.

"Yes, there," she commanded.

Murph proceeded to pull down his pants, squat, and defecate in the middle of the room.

"No," I gasped, putting my hands over my eyes in horror, buckling over in the opposite direction.

"Oh yes," Dinah said.

Dinah laughed at my reaction. *Crazy, crazy bitch.*

My gut wrench did a somersault and a backflip. I could smell the toxic fumes and I was going to vomit. She laughed at me as I ran into the bathroom to wretch.

"Don't run away Ma'am, where do you want the smears?" Murph yelled at my back.

The smears? Dear God, what was that? And why was he asking me? I didn't know what was going on.

I returned to the scene in shock, utterly speechless from the bum who shat on the floor before me.

"On the lovely, expensive paintings, which come with the building, and the white walls over there, please," Dinah instructed.

Like a hired contractor working with spackle, he grabbed a load of his fecal matter and began to do what he referred to as *The Smears.* I thought I was going to be sick again, feeling dizzy.

Breathe Cecelia, breathe.

Yes, I felt better, but the smell was making me nauseated again. When Murph was finished he used the bathroom to wash his hands.

"Hey, there's no towel in here," he complained.

"You shit all over the floor and smeared it on the walls and you're concerned about a hand towel?" I asked in amazement.

"Hey, just because I'm a street person, doesn't mean I'm not used to certain things when I go places," he defended.

"I have paper towels in the car. The less evidence in here the better. Let's go," Dinah rushed us out as she handed him the wad of ten-dollar bills.

Before we left, Dinah busted the door jam, making

wood jut out in splintery pieces around the lock. Much like my classical woodworking at my home, it saddened me the dug-in entryway could never be fully restored to its original historical beauty.

This poor buyer was going to feel intrusion before he ever got a chance to move in. And Mitchell was going to be handed one crappy deal. I'd give anything to be a fly on those shit-stained walls when Mitchell and the buyer returned for the final walk through.

The satisfaction I'd hope to gain from these treacherous acts wasn't sinking in the way I'd imagined. Dinah said destroying Mitchell's work would hurt him in the worst possible way, and destroying him was the goal, but it wasn't completely doing the trick for me. Broken business deals weren't a match for broken hearts. I could only hope all of our efforts would at least get rid of Katelyn somehow. Maybe, if I saw him penniless without a girl on his arm it would make me the happiest.

This latest assault could definitely move us toward the desired goal. Katelyn was his assistant. She'd assisted him in all of his recent failures. Mitchell and she could share in the depressive outcome of all of their hard work. Tension would float over every charming sconce in their swanky brownstone, boil over in nasty fights on their kitsch little stove she never used to cook him meals. Now, that was a pleasing thought.

"Why're you destroying the entryway?" I asked as I watched Dinah scrape into the wood harder. I stood watch in the hallway with Murph.

"The bum had to get in some way," she explained.

"Can I get a lift back to the park?" Murph asked.

"Sure," Dinah said.

203

I glared at Dinah, but knew there was no fighting her. With Murph safely back inside my vehicle, the aroma was now a rancid mix of urine, whiskey, and shit. I held my breath to quiet the bile rising in my mouth. I started to sweat, my scalp prickling as my lack of oxygen made me woozy. I was worried I might pass out but Dinah hollered at me to keep driving. We dropped off Murph, but his stench lingered on. I began to gag as the cool March breeze sent Murph's backdraft into the car as he shut my door.

"You'll thank me later," Dinah reassured.

Words wouldn't come to me when I attempted to speak to Dinah. I couldn't even look at her as I sped back to the diner with my window open, gulping for air like an overheated Golden Retriever.

"You're not cut out for this type of work. I thought you were tougher than this," she grumbled.

"You're insane," I squeaked.

"Do you think the property will pass inspection on Monday?" Dinah asked.

"Hell, no. But, I'm more worried about the police catching us this time. What we did was atrocious." I yelled.

"What we did? You mean what Murph did. We didn't do a thing. All we did was let him in. And we wore gloves, so the only prints will be his."

"What if he gives us up?"

"You're assuming too much. You're assuming he's in the legal system's computer and they will be able to track down a homeless man. How do you track a man who has no home? I didn't give him our real names. The only thing he has is your car, but I doubt he even noticed it was a Mercedes. All he will likely remember was the white car with the grope-worthy, creamy interior." She laughed.

I glanced in my rearview mirror in horror to see his smudged fingerprints on my backseat.

"Ugh," I gulped, swallowing a little throw-up as I did so.

"He was a filthy animal, but he did a great job," Dinah said with pride.

"How does a person even think of such a sick plan?" I asked.

"I'm creative. And ze' stench plan worked so well da first time, I thought why not try it again? Next week will be a more extreme measure. I will need you to put on your big girl panties for the next one. It won't be so easy."

"I don't know if I can keep this up. The first one was kind of fun. Today was horrible and if it gets any worse than this, I don't think I can do it. I don't even like dirty fingerprints on my windows. Human shit smeared on windows, uh, no way," I freaked.

"Breathe Cecelia, and you vill be fine," Dinah reasoned.

"How do you know I need to breathe?" I asked her.

"I noticed your little quirk of holding your breath when your nerves get you. It's pathetic," she retorted.

"Thanks for the vote of confidence."

"I'm not here to boost your self-esteem. I'm here to get your life back," she snapped.

As I was dropping her off she said, "Vill I see you here next Friday?"

"What time?" I asked.

"Eight o'clock and don't go inside, meet me out here," she said.

"Okay," I answered, not sure why I wanted to continue.

****

After the kids went to bed, I scrubbed the interior of my car for two solid hours. I was an image of my mother—surgical mask, long rubber gloves, hair pulled back in a net. After I was done scrubbing the inside, I decided the filth could have permeated to the outside of the vehicle. Heavy thoughts of dirt-smudged fingers on my passenger side door filled my mind.

As I pulled my car out of the garage and began to burnish the exterior, the crisp, spring air nipped at my thin pajama bottoms. But I scoured every last inch and even threw on a coat of wax. There was nothing like polishing your car by the waxing and waning of the moonlight. My neighbor was a physician who often kept odd hours, and when he pulled into his driveway at midnight, his look said it all—*crazy woman.*

I was so overwhelmed with anxiety, my night ended with a ripping headache, which had been trying to surface all day, followed by a shower I didn't remember. I only knew I'd bathed because I woke up in my robe—again.

When I awoke, my body ached strangely, my thigh muscles overly tight, probably from standing on my tiptoes to wash the roof of my car. When I used the bathroom, my bladder hurt from holding my urine too long, the stinging sensation in between my legs making me feel as though I'd given myself a urinary tract infection. My anxiety was getting so bad it was making me forget basic human functions.

When I arrived for my early morning shift at *The Coffee Bean*, the door was opened, but Sam was nowhere to be found. Odd, but I started prepping the machines and organizing the paper cups like I always did. I liked my job. It was mindless and it quieted the demons. The stinging had alleviated between my legs, and I decided it was now okay to toss my cranberry juice and move onto bottled water. My thirst was insatiable, my mouth feeling as dry and strangely sweet as a stick of cotton candy. My dehydration was evident by my bloodshot eyes and patchy dry mouth. My double-life was wearing on my health.

I was so tired from my clean-a-thon and enjoying the ice cold water so much I barely noticed Sam stumble into the door. I took one look at him and registered he was high as a kite. It was nine a.m. and his eyes looked as pink as the strawberry frappes I was so good at blending.

"Sam, you look like I feel. No, you look much worse than I feel. You should go home. Customers don't need to see you like this," I preached.

He wasn't only high; he was completely stoned out of his gourd. His mouth tried to smile, but it hung open in a surly, dazed manner, which made me want to slap it shut.

"Oh sure, pretend like everything's normal," he said, squinting at the light.

"Nothing's normal. You're totally baked, and you smell like shit. Go home," I said disgusted.

"You want to play this game, like nothing's going on between us. I can dig it, doll. I can play. Yeah, let's play the no strings attached game. Free love, Cece, I'm all about it," he babbled.

"I don't know what in the hell you're talking about, but you need to go splash some water on your face before a customer arrives. It's going to hurt business for people to see you like this, Sam," I scolded.

"Ignore it, it will go away. You're a Republican," he slurred.

"I'm serious Sam, you reek, bad!"

"You didn't mind how I smelled the..," he coughed a stinky breeze, "uh-other night," and stammered, swatting his hand at my ass and missing.

"You didn't smell bad the other night. You can't even see straight," I said, disgusted.

"You deal with your problems with your meds, I'll deal with mine with my meds," he said, his voice squeaking up at the end.

"Your problems? What problems?"

"I didn't know what to expect today. I needed some reinforcements," he said, giggling.

"You're making no sense. Can you just go home?" I asked.

"I'll let you kick me out of my own business, sweetheart. But only because it's you," he said as he tripped on his way out the back door.

I shook my head as my train-wreck boss exited the building. *What a fuck-up.*

Callie and Julie padded in an hour later, serious expressions on their little round faces. They were like a two-man army of blonde *Bratz* dolls, oversized eyes too big for their heads.

"Two non-fat lattes, Cece. How are you?" Callie asked.

"Fine, I guess. What's up? You girls look worried," I said.

"So Mitchell didn't tell you about Monte?" she asked.

"Mitchell and I aren't speaking much these days. What about him?" I asked.

"Right," she eyed her sister and looked down guiltily, "Monte's surgical center burnt to the ground last night and his office safe was stolen. It was arson," Julie whispered.

Monte owned his own plastic surgery center in West Orange, NJ. It was a beautiful, multi-million-dollar, light-brick building with state of the art floor to ceiling windows. I imagined the large edifice in a pile of ashes and bricks.

"Jesus. Do they know who did it?" I asked.

"No. Monte didn't have any enemies. However, many of his patients paid in cash. When I asked Maeve why, she said a lot of wives and husbands didn't want their spouses to know they were having work done. A lot of it was Botox injections and laser procedures, but Maeve said there was enough money in his safe to support them for an entire year," Julie whispered again.

I knew Maeve's lifestyle, so there must have been a lot of money in his safe.

"Who knew about the safe? Why not just steal the safe? Why burn the whole damn building down?" I asked.

"Maeve said when patients paid in cash, he would swing around in his chair and place the money into the safe embedded into the wall. Many patients saw it. They aren't sure why they burned down the building. Making a statement, I guess," Callie added.

"It's all so awful. We're all hitting a rough patch lately. Did you hear about my dolls?" I asked.

"Yeah, I'm sorry I haven't returned your messages. Things have been crazy. Dare I ask if they got chicky number one, your dream girl? Didn't know if you might have had her stashed somewhere special," Julie questioned, with a hopeful smirk, which almost passed as genuine.

"Oh no, they got her and all my other ones I've been collecting since I was like six," I lamented.

"I don't know any six-year-old who can resist taking a toy out of its box," Callie remarked.

"It was my mother. She told me they would be worth more, kept neatly in their boxes, but I learned later her real motivation was so I didn't make a mess. She hated all the little shoes and accessories they came with," I said.

"Imagine that," Julie said, raising her eyebrow at me.

"Hey, I'm not so bad. This divorce thing has loosened me up. I even drove the kids to school without showering the other day," I announced.

"Oh, no you didn't," Julie gasped.

"Oh, yes I did," I said.

"Wow, that's quite a breakthrough," Julie said.

"Or a breakdown, whatever you want to call it." I sighed.

"Well, Robin and Maeve don't like her if it makes you feel any better," Callie said.

"Callie…" Julie scolded, nudging her sister in the ribs.

"They don't like who?" I asked.

"What," Callie said, shrugging her sister off. "Mitchell and his girlfriend had dinner at Robin's with Maeve and Monte the other night."

My own internal emotional latte began to brew as my eyes filled with steam and water. *What traitors!*

"Don't be upset. They absolutely hated her. They said she was classless, kept stuttering, wouldn't make eye contact, couldn't hold a conversation. Maeve called her a bumbling fool and a preschooler," Callie laughed.

Hearing this from my friends made me happy. At least they weren't welcoming her with open arms, replacing me at the flip of a coin. But I was pissed they would invite her over at all.

"Where's Sam? He's never here. They should call this place, Cece's Coffee Bean," Julie said, obviously wanting to change the subject, her loyalty to Maeve unwavering.

"He was acting really odd this morning and was so high he couldn't see straight, so I sent him home." I laughed.

"Ugh, what a loser. Well, there was a Dave Matthews Band concert last night. He was probably still hung over from the night before," Callie said.

"He probably was, I guess. Wasn't in the mood to deal with him today," I said.

"I can't imagine all you're going through. I'm sorry about everything. We'll try to keep in better touch," Callie assured.

"Hell, every time you come in here, you have bad news. Only come back to see me if it's something good," I joked.

"Will do. Hopefully, there will be some good news to report soon," Julie commented.

"I hope so too," I said.

Julie and Callie were added back to my Christmas card list this year. At least they were trying to keep me in the loop. Between robberies, arson, and my own string of criminal activity, I would say everyone had

211

good reason to keep to themselves these days and I needed to make a better effort to tramp out my pity party. I also had major doubts about our local police department. So far no leads on my dolls. I realized finding missing baby dolls (as they had called them) was probably not at the top of their priority list, but I would have appreciated not being laughed at when calling in to reference my case.

I had dreams of being reunited with my stolen treasures someday. One fantasy played out where the thief was not able to unload the dolls in time and they were found untouched in an abandoned warehouse. Another had them all posted for sale in one lot on eBay. I would discover the post and immediately have the seller apprehended and the dolls would be returned in their pristine condition. So far, none of my fantasies had come to fruition.

Chapter 17
Bam, Bang, Pow

Monday morning started off with a bang. Well, not exactly, thank God, but it could have. Mitchell and I both received the call from Camdyn's school about the mishap with the grenade.

"*Shit*," I yelled, as I threw my cell onto the passenger seat and hammered down on the accelerator in my car.

I knew where he'd gotten it, but why he thought it was okay to bring it in for his sixth grade Social Studies family heirloom *Show and Tell* was beyond me. The school was on lockdown when I got there, police swarming the perimeter and news helicopters circling the grounds.

The principal's office was Camdyn's temporary jail cell. I stalled his incarceration, pleading for them to wait until my husband got there. Camdyn sat in handcuffs wincing as the metal cut into his small wrists, hot tears on his cheeks. I had never seen Camdyn cry past age five, not even when his grandfather died. It was ripping a hole through me to watch my private child in remorseful agony. He had the expression you wore when you made a really big mistake and knew you were in deep shit; the kind you'd give your left arm for to have a do-over. Only his left arm belonged to the apathetic juvenile officer gripping his elbow, ready to whisk him away. The only thing the official saw was another kid ready to shoot up a school. The officer was waiting for the principal to give him the green light. There was also a state trooper and a local cop on the other side of the door.

Dammit. I knew the cop. Officer Marlow gave me a suspicious nod of his head as to say,

Missing baby dolls and a kid with an assault weapon, eh? The Laramie family is a bunch of whackos.

Mitchell arrived shortly after me; still buttoned up and sharp from work, beads of sweat sprouting on his brow. There was a question as to whether a law was broken. The grenade was over one hundred years old, had no pin attached and was in a memorial case. The case may be what could save Camdyn's ass, because it looked like it was plucked straight from a museum. My pleas with the administration had kept my son sitting there a few minutes longer, but we were on borrowed time now.

"Principal Riley, please, please don't expel him. Don't take him to the detention center. He's a good kid. He meant no harm. My family collects military relics. His uncle gave the grenade to him. He fought in desert storm, his grandfather in Vietnam. He looks at those things like a collector's item, not weapons," Mitchell pleaded.

The principal, a stout, short-haired woman in her late forties, seemed to resonate with this line of thinking, shaking her head from side to side, glancing sideways at an American flag plaque on the wall which read: *In loving memory of David Riley who bravely gave his life to save others.*

The plaque was the second thing to maybe save Camdyn, I was sure of it.

"Camdyn, what were you thinking?" Mitchell yelled.

"Mitchell," I put my hand up, pointing to our son racked with tears in the corner of the room.

"I-I'm sorry Dad. I-I made a mistake. I thought it was neat for *Show and Tell*," he cried.

Mitchell's face softened as he observed his son. Camdyn was afraid—a feeling we'd never observed in him before. I nudged Mitchell, averting my eyes upward to make him look at the plaque. He was better at winning arguments than me. Mitchell was one hell of a salesman when he wanted to be and I needed him to sell the school's principal on our son's freedom right now.

"Principal Riley, he honestly didn't see this as a weapon. His Uncle collects military items, especially antiques…" he started.

"I got it. Your wife spelled it out for me. Your family doesn't regard military weapons as real weapons. Which is bad education, sir. Teaching your children to view weapons as anything other than what they are can only spell trouble for everyone involved," she lectured.

"I couldn't agree with you more. Camdyn made a mistake, but I think you would have to agree he in no way meant any harm. He's never been a problem before. He doesn't fit the profile of the child you're making him out to be," Mitchell reasoned.

"I'm afraid we take this kind of thing very seriously and there is no way I can…" Principal Riley began.

"Look, you've had a family member who was in the military. I happened to see your plaque and I'm sorry for your loss. You have to understand how a young boy can see these items as symbols of honor and courage. He idolizes his uncle and worshipped his grandfather before he passed. You can't look me in the eye and tell me you actually think he meant to hurt anyone by bringing this here today? He made a mistake. Please don't make him pay for it by removing him from school. Cecelia and I are also going through a divorce right now, and I haven't been around. He's obviously having a hard time. I promise I will make an effort to supervise him more if you can drop these charges, please," Mitchell pleaded.

I watched as Principal Riley took note of the tan line on her left finger where her wedding ring used to be. It must've been a very recent separation per the white circle of flesh. Bingo, we had another personal commonality with the bulldog lady who sat before us, and possibly the tertiary driving force to getting Camdyn off. Divorce could be hard and Principal Riley knew all too well.

"This is a warning. If he so much as sneezes in the wrong direction the rest of the year, we won't be having another conversation like this," she said gruffly.

The detention center officer released Camdyn's elbow with a disapproving snicker. He unlocked the cuffs and Camdyn immediately grabbed my hand. My little boy needed me.

Mitchell followed us home. We sat Camdyn down and talked about the consequences of his actions. It didn't take much convincing. He understood what he did was wrong and the whole experience had scared the crap out of him. I wanted to let it go as a lesson learned, but Mitchell thought he needed punished.

"No video games for one week." Mitchell ordered.

"Okay," he said, not arguing.

"Can I go to my room now? I'm really tired," Camdyn asked.

"Yes, baby. Come down for dinner, okay," I said, giving him a little kiss on the forehead.

"Okay, Mom. Thanks for helping me today," he said.

"Absolutely. We'll always be here for you," I said.

Camdyn ran upstairs. My forehead fell into my hands. I let out the deep breath I'd been holding in, tears running through my fingers.

"How could you let him take a grenade to school?" Mitchell asked with rage.

"I've never seen it before. What am I supposed to do, check his backpack every day for weapons before he leaves? Are you seriously blaming me for this?" I asked exasperated.

"No, I'm sorry," Mitchell began, "but I want to kick your brother's ass."

"You'd surely lose."

"Cece, are you going to talk to Dom? Are you fucking kidding me he gives our kid a grenade?" he asked.

"I didn't even know they'd been in contact. Yes, I'm going to yell at him. He probably didn't think anything of it because it was in a case. Dom probably saw it as an innocent gift."

"Please get over defending your crazy brother. He's a maniac."

"He's not so bad."

217

"He's a cokehead, war-obsessed, piece of shit who almost got our son expelled. I don't want him around Camdyn anymore."

"He doesn't come around much, Mitch."

My headache was seizing me right out of this argument.

Grenades and annihilation.

Annihilation and dirty linens.

"Shh," I told the voices. Not now.

"Still having headaches? Is the medication not working?" he asked.

"Yes, I am and no it's not."

"Go back to Dr. Gibbs."

"I need to, but I've a feeling it's from increased stress lately," I said, looking straight at him.

"I guess you're blaming the added tension on me."

I didn't answer, only leering at him with tired eyes. I was so very tired.

"I'm sorry you're still having headaches," he said.

"Doesn't look like they'll be going away anytime soon. You did a great job today, by the way. I never could've done it without you. Our son would be sitting in a juvenile detention center terrified right now if it wasn't for you."

"She might have buckled for you. You were the first line of defense," he said, a smile peeking up on his ego-driven face.

"We made a good team," I commented sadly, "but I think her mind was made up to kick him out until you got there. I knew you could do it, it's the reason I stalled them."

"Yeah, we did do okay getting him out of that jam. It could've gone very badly," he said smirking the way

I used to like.

We stared at each other across the table, a husband and wife coming together to save their child. A connection we'd always have even though every other one had been broken, making my motivation clouded. There were times I almost liked Mitchell again, but it displeased the other part of me, the ugly part. The one growling so loudly in disapproval right now, I could hardly hear myself think.

"You're quite the salesman," I commented.

Mitchell's face crumbled, a look of anguish turning his lips into a frown.

"No. No I'm not. I have something I wanted to talk to you about." He sighed.

Thoughts of Murph and the Soho smears crossed my mind for the first time today.

"Things not going well at work?"

"I haven't sold anything since January, Cece," Mitchell stated.

Oh shit. I thought Dinah was exaggerating about him not making any big sales, but no sales at all was *really bad.*

"I'm sorry. And to think you were a top producer last year," I jabbed.

"Thanks for reminding me. Last year's peacock, this year's feather duster," he coughed out.

"You'll make a comeback the latter part of the year. Spring and summer are always big for you," I said reassuringly.

Josie stormed in then. Her gaunt face, runny and streaked, staring at us sitting casually at the table like the picture of the hauntingly loving couple we once were.

"I knew something like this was going to happen," she said, panicked.

"He's okay, Josie. Your dad talked them out of arresting him. He wasn't expelled. They dropped the charges," I said cheerfully.

"No, no, Mom. There're things you don't know. I've been keeping his secret, because well, I didn't think he would do anything. But now I'm not so sure," Josie cried.

"What're you talking about, sweetheart?" Mitchell asked.

"I caught him looking up things on the Internet he shouldn't have been looking at," she said in a hushed tone.

My first thought of what it could be was— pornography.

"What kind of things?" Mitchell dared to ask.

"I saw searches for things like bombs, weapons of mass destruction, school shootings…" she trailed off.

Oh porn, would have been so much better.

"Well, when, how?" Mitchell asked flabbergasted.

"Honey, what your dad is trying to say is how did you come to find this information?" I asked.

"I needed to use the computer one day for school and I was looking over his shoulder. He didn't see me," she confessed, "And then I looked in the web history and saw all of the things he'd searched."

"Josie, why didn't you tell us? This may have all been prevented," I scolded.

"Because he asked me not to, said it was no big deal and that he's just interested in that stuff and the things going on in other places," she whined.

"And you believed him?" Mitchell asked.

"Yeah, I believed him. He's quiet, but he's not crazy. At least, I didn't think so," she said.

No one saw Camdyn hanging out midway on the spiral stairwell listening to our conversation.

"She didn't say anything because she didn't want anyone to know her little secret," he hollered down the stairs, pointing at his sister.

"Camdyn, we're all worried about you, don't you—" Josie started, half chasing him up the stairs.

"Josie pukes in jars and hides them in the backyard." Camdyn screamed.

Josie's face turned bright red. So did Mitchell's.

"Josie, is this true?" I asked, in shock.

"No, Mom, he's lying. You little bastard," she swore as she chased him up the steps.

Josie's fists came down hard on the back of Camdyn's head. Before we could stop them they were a wrestling, scratching, hair-pulling mess. Mitchell darted up the stairs and ripped Josie off Camdyn, holding her scrawny arms behind her back.

"Go to your room, Camdyn." Mitchell yelled.

"But I didn't do anything," he whined.

"*Go to your goddamn room*," Mitchell roared.

"*Let go of me*," Josie wailed, through tears.

"Can we talk about this?" Mitchell asked Josie, still holding her in a deadlock.

"*No. Let me go,*" she cried.

"*Mitchell, let her go.*" I demanded.

He let Josie out of his hold and she flew into her room and slammed the door.

"For God's sake, Cece." Mitchell exploded, as he flew down the stairs and out the back door.

I didn't know what Mitchell was doing at first,

until I saw him heading for the backyard with a shovel. I guess he needed proof. I didn't. I knew Camdyn was telling the truth, but Mitchell needed to see it for himself.

I let out a deep breath as my belly churned with nerves. How could I have been so blind? So, that's where she was hiding all of the carefully planned meals I'd prepared for her—in jars in the backyard. Tears stung my cheeks again as I placed my head down on the kitchen table and wailed. The monster in my ear had given me a moment of silence so I could hear myself sob in defeat. Being a good mother was my absolute number one priority and I'd just witnessed the ultimate marker of failure today. There'd never been a greater moment of desolation than this.

Stunned into shock, I couldn't help Mitchell, but I could watch him. He'd ripped off his tie, threw it on the ground, collar unbuttoned, dress shirt rolled up. His day had really gone down the drain. It started with a shit-smeared apartment and ended with jars of vomit in his backyard.

The jars weren't buried very far, which didn't surprise me. Josie had the strong, muscled body of a dancer, but her slight frame wasn't made for digging ditches. When he pulled out the first jar, he lost it. He sat right down on the ground, put his head between his hands, and had himself a nice little cry. At least, he was admitting he'd failed too.

Our backyard was fenced in so no one could see him. I watched Mitchell through the kitchen window, questioning whether I should go out there, but let him have his own silent moment, mourning the family, which had fallen apart since he'd left. He got back up and dug some more. I watched his lips mouth curse words as the sweat poured down with a few stray tears. He was in that state; the one where you get so mad you cry and then get mad again, making the tears go away, until you start crying all over again.

There were at least twenty jars. I was disgusted. My OCD went *tick, tick, tick.* It was almost spring and the jars were probably thawing from the winter. I recognized them. They were the mason jars I'd bought to can peppers, but had never gotten around to it, side tracked by one of many other stupid projects I'd probably picked up on one of my many online decorating sites.

I appeared with a box of trash bags after he had gotten all of the jars unearthed and threw them at his feet. He still needed a moment to himself, as evidenced by the waving of his hand, so I walked away and made myself a cup of coffee.

"Not now, not now," I heard him mutter to his incessantly beeping phone as I strode away.

No one needed to tell me Camdyn wasn't lying, just like no one needed to tell me the person who was buzzing his phone was Katelyn. She would always play second fiddle to us. Why hadn't she figured it out yet?

There was no way I was going to let her parent my daughter now. My daughter was sick. She shouldn't be spending weekends under the influence of that little whore.

I put a roast in the oven for dinner, sat down, drank my coffee, and waited. I wasn't sure how Mitchell wanted to handle this. What's the appropriate punishment or should I say therapy when you find out your son is a wannabe-terrorist and your daughter is bulimic? No parent rulebook for that one. I knew Josie needed help, but I didn't know how to make her get treatment. If I pulled her out of dance, she would never forgive me. It may also worsen her condition, because she lived for dance, and if I took it away, she wouldn't have the ambition to get better. And, if I pulled her out now, it could affect her chances of getting into a good dance school, like Julliard. As for Camdyn, I never knew his passion for video warfare trickled into reality. He couldn't be one of *those* kids, not my son.

Mitchell entered the house a soiled mess. His dress shirt and pants were covered in mud, his face streaked brown from where his dirty hands wiped at his watering eyes. I had a pair of NYU shorts, a matching t-shirt, and boxer briefs sitting for him on the marble kitchen island. He glanced at them and chuckled.

"Well, did you check the computer?" he asked as he washed his hands in the sink.

"No. Camdyn didn't deny he'd made those Internet searches, Mitchell."

"Really, Cece? I've been out there digging up jars of puke and you are, what? Sitting in here, drinking coffee and cooking? Our kids are sick, and what're you doing about it?" he asked.

"Look at what happened today. Obviously, Camdyn was doing some inappropriate research. And, I believe what Camdyn said about Josie. I don't need to know exactly what it looked like. I don't think I want to know," I said honestly.

"And you don't think that's how we got into this predicament in the first place? Ignoring there was a problem. Time to face this head on before we lose our kids," he said through strangled sobs.

"It's going to be okay. Look, I've been researching treatment centers on my phone for Josie. I've written them down. It's getting her to go there that'll be the hard part."

"Oh, she's going. She's going tonight," he insisted.

"Mitchell, we can't simply ship her off. We have to get her buy-in or it's not going to work. Most of those places are voluntary admittance. They can't force her to stay there, and then where will we be? We don't want her to run away," I argued. Forcing Josie into action was always Mitchell's poor solution to her problem.

Well, make her go the therapist.

Make her eat the sandwich.

Eating and therapy weren't things you could force on someone. I'd never seen Mitchell successfully execute any of his bright ideas. Hell, I'd never even seen him try. All I did was try.

"My little girl, my little girl," he tried twice, but it caught in his throat.

"Look, here're some clothes. You're filthy. Why don't you get washed up and calm down and we'll talk about it later," I suggested.

"Where did you find those?" he asked, pointing to his old clothes.

"They were in the garage in your gym bag from when you made a brief, um effort, to go to the gym."

"Right, that delusional time," he said with a cackle.

He took the clothes and charged upstairs to shower. The kids had not made a peep and I was grateful, unsure of how to make things better. Mitchell left his cell phone on the island while he showered and it was lighting up again. I couldn't resist the urge to pick it up. It beckoned me like an electronic Pandora's box, begging to be opened. There were two threads of interest. One was from Nikolay. And one was from her.

Mitchell's Text: *I have a family emergency, you need to try to bring this buyer back, we need this sale.*

Nikolay: *He's walking. He won't reconsider even if we offer to cover all cleaning expenses. He's artsy, says the place has bad karma or aura, one of those two American words.*

Mitchell: *Offer to lower the price.*

Nikolay: *I did, he wants nothing to do with the property. I've tried. Really I have.*

Mitchell: *What did the police say?*

Nikolay: *Nothing. The cameras were disarmed, the door shows a break-in, and they grabbed fingerprints from the walls, but no match. They are assuming it's a homeless person. Didn't sound confident in catching him.*

I didn't know we disarmed cameras. Dinah must have done it earlier. She thought of everything. She was brilliant, I had to give her props for her foresight.

Mitchell: *Damn. I'm dying here. What about the West Village? Did they fumigate?*

Nikolay: *They fumigated, but the smell is still there!*

Even though my chest ached with the pain of failing my children, I was succeeding fantastically at my other venture. It was a time for suffering. Mitchell needed to feel it too. He'd made me suffer by his unscrupulous actions, shaming me across town. The kids were obviously acting out because of his absence, and now his business would suffer as well. It seemed like proper vindication. But somehow it still didn't seem like enough. Katelyn needed to go too.

The second thread of texts was from Katelyn. It was miles long and accompanied five missed calls in the last half hour.

Katelyn: *Where the hell are you? Better be on your way home.* (20 seconds ago)

Yep, threaten him, it'll bring Mitchell right to your doorstep, stupid twat. She didn't even know him. I guessed she believed in blunt force orders as well.

Katelyn: *Mitchell, you said you were leaving fifteen minutes ago?* (5 minutes ago)

Katelyn: *What is going on, I demand to know!* (10 minutes ago)

Oh good, now you're demanding, ordering him will make Mitchell jump right in his car. Didn't know she had it in her.

Katelyn: *Are you still at your old house? Why have you been there so long? What is going on?* (20 minutes ago)

Katelyn: *Is everyone okay? Anyone hurt? Your noodles are getting cold.* (30 minutes ago)

Mitchell: *Family emergency honey, have to run back to Jersey for a bit!* (11:45 p.m.)

Mitchell: *Sure. Curry noodles with chicken for me, #7. Thanks.* (11:15 a.m.)

Katelyn: *Pad Thai for dinner? Thai Palace? My morning jog has me thinking about dinner already!* (11:00 a.m.)

It was all I could snoop before I heard Mitchell tromp down the stairs, but it was enough. She was threatening, nagging, and demanding him via text message of all things. She didn't cook. And he hadn't felt close enough to her to divulge his missed sale this morning. He was afraid to disappoint her, I'd guessed.

None of this boded well for their relationship. He picked up his phone, scanning me as I set the table—four plates.

"I won't be eating," Mitchell said briskly.

"Well, you want to talk to them before you leave, right?" I asked.

"Well, yeah," he responded.

"We're eating dinner, I made a roast, why not just eat it?" I questioned.

"Roast?" he said, involuntarily licking his lips.

"Yep, a big ole meaty one with potatoes and carrots."

I could see his mouth begin to salivate. Something told me he hadn't had a home-cooked meal since he left here.

"Okay, what's the harm," he said, convincing himself.

"Oh, did she have supper waiting for you?" I asked.

"Takeout," he said.

"Not the cook?" I asked.

"Not really," he admitted.

"You want to go get them for dinner or do you want me to?" I asked.

He flapped his right hand around, as to say, *It's all yours.* I approached our wide wooden staircase and screamed upstairs, knowing I'd be totally ineffective if I approached them individually.

"Kids, dinner."

I reentered the kitchen and Mitchell held his head in his hands.

"They're never going to come down with one soft holler," he snapped.

"They'll come down when they're hungry."

"So for Josie, that means never."

"She eats, Mitchell, she just doesn't keep it down."

We glared at each other across the table again like earlier, each of us taking a good look at one another. My husband's brown hair lie wet and all messed up on his head, like I had seen it so many other times. I could actually remember him wearing the old clothes he had now from when he was in his twenties.

"What're you looking at?" he asked.

"You, in your outfit. Brings back memories."

"These clothes are so old they're threadbare," he said. I thought I saw a creep of blush touch his face.

"Do you remember running back in the rain from the movie in the park? What was the name of the movie?" I asked.

"Oh come on, you don't remember?" he asked, insulted.

"I really don't remember," I said. I remembered. But, I wanted him to recount the night for me.

"It was *A League of Their Own*. About the female baseball players, you loved it. You were so mad we had to leave early and you made me rent it the day it came out so you could finish it," he mused.

"Oh yeah, now I remember."

"Cece, what does the movie have to do with my shirt? I wasn't the most stylish guy back then, but I know damn well I didn't wear this on a date."

"No, Mitchell. You didn't wear it on the date, but we did run back to your place. We got all wet in the rain and after we...yeah know, and then you jumped in the shower and put it on afterward," I said, a sly smile playing on my lips.

"Oh, right," he said awkwardly.

"Well, I'm surprised they still fit. Although the shorts are a little snug," he laughed.

"All that greasy takeout is going to make them tighter."

"She's a good person, Cece. You don't have to take a stab at her every chance you get."

I liked the wording "stab at her". He shouldn't say such things to me. I tried not to think about it.

"I'm not the one inflicting injury here."

"It's not like I'm doing this to intentionally hurt you or the kids," Mitchell stated.

"Why are you doing it then?" I asked, suddenly wanting to know the answer to the question.

"What do you mean?"

"Why? What do you have to gain by leaving us and being with her?"

"It's not a matter of gaining anything. I love Kate. I want to be with her."

"And what? Leave your family to start a new one with her in Brooklyn, until she nags you enough to leave her and start over with someone else?"

"Kate doesn't want kids," he spit out.

"Oh, well how very convenient for you. You can run off, leave all of your responsibilities behind, be a part-time father every other weekend, and live it up in the city with your new, young lover. And, how do you think your part-time dad duties are going to rub off on our kids if she doesn't like children?"

"She'll be fine. And, you know I'll be here in a minute if those kids need me. Look, I'm here now," he defended.

"But you're going to leave again. And they need

you right now."

"I'm not arguing about this. I can't stay here. You know that."

"Don't answer me, but think about this. Is it worth it? Everything you're trading for her. Your whole life here. All your old friends you don't see anymore. Spending time with your children. Paying two mortgages. Meeting the demands of two women. I hate to tell you this, but just because we're going to be divorced, doesn't mean I'm not going to call you when the heat goes out in the middle of the night, because we both own this home. And just because you're not here, doesn't mean you're not going to get a phone call when I'm sick and the kids need picked up. So ask yourself, do you really want to be spread so thin? And, at what cost? Because I can assure you for every pedestal you've placed her on, over the years she will be bumped down notch after notch until all you're left with is a normal girl who can't cook."

Mitchell was about to reply when the kids actually appeared, nixing our spat, giving me the last word. They sat down soundlessly, waiting for us to say something. I started cutting the meat and handing out the portions, waiting for Mitchell to start our family talk. He looked at me apparently waiting for the same thing. He was Mr. Wordsmith and he needed to step up to the plate. After I didn't say anything and raised my eyebrows at him he finally got the hint he would be the moderator tonight.

"Kids, we need to come together here and help each other. Everyone has problems and no one should be ashamed. Your mother and I love you both very much and we want the best for you. Josie, you're going into a treatment facility no later than next week," Mitchell said.

"What about dance, you can't make me miss it. I promise I'll eat and not throw it up. Please, just don't make me miss dance," she cried.

"Your mother is going to try to arrange a way for you to stay in dance, but this eating problem is way out of hand, and I want you in a rehab center. You can't stay here," he said.

"I'll go if I can dance," she agreed.

"You're going regardless," Mitchell said.

Josie burst into tears, her head shaking back and forth as if she couldn't fathom the idea of not dancing. Mitchell didn't know how to talk to her. She'd agreed to get help for the first time, damn it.

"Honey, I'm going to do everything I can to find a place which will let you out for your lessons, okay? I will research every one until I find one," I reassured her.

"And what about you, buddy?" Mitchell asked Camdyn. "What're we going to do about your little hobby?" he asked.

"Dad, I never wanted to hurt anyone. I promise. I'm just interested in weaponry and current events," Camdyn said.

"Interested enough to do an Internet search on how to use the weapons against your classmates? Scary stuff, Cam," he said.

"I was checking a story from the news. I won't go near the computer, only for school use, as long as you let me continue my games in a week. Longest week of my life," he reasoned.

"You almost got kicked out of school today, kiddo.

I assure you, your first week in kid jail would have been the longest week of your life. Pretty sure it would've trumped missing a week of video games," Mitchell chided.

"Dad, I know what I did was wrong and I'm sorry about the stuff I was looking up online. I won't do it again," Camdyn promised.

"Honey, if you get feelings like you want to hurt someone or anyone at school, will you please come to us first?" I asked.

Cam threw his hands up in frustration.

"I would never hurt anyone. It was never about hurting anyone. I find it all fascinating, especially when it happens for real. You know how some people like to read about serial killers and own all kinds of books on them, but would never be a serial killer. It's how I am with explosives and stuff," he explained.

"And who do you know obsessed with serial killers?" Mitchell asked.

"I don't know anyone personally, but I saw a show on this guy who owns like every book on them, doesn't mean he wants to be one," he said.

"Okay, okay, we get it, honey. But, if you start having strange thoughts to put your weapons knowledge to real use, we need to know about it," I said.

"I got it," Cam said.

Mitchell left as soon as dinner was over without saying another word to me. Maybe he would think about what I said. Maybe he wouldn't. But the most important thing was she wanted him home for dinner and he ate dinner with us instead. I win again, bitch.

Chapter 18
Fire Engine Red

My Friday night grocery list made me blubber like a fool in the eight-items-or-less line of the supermarket. A woman waiting to check out behind me adorned in a Burberry scarf and too much red lipstick offered me a tissue. She looked like she'd run into the store to snag something on her way to a hot date only to be railroaded by the likes of me. Maybe she thought I'd hurry up if she were polite.

"Thank you, I'm sorry," I whimpered, as I turned my attention back to the sparse items in my little red basket.

One filet of salmon. One lemon.

Salmon would always be the fish to remind me of rejection. I don't know why I'd tortured myself, choosing it for my meal tonight. The pink healthy piece of protein took me back to my conversation with Maeve on her doorstep.

I'm sorry, I only bought enough salmon for the five of us.

The remaining items mocked me as they slid along the black plastic conveyor belt.

One bottle of wine. Drinking alone tonight.

Some string green beans I knew I wouldn't eat, and a single box of Raisinets. Chocolate would be very necessary tonight.

It was joint custody weekend—my first weekend alone of many to come if Dinah's plan didn't work out. Now more than ever I was compelled to do whatever Dinah wanted so I never had to feel this way again. It wasn't fair. I'd done nothing wrong, yet he was permitted to take them away from me on the two days I actually had a whole eight hours to spend with them. Divorce was a rotten deal.

Mitchell arrived to pick up the children for their weekend visit. Josie would enter a private facility for her eating disorder on Monday, so she only had to spend one weekend with Mitchell and Big Red before going in for treatment. I felt bad Camdyn would have to face them alone in the coming months.

"He's here," I announced up the stairwell with dread.

Someone might as well have grabbed every damn one of those family portraits lining my stairwell and taken a sledgehammer to them. My perfect family picture shattered as I watched my children run down the stairs with their weekend bags, leaving me for the first time. The front door opened and the kids ran past their father on the stoop and climbed into his car. Mitchell was kind enough to greet me at the door. It felt so odd, almost funny, for him to be knocking on his own front door, but there was nothing comical about it.

"How have you been?" he asked.

"Okay, I guess," I lied.

I'd dressed up for my own husband: snug, ass-jeans, (as he always liked to call them), a deep purple v-neck sweater I knew he liked, did up my hair and full makeup. I looked good. Mitchell's eyes wandered nonchalantly from the deep crevice of my v-neck to my stilty heels. Katelyn didn't wear sexy footwear, and as much as he'd complained about my shoes, I knew they turned him on.

It was all part of the plan. I'd rehearsed the speech. I'd been waiting for this moment all week. The hard part would be getting it all out and making my scripted lines believable.

"Can I ask you something?"

"Cece, what is it?" he asked. My confliction was constricting my speech. But, I needed to get this out. And, I needed him to really think about my words after he left, and realize she really wasn't worth all the trouble. She was just an ordinary girl who couldn't cook.

"It's hard for me to see them go with you when we used to be a family. I don't believe you don't love me anymore. I feel like you're making a big mistake and you're too proud to admit it." It burned coming off my tongue, but hopefully he'd perceive my strangled speech as nervousness.

"I love her. I do. Let it go," he said as he backed down the stairs, putting his hands up in defense, pumping them with each backward step.

"You say you love her, Mitchell. But you've never said you didn't love me anymore. Think about it," I spat as I closed the door, sinking to the floor in my foyer. As the car pulled away with my family inside, I turned into a watery mess on my pristine hardwood floors.

****

I met Dinah at eight o'clock outside of the diner like I said I would. She was wearing all black, a dark backpack slung over her shoulder. The thought of what could be in there scared the shit out me. I didn't think about wearing black. She should have told me if we were supposed to be in disguise. I wore jeans, a navy sweater and brown leather boots.

"This address," she said, throwing a piece of paper at me.

"Well, hello to you too," I said.

"I'm not happy with you."

"Excuse me?"

"You act like coward."

"You cannot be mad at me. You need to tell me what's going on if you don't want me to be surprised when you tell me to pick up a bum off the street corner. Please tell me we aren't picking up anymore bums tonight?" I asked.

"No bums, but you need your big girl pants on tonight."

"You said the same thing before. I hope my Ann Taylor skinny jeans will do," I joked.

Dinah glowered at my humor.

"You know the police are investigating the Soho break-in?"

"I would hope so," she said sarcastically.

"Don't you worry about getting caught?"

"What did I do? Nothing. I watched another man do something,"

"And drove him to the place to do his something, and paid him money to do his something." I sighed, repeating her words.

"If you want to quit, drop me off and I can finish this on my own. I'm sick of hearing you complain."

"I'm fine. You just need to tell me what we're doing. No more surprises. We're going to Tribeca, in my opinion, the richest part of Manhattan. And every property has a doorman. What do you imagine we can pull off there?"

"There's a new building under construction right now. When it's complete it will have forty units. Right now, there are two units on display, acting as the model to sell out the rest of the building. Keep in mind, right now, no one lives in this complex. So, to answer your question, there is no twenty-four hour doorman because it's vacant. There's a buyer interested in purchasing the two bottom units on display, knocking out the wall, and making it one big loft. The apartments on the bottom level go for five million dollars a piece and the price goes up as the floors climb. Better views, higher price. This guy wants to get in for cheap on the ground level and make one large unit. He's a serious buyer. He's meeting Mitchell tomorrow to put in an offer."

"So that would make it a ten million dollar deal." I shouted.

"Yes and Nikolay found the buyer, so naturally they're splitting it."

"I'm nervous Katelyn will try to double-check the listing tonight for nuances, since the last two buyers she set up failed miserably."

"It's the weekend. He's probably wining and dining the bitch right now."

"Actually, they have my kids tonight," I said with a gulp.

"Oh, see. She's already moving in, taking over, replacing you. She's the young, fun mom and you're the mean one who yells at them to do their homework and their chores. See what is happening here?"

Those were fighting words. Dinah knew how to get me going. Could they really like her more than me?

Those were thoughts I hadn't considered. She was younger, maybe Josie and Camdyn would relate to her better, because we sure weren't connecting lately.

"You're right. Let's do this."

I parked and realized Miss Long-Winded never did tell me what we were doing, only the background on the real estate. I recognized the street I was on. It was the same one where I woke up a few weeks ago after passing out. The one responsible for all of the parking tickets. The building on our hit list was gorgeous. It was a tall, glass, modern complex with different wings jutting out in all different directions. It looked like a perfectly balanced Jenga puzzle. All of the units had floor to ceiling windows, giving it a very cutting-edge appeal. I could see the construction scaffolding and the two completed units on the bottom floor. Dinah was tinkering in her bag for a minute, but I couldn't see what she was doing in the darkness.

"Okay, it's ready, let's go. We're going to climb onto the scaffolding," she said.

"People will see us," I said.

"We'll wait until the street is calm and then climb up."

I rolled my eyes thinking we would be there all night if we were waiting for the street to be empty. But the area was residential and surprisingly not busy. When there was no one in sight we climbed the scaffold until we were facing the window of one of the new apartments.

It was tight up there. Half of the scaffolding hinged downward from the middle, hanging like a half-folded piece of paper. The men working on the building would have to snap it together to get their footing and I didn't see how we were supposed to balance on the tiny half-landing with my foot wedged between two metal bars and the complex. Dinah moved with grace as I shimmied behind her. After we'd scooted along enough to meet her specifications, she placed her leather, gloved hand on one of the windowpanes and jiggled it until it slid open. I realized then how much recon she actually did before a "mission." She knew the window would open before we got there.

Dinah pulled a long cylindrical metal pipe from her bag. It had what appeared to be a wire sticking out of the top of it. My gut wrenched doing triple somersaults and I started to fall backward. She grabbed me at the last minute before I tumbled over the edge. Dinah looked at me then, her bright eyes shining in the dark night. She could have let go and I would have fallen backward, crashing my head onto the concrete. She could throw her device, ruin her husband, and have an alibi all figured out for her. But she didn't. She reeled me in like the flailing fish I was.

"Breathe, Cecelia, now," she demanded.

A deep breath sputtered out as she pulled me to my feet. At the same moment she dropped the pipe in the building.

"Nooo," I shouted in what seemed to be slow motion.

"We have to go. Don't shout another word loudly unless you want to go to prison for a very long time," she instructed in a whisper.

My legs jelloed beneath me and I felt her sharp fingernails dig into my skin, steadying me again.

"Think about your children. If you don't want to die, you need to move," she said in a hushed, urgent manner.

I was behind her on the platform, twenty feet above the sidewalk. If I didn't move she'd die too. I was now in front of her on our way out. My legs started to tremble backward toward the makeshift construction ladder. My limbs were going too slowly, but I couldn't seem to control them. I was grateful they were moving at all, but Dinah urged me faster.

I heard a hushed, "Go, go, go."

Climbing down was the hardest part. Shaking feet on metal rungs. *Clank, clank, clank.* It reminded me of my father's coins whizzing down the heating register. But my punishment for this offense would be far greater than the lash of a leather belt.

Once descended, Dinah grabbed my arm and pulled me to the car. My feet felt like they were being trudged through mud. Dinah threw me into the cold passenger seat and hopped into the driver side, speeding off. I wasn't sure if she knew how to drive by the way she was swerving around the city streets, clipping curbs, and nearly taking out civilians. She seemed to get the hang of it by the time we reached the interstate. *Thank God!*

"Coward! I knew you would mess this up for us," she yelled.

"Where's the explosion? I didn't hear it," I mumbled, still in shock.

"There's no explosion. Did you think I wanted every cop in New York looking for us? We can't be made a priority case. We would surely be caught then. I like keeping the theme of our work—prank/crime, then we only remain in the middle of their never-ending pile of criminal cases," she reasoned.

"Oh, we have a theme? That's nice," I said in a too-high-pitched voice. "Well, what was the can you threw inside then? It was a bomb right? It sure looked like a bomb!"

My mouth was dry and my lungs hurt from holding my breath so long.

"What's the theme, Cece? What's been the theme of all of our little acts of destruction?" she asked.

"Quit asking me fucking questions and tell me what you did. Jesus Christ, you can't ever give me a straight answer. It's like you feel the need to setup every conversation with a dramatic ending. Well, guess what, Dinah? Your actions are drama enough," I said.

Her eyes seared laser holes through my body. I thought she was going to hit me or kill me or push me out of the car. At this point, I almost welcomed it.

"It was a giant stink bomb," she said, her Russian accent extenuating the "ink" in *stink*, baring her flashy teeth, making me flinch back in my seat.

"A stink bomb?" I laughed.

Then I started laughing uncontrollably, so hard I started to cry. She was going to drive me mad.

"Well, there's a little more to it than stink."

Here we go.

"Oh, tell me. I have no more patience for your stories so tell me about it, please," I pleaded, weary now.

"It's a stink bomb. But it's also going to release a gas which will make it hard to breathe and see," she explained.

"So, it's tear gas. Oh , that's great, that's also terrorism, Dinah. We're fucking terrorists now," I panicked.

"Not necessarily. It's definitely the worst one yet, but this is for a double deal, we had to go big."

"Go big or go home." I screamed.

"Calm down, we'll not be caught," Dinah insisted.

"Wait. Why did you tell me I was going to die? What the hell was the dying part about?"

"I needed you to move. If you knew I hadn't detonated the bomb you would have gone back in to get it like an idiot and gotten us caught."

"It's not detonated yet? Turn around, Dinah," I said vehemently.

"The effects wouldn't have been as present by tomorrow and the impact not as grand," she said with excitement.

"Turn this car around, we're going back to get it!"

"No. This is it, Cece. No more mischief. Not in the city, at least. There's one more final act which will bring it all together, but timing is everything," she said in her flat monotone.

"I can't do this anymore. I'm out. I'm done. Turn the car around or I'll call the police," I threatened.

"Don't call the authorities. Remember this. You tell no one about me. If you tell anyone about me, it will only hurt you. I'm like ghost. Besides, how well do you think you will be able to care for your children from behind bars? It's where you'll go if you tell the police about me, because you're an accomplice to everything I've done," she said.

This crazy Russian bitch had me backed into a corner and there was no getting out now. Hot tears hit my face as we pulled into the empty parking lot of the diner. Where was Dinah's car? I turned my head to scan the parking lot and then—w*hack*, my jaw clapped together, knocking my teeth and tongue in a forced bite.

Holy hell, did the bitch just slap me?

I was so shocked, my cheeks sucked together in disbelief, my face stinging from the wallop.

"Pull it together. You're going to be the only reason we don't succeed. You need an alibi tonight. Go somewhere you can be seen. Mitchell is no dummy. He's going to figure out after this one they're all connected. See you next Thursday," she said plainly, as if she hadn't belted me across the face.

I watched her dark, lithe body sneak off into the night. She barreled around the corner by foot and seemed to vanish into thin air as my vision flickered in and out from the pale yellow lights in the parking lot.

An alibi? I needed an alibi. This was really bad. I took a good look at myself in my rearview mirror and gasped. There was a sizable red hand mark on my right cheek. If she wanted me to be in disguise, not imprinting my cheek with her palm would have been a good starting point. My own right hand stung as I clung onto the steering wheel. I sat there staring at the dumpster in the parking lot, realizing I might end up in one if I tried to cross the violent woman again. I was terrified of her stealthy fearlessness but admired her precision to carry out a plan. She was the collaborating force who would bring me victory.

Since I had no friends to visit, I drove to *The Coffee Bean*. Sam was wiping down the counters getting ready to close up for the night when a slew of teenagers bopped in, fifteen minutes before closing time. Sam would serve them though because it was the type of businessman he was. Despite being a pothead, he was serious about his shop. He sighed as he saw me.

I threw on an apron, gave him a wink, and started assisting the late night rush. Sam gave me a raise of his eyebrows back, saying *thanks*, and started taking orders. To my surprise, Callie and Julie staggered in next, drunk as twin sister skunks.

"What is this?" Sam sighed.

"Friday night," I chirped back, wishing I'd gotten there earlier.

Work had a way of calming me down. I found peace in scouring things until they sparkled. If I was obsessively cleaning at home, people thought I was nuts, but at work I was just doing my job.

"Having fun ladies?" I asked them.

"Hi, Cece, we miss you," slurred Callie.

"I miss you too, girls. Where've you been getting into trouble at tonight?" I asked, irony ringing in my voice.

They were all dressed up, in almost matching, short black party dresses.

"Robin's charity thingy. Something about infusing good juju back into her home. The cops still have no leads. She says she's very disappointed in them so far," Julie said.

"Yeah, they're incompetent. No leads on my dolls and they don't even care," I said flustered.

"As much as I enjoy your company, may I offer you ladies some black coffee to sober up? We're closing in a few," Sam interrupted.

"Got a hot date, Sam?" I asked.

"Only if you're coming over later," he whispered in my ear, making me half-smile in my shocked state.

Sam was courteous to the teens, but had a special hatred in his heart for Julie and Callie.

"Two waters please. Mouth dry," Callie managed.

Sam pulled two bottled waters out of the cooler and handed them to the girls.

"May we escort you out?" Sam said in his most gentleman-like voice.

"Sure," Julie said.

"Did you have a good night working?" Callie asked.

"It was a rough one, but we pulled through," I said, giving Sam a wink.

****

I sat in my drawstring, striped pajama pants, sipping my coffee, and watching the breaking morning news unveil a suspected terrorist attack in Tribeca. *Terrorist.* I knew the media would call it an attack. I didn't think it bordered on a prank. This was going to notch up the investigation more than Dinah thought. I should have never trusted her. My coffee sloshed over the sides of my mug, burning my hands, as I suddenly realized I was shaking from head to toe.

"*Shit.*" I swore as I fumbled my cup onto the coffee table.

There were a dozen fire trucks, multiple police cars and a couple ambulances. *Ambulances, oh no!* Then I saw Mitchell on the television being wheeled out. I recognized the bright, purple, argyle tie I'd bought him for Christmas flapping off the stretcher. I inhaled sharply, sitting back down as the bile rose in my mouth. I sprinted to the bathroom and vomited my breakfast.

Oh My God. What have I done?

Annihilation and dirty linens.

Was Mitchell lying half-dead on filthy hospital sheets? Why did the vision make me slightly gleeful.

Stop. That. Now.

Upon googling the effects of tear gas, I saw words like: *Blindness, Cardiac Arrest, and Severe Burns of the Skin.* She never told me it could hurt him. My blood bubbled and the heat touched my face and scalp. I wanted to call her and scream at her, send her a nasty text or a scathing email, but I couldn't. Because she had sworn off any type of communication, which could link us together if the *shits hits the fans.* Well, I believed it just had. I jumped, all-ants-in-my-pants, as Josie buzzed my cell.

"Mom, did you see the news? Dad's been hurt," she said.

"I saw it baby, is he okay?"

"I don't know. We're on our way to the hospital now," she said.

"I'll meet you there," I said.

Chapter 19
Just a Prank

When Dominic strapped the beak shut on Mrs. Avon's class parrot in third grade because he was sick of it repeating itself, it could've been perceived as a prank. And when Mitchell stopped paying attention to our synchronized digital calendar, and I'd made it auto-alert him it was our anniversary when it wasn't, that was a pretty good prank, too. Although, I did feel guilty about receiving ruby earrings for no good reason at all. At the very worst, the heinous acts performed on my dolls could be seen as a vicious prank by the more depraved individuals of the world.

But what we did to Mitchell during his listing appointment—was not a prank. It was something much worse. And even though the earrings were expensive, I had a feeling this prank would cost him far more.

I gathered myself together and dashed to the hospital. It would look suspicious if I didn't go. Plus, I couldn't stand the thought of Katelyn comforting my children. They were probably scared as hell. I swallowed hard at the men in blue surrounding the hospital, and then I shook it off. The city couldn't be on this high of an alert over a little tear gas.

When I'd reached Mitchell's room, he looked like he'd fallen face first into a wasp's nest, with his puffy eyes swelled shut and red flushed skin. If I'd only gotten rid of the pest problem sooner, this could have all been avoided.

He was salivating too much, reminding me of a teething baby, making me want to give him a bib. Maybe I could make him one that said: *My wife gassed me,* so they would know what happened to him.

I wasn't sure if Mitchell could see me through his swollen lids. Katelyn had latched onto his hand with her pale, long, talon-like fingers. She was trying to be a comforting girlfriend, but she was squeezing his hand too tightly in my presence. She didn't look like she fit the part to me. They looked mismatched somehow, like a couple trying too hard to be in love. It was the first time I'd seen them together since the restaurant, but something was off.

Katelyn wore black yoga pants and a zip-up sweatshirt; her raggedy hair pulled up in a tight, wild ponytail, no makeup or lip gloss to separate her nude mouth from her skin.

She looked more like his niece than his girlfriend. Katelyn sensed my skepticism and whispered something into Mitchell's ear to alert him I'd arrived.

I scooped up my children in my arms and clenched them tightly to my chest.

"Cece," Mitchell croaked.

"Yes. Hi, Mitchell, I'm here. What the hell happened?" I asked.

Mitchell propped himself up on his elbows, as his attentive girlfriend tried to convince him to take it easy.

"Someone gassed my listing," he said, his voice raspy and dry.

"Jesus. Are you okay? Any permanent damage? Was it a terrorist attack? Should we be in this room?" I

249

asked, trying to act erratically like I normally would.

Katelyn's nose wrinkled at me. I saw the corner of Mitchell's mouth perk up, because he knew what was supposedly going through my mind.

"No, it was only tear gas, relax. You aren't catching a flesh-eating virus right now," he commented.

"Thanks for the reassurance," I said.

"Cece, where were you last night?" Mitchell asked.

"I helped out Sam," I said, which was not a lie.

Mitchell's mouth went slack again as he turned to Katelyn trying to finagle a disconcerted look.

Why won't someone give him a bib? The drool was killing me. My OCD—t*ick, tock.*

Katelyn didn't try to hide her frown and I knew she'd planted a seed in his head. A seed sprouting with thoughts of me linked to the attacks on his listings.

"Oh, I didn't think you worked Fridays. Did you see anyone out?" he asked.

"Needed to keep myself busy," I said sharply, "Callie and Julie stopped by after a charity event at Robin's I wasn't invited to."

My not being invited comment shut him up. I knew he wouldn't talk to Sam, but he could always call Callie or Julie's husbands to verify they'd seen me. The girls had no idea I didn't work all night.

Bam. Alibi. Suck it.

Katelyn, obviously agitated, rolled her eyes, her pale cheeks turning as red as her hair.

Josie shot Katelyn a nasty look, but Katelyn was too self-absorbed to notice.

"Why the sudden interest in my evening?" I asked.

Then, a police officer entered the room, pointed at me and said, "This her?"

"Never mind, she was working last night," Mitchell said quickly.

"What's going on?" I asked.

"There's been a lot of strange things going on lately, Cece. The police asked me where all of my family members were last night," he said.

"Glad you still consider me family," I beamed.

"Of course," he said.

Katelyn's eyes and tongue went-a-wagging as she turned her head trying to hide her alarm.

Camdyn seemed oblivious, but, again, I watched my daughter's reaction, and her slight smile told me she was pleased with her father's answer. I wondered what happened to turn Josie so sour toward Katelyn.

"Can I take the kids now? We can come back and see you later, give you two a moment," I suggested.

They both looked at me surprised.

"Oh, you know I'm not buying it's simply tear gas," I said, nervously squeezing myself tighter in a self-hug.

I thought I heard a stifled laugh from Mitchell, until Katelyn gave him a good punch on the shoulder.

"Ugh, come on, Kate," he complained. "Okay, see you later kids," Mitchell said as they kissed him goodbye.

Dinah covered her tracks well. The owners of the complex were in cahoots with the mob. Eyes were totally off me and now the focus had shifted to the Rocco Family. There was probably a new mob war going on in the city right now because of me. Or there was a mob family who would soon be replacing my Louboutins with cement boots. I was hoping it was the former and not the latter.

251

The kids were shaken by the attack on their father, but Camdyn was more enthralled by the militia weaponry used than the assault itself.

"Do you think it was a terrorist attack?" Camdyn asked me.

"No, no, honey," I answered him. He looked disappointed by my answer.

"Josie, I noticed you making faces at Katelyn. How was your first weekend with her? Did everything go okay?" I asked nervously.

"Not really." Josie said.

My stomach knotted.

"What happened?" I asked.

"She was mean to Josie," Camdyn answered for his sister.

"Shut up, Cam." Josie argued.

"Tell me what happened," I demanded. My tone was angrier than usual and both of the kids stopped fighting and straightened up in their seats.

"I don't like her. She wouldn't cook anything edible. She told me I needed to eat a cheeseburger and said I looked gross and none of the boys would like me because I was too skinny," Josie spat.

What?

It was everything I could do not to turn my car around, reenter the hospital and blast the stupid twat across the face. My daughter wasn't a picky eater, she had an eating disorder; there was a difference. Katelyn sexualized her by telling her none of the boys would find her attractive. What kind of thing is that to say to a teenage girl? As if all of her life's aspirations should be to appear attractive to the opposite sex, and if she didn't achieve this look, she was gross. I was horrified.

252

"It's not true, Josie, you're beautiful."

"You're beautiful," Cam mocked me in a dreamy tone.

"What did your father say?" I gasped, ignoring my son, grasping the steering wheel tighter.

"He was showing an apartment."

"So, what did she feed you?" I asked, scared of the next answer.

"She put the cheeseburger and fries in front of me and told me to eat like a normal kid and to stop being such a freak," Josie said quietly. It sounded like Mitchell's warfare tactics on Josie's eating disorder coming out of Katelyn's twatish mouth. This was unacceptable.

"The cheeseburger was good. It was from this place called Thistle Hill," Camdyn added brightly. God forbid Katelyn attempt to cook the burger. A slow, steady burn started between my temples.

"So, what did she make you eat instead when you wouldn't eat the burger?" I asked.

"Nothing. She said I was only going to throw it up anyway, so what did it matter." Josie sighed. "She said I might as well at least enjoy it on the way down."

"*Ugh.*" I was so revolted I couldn't speak for a moment, choking on the venom pooling in my throat.

"So, she let you eat nothing?" I asked furiously.

"Yeah, she told me she was brought up to eat whatever her mother was kind enough to bring to the table, and if not, to starve. And that you had spoiled me," Josie answered sadly. Her head was bowed down in embarrassment, and I'd never hated anyone in my entire life more than I hated Katelyn right then.

"So, she thinks preparing healthy meals is spoiling

253

a child? Someone should put her down so she's unable to procreate."

"Wow, mom," Josie said.

Then, the monster roared so loudly I veered off the road. It startled me like a semi-truck blaring its horn in my ear. She told my bulimic daughter to starve because she couldn't eat like a normal girl. Then, she let her famish? And, Mitchell let her starve too? I was going to kill her. I was going to kill both of them.

Pieces of skull mixed with red blood and hair.

Annihilation and Dirty Linens.

"*Mom.*" Camdyn screamed.

I steered the car back on the road, but my tears were coming fast now, and I didn't care if my kids saw me crying this time. All that mattered was I got them home, safe and sound, so they never had to spend another moment alone with that awful bitch.

****

I checked Josie into the inpatient treatment facility on Monday morning. As I hauled my daughter's suitcase into her little dorm-like room, I began to cry again. My emotions were out of control lately. I wanted to be strong for her, but the facility was basically a hospital with nicer rooms. I was leaving my baby girl in a hospital because she was trying so hard to be perfect it was killing her.

Of course, I blamed myself. But like Mitchell said, she had *It* too. I wrapped my arms around her bony shoulders and told her I would see her on Wednesday evening for her dance lesson. I'd worked out a system with her teachers to have her attend school via the Internet and return to classes in the fall without missing a beat. It was almost April, so she would only be out a couple of months.

The facility also agreed to her dance classes, as long as I picked her up, took her straight there and back and did not let her eat while in my supervision. The inpatient program was ten weeks and I was allowed to visit anytime I wanted. Josie seemed okay with the arrangement, taking everything in stride, realizing it was time to get some help for her problem.

Mitchell wasn't able to make it to the hospital to drop Josie off because he still wasn't feeling well. He didn't have any permanent damage, but was still having nausea from the gas. Camdyn had become obsessed with the potential for a terrorist attack and had been talking to my brother about the dynamics of the incident. Wouldn't he be floored to find out who'd really done it.

I dropped Camdyn off at Dom's place in Queens for the day because he did not want to see Josie off. He felt guilty for ratting her out and their relationship wasn't repaired yet from their scuffle in the upstairs hallway. On my way to Dom's, Mitchell lit up my phone. I picked it up reluctantly; still afraid they might catch on to my shaky alibi.

"How'd it go?" he asked.

"She was okay. Not thrilled to be there, but as long as she can still dance, she'll be okay." I sighed.

"Good. I'm sorry I couldn't be there. I feel badly about missing her first day."

"She understands."

"Listen, Cece. There's something I need to talk to you about," he began, his voice still a dry raspy mess.

I winced, preparing for the worst.

"Yes?"

"I've cancelled your American Express card."

"You what?"

"Cece, we're not going to be married anymore. I can't have you going on shopping sprees and expecting me to pay for them."

"I haven't been on any shopping sprees, Mitchell."

"I know, but you know what I mean."

"No, I don't know what you mean. Please explain to me how I'm supposed to feed our children with no money. Speaking of feeding our children, I heard Katelyn told Josie to eat a cheeseburger or starve. Did you know she told her she was gross and none of the boys would find her attractive?" I seethed.

"I talked to her about what she'd said."

That's it! You talked to her about it.

"Mitchell, how can you be with someone who talks to your daughter like that? She told her she was a freak."

"Kate's learning, Cece. She's never been a parent before."

"And thank God for that, because she's pretty terrible at it. Our daughter is sick, and she tells her she's gross. She told her it didn't matter if she fed her because she was going to throw it up anyway."

"Kind of true," Mitchell chimed.

"*Mitchell.*"

"Look, she'll never go hungry in our house again. Kate made a mistake. She knows she did," Mitchell conceded.

"How many other mistakes is she going to make and at what cost to our children?"

"Look, Cece, I'm going to give you a credit card with a monthly five hundred dollar credit maximum.

I'm shutting off your access to the checking account, as I will be paying all of the bills for the house," Mitchell said, avoiding my question.

"You have to be joking me, Mitchell? Do you know how much groceries are? No you don't, because I do the shopping. Five hundred isn't going to cut it. What if the kids need stuff for school? What if I have an emergency?"

"Cece, we're separated. You can buy things nonorganic, and save a dollar. I cannot support you anymore. You will receive child support to cover the kids' expenses. Consider yourself lucky I'm paying your mortgage. After the kids go to college, it will change. I suggest you start figuring everything out," he preached.

"Oh, you make me feel so lucky. What do you expect me to do, Mitchell? I haven't worked in over a decade. How am I supposed to support myself, when I've spent all my time supporting our family instead? And you're going to leave me high and dry?" I asked.

"Again, I'm paying for you to live in your very expensive home and giving you limited spending money and child support. It's a lot for an ex-husband. A lot more than most. I think I'm being generous. You have six years before Camdyn goes to college to figure out the rest."

"Oh, aren't you the best?"

"Time to get a job, Cece. You've sponged off me long enough. Put your interior decorating talent to work, open up a cleaning company, do something."

"You're such an ass. I suppose you don't recognize the years I've spent working to take care of our family? This is just so you can afford your second mortgage with your ten years younger, child-abusing, gingersnap of a mistress. I bet she's not even there right now and doesn't know a thing about your money problems. How attractive would you be to her then? I lived with you in a two-bedroom apartment. Ask yourself if she would do the same."

He didn't say a word.

"Oh, she is there."

"No, she actually went north, I mean, she's not here," he said.

"North where? You said north."

"It's not what I meant. She's an aspiring novelist, she travels to get inspiration for her writing."

"Well, isn't she charming."

"Stop it, Cece. I appreciate how well you've taken care of our family, but my business has been bad, to say the least. Money is tight and I have to make cuts."

Dinah was right. He cut me off.

"Fine, I have to go."

"Well, I will have the card to you in a couple of weeks. Please try not to go overboard on purchases with the old American Express in the meantime. It's still good till then."

I hung up on him, totally unsympathetic of his financial problems. I hoped his eyes were still swollen like bruised plums and his stomach was so sour he'd be barfing up takeout for a week. Katelyn probably didn't even know their money was tight. He was doing this to keep her happy. It made me sick.

At this point, I was very interested in hearing the rest of Dinah's plan, despite the whole "terrorism" thing. I needed to get rid of Katelyn. Mitchell's first priority obviously wasn't our children or he wouldn't be defending her. She could not be a part of their future.

Dinah was right, I had been a coward, and now I had a new sense of bravery fueled by protecting my family, and making sure Mitchell and Katelyn paid for hurting my kids. I had so much more motive to inflict harm than ever before.

I found it peculiar Mitchell said Katelyn had gone Northeast. As in to East Hampton? Why was Katelyn already heading up to the cottage? I thought they weren't renting it until June. Now I knew where the extra pinch in his wallet was really coming from. The little wholesome twit from middle-of-nowhere Ohio was turning out to be more high maintenance than I expected. Mitchell would've been better off with my revolving bill at Barneys. Would've cost him far less than two additional mortgages a month.

The loss of my little plastic friend, which had seen me through every one of my small tragedies would be a setback. While street-parked in front of Dominic's dump of an apartment, I stirred another ladle into the shit soup of my life. I knew I should have anticipated this, but I really thought he would do me the justice of letting me continue my lifestyle as retribution for all my years of service. I felt like I was being robbed of my housewife pension. There was a part of me who believed he would take care of me; as long as he could have her too, but it was another fantasy I'd been led to believe.

He was screwing me—*bad*. I would do whatever it took to make sure they were the ones who were hurt in the end. Mussels, bums, terrorists, throw in some prostitutes, piranhas, guns, whatever it took—I was down.

I rang the doorbell three times and no one answered. I checked the address Dom gave me again and confirmed I had the right one. He wasn't supposed to take Camdyn anywhere. Dom knew he wasn't allowed to drive my children places, because of his dependency issues. I became panicked. I had dropped my daughter off at a treatment facility, found out I was financially paralyzed, and now my son was missing. Combined with the fact half the law enforcement in the city was looking for me, I was well on my way to a mental breakdown.

The chipped blue paint of the cruddy stoop prodded my leg as I sat down to call Dom's cell. It went to voicemail, which only heightened my panic. I couldn't see through the dirt-smudged windows of the apartment, but everything appeared dark. Where the hell had he taken him? Dom was an irresponsible adult and often lost things like his car keys and his wallet. I knew he probably had a spare key stashed somewhere, so when he came stumbling home from a drunken night on the town, he could get into his place.

There was a red flowerpot, which housed a wilted plant. Dom was not the type to care for anything green. I stuck my fingers into the soil about an inch and felt the black, smooth box. I grabbed the plastic holder and quickly keyed myself in.

Well, that sight wasn't what I needed to see to calm my nerves. There were more gun safes than dishes in his pantry. The tiny apartment included only two rooms and one of them was all weaponry. I appreciated the fact Dominic had them locked up, but there must have been twenty gun safes piled on top of one another and a slew of ammo to go with them. He had milk crates full of grenades, which was alarming enough. There was one grenade set off to the side, which caught my attention, because it wasn't with the others. It reminded me of a pineapple with its shape and indentations on the sides. It appeared markedly older than some of the others, but there was a metal clip fastened to it which made me take another look. Upon closer inspection, I noticed it did indeed still have the pin in it. I started to get sick at the thought of my son being here with a live grenade.

Two flipcharts with maps were stationed on top of the couches with circles highlighting the area of the gassing in Tribeca. There was an internet print-out of what tear gas was and its side effects, along with a box of Dom's military stuff laying wide open, war paraphernalia spilling out of the box.

My head was pounding and I needed to lie down on the rumpled, stained couch for just a moment until the pain stopped.

****

"Mom, mom, wake-up," Camdyn said.

"Hey, uh, Cece, you might not want to lay there," I heard Dom mutter.

"Huh," I said.

"I had a special friend over the other night, you might not want to lie there," Dom repeated.

"Oh, God," I said as I tried to get up.

"Sorry, Mom. I was hungry and Dom didn't have anything here so we walked to this great Korean restaurant and they had the best barbecue ribs I've ever eaten," Camdyn said excitedly.

"Why didn't you answer your phone, Dom?" I asked.

261

"I'm sorry. It died and I haven't charged it in a couple of days," he said.

"Okay, well I broke in because I was worried," I explained.

"Flowerpot, dead giveaway, huh?" Dom asked.

"Definitely."

"Well, I gotta lot a loot in here. I'll have to do a better job of hiding it."

"Yeah, Dom, I need to talk to you about what else you're hiding here, too. I'm not sure Camdyn needs to see all of this. I wasn't aware you had so many dangerous weapons for roommates. Perhaps, you should consider getting a storage unit. It looks like you're stocking up for the end of the world here," I joked.

"You mean the Zombie Apocalypse?" he asked.

"The what?"

"It's going to be the end of the world and I will be ready for those fuckers," Dom declared.

"Language. Can we not cuss in front of him?" I sighed.

"He's twelve, almost a teenager. He's heard it before," Dom said, as Camdyn rolled his eyes at me.

"But he doesn't need to hear it from his uncle."

"You don't look so good. Your cheeks are all red," Dom said, ignoring me.

"I had a headache. Which is why I laid down. I never meant to fall asleep. We gotta go buddy. Tell your uncle thanks for whatever weird plots you two were coming up with down here," I said.

"We figured it out," Dom said.

"Oh yeah, what? Terrorist attack or mob hit?" I asked.

"Neither. It was someone no one would ever suspect," Dom said.

"Do tell, Colombo," I inquired.

"It was a woman," he accused.

My heart sank to the gun trodden floor, and then—*Kaboom*—went the mental dynamite in my brain. My vision wavered for a moment. There were too many people in the room.

"Why do you say it was a woman?" I asked, rubbing the spot above my eyes back into focus.

"Well, I went down to the scene to observe and picked the brain of a few ex-military police officers who are buddies of mine. There was no forced entry, but an open window was found. It's where they made the drop. Therefore, someone had to have gotten up on the scaffolding, which was only partially built. It wasn't really ready for anyone to work on yet," he said.

"So?" I asked.

"So it was very narrow. Too narrow. And the platform for the footing was maybe a half a foot and it was even skinnier through the passage to the window. It also wasn't reinforced from the bottom. It had to be a small person, who didn't weigh much and had small feet. Any person of substantial weight would have crashed right through. So, it was a chick. One badass mamma jamma," he concluded.

"Did the police tell you this?" I asked, feeling tingly all over.

"Nope, just my power of observation. We all have it, I think. Me, you, and Natalie, although you probably think I'm a fucking idiot," Dom said.

No, I think you're fucking brilliant.

"Did you mention your ideas to the police?" I

263

asked again, in a state of shock.

"Nope, they ain't paying me. They'll figure it out."

"You're right. Why do their work for them?" I laughed.

"Wow, not the response I would expect from you," Dom said.

"Yeah, well, I'm having a bad day," I said. Which was the understatement of the year.

"It was probably rough seeing Josie off, but it was the best thing for her. I hope you told her Uncle Dom loves her and skinny bitches aren't what's up."

"Not in those exact words, but I passed along your support."

"All right buddy, well your mom looks tired. It's been a joy. I hope you learned a thing or two from your Uncle Dom."

"But not too much," I joked, but not really.

I hope you don't figure out it was your momma, Cam.

Chapter 20
The Big Plan

When I arrived at the diner, I noticed there were no other cars in the parking lot. This was odd for the lunch hour. Had I beat my callous accomplice to our meeting spot this time? Upon entering, I was surprised to see her sitting in our booth waiting for me as usual.

"Where's your car, Dinah?" I asked, taking a seat.

"I had to sell it. He cut me off. I won't sign ze' divorce papers, and until I do, I'm broke. He's trying to force me into signing, but I won't. The Lexus dealership gave me twenty thousand dollars in cash. He's so stupid. I can live off that money for months if I have to."

"And then what?"

"It won't matter because in a couple of weeks it vill be all over. After *The Big Show*," she said with a scary grimace.

"Well, I hate to tell you we might not make it a couple more weeks. My brother figured out a woman did the Tribeca gassing," I whispered.

"And there're lots of women in the city. Does he have anything else?"

"Well no, but he's not a cop, and I'm sure they might be able to figure out the rest."

"This pessimism cannot be allowed in the grand finale of our plan, Cece. You either believe in us or you don't."

"Okay, I'm sorry. I like to be careful. Now what's our next move?"

"I thought about making this our last meeting. You've been some help, but this one might really be too much for you. You've been quite the disappointment."

"You've mentioned your dissatisfaction with me several times. It seems to be the running theme in my life right now. Look, I'm ready now. I wasn't before, but I want to destroy the bastard and she needs to go away and I don't even care how anymore."

Dinah looked up from the menu she was perusing, but never ordered from, her long eyelashes giving me a flutter of interest, her skin glistening in an iridescent dreamlike flawlessness as the sun shone through the half-drawn blind of the diner window.

"What brought on this change of heart?" she asked.

"Oh, you were right. He cut me off too. But at least I got a stipend of five hundred dollars a month and free rent. He told me I was lucky. Huh, simply won't do. I'll never be able to get a manicure again with that type of budget," I said, exasperated, looking at my fingers almost due for their treatment.

It was my beauty ritual to have my nails filled every three weeks to the day, and to have a paraffin wax treatment every other month to calm my chemically abused flesh. Brandi, my nail technician, expected me on the third Friday of every month. It was another thing I was obsessive about. I'd be pouring coffee just to pay for my hair and nails.

"Oh, you poor baby. Try having to sell your car to pay for your rent," she said bitterly, making me feel stupid. Maybe I was luckier than I thought, but it sure didn't feel like it.

"Yeah, you're right. Sorry," I apologized again.

She sucked her teeth at me, fighting back vicious words.

"So what's the grand plan?" I asked, changing the subject.

"You have to understand, Cece, there are some details I can tell you and others I have to keep to myself until it plays out. Your weaknesses compromise our endeavor and this one has to be done perfectly. There cannot be a false move here. This one doesn't deal with their listing. It's more of a personal vesting taking even more money out of Mitchell and Nikolay's pocket."

Here goes the build-up. I sat back in the vinyl booth. If this was *The Big Show*, it was going to require a long explanation from my Russian orator. I ordered a coffee to go with today's lunch and sat back anticipating the epic saga, taking a nice long sip.

"No one is going to be killed," she started.

And I spit it right back up on my lap.

Ow—damn it. How many times could a woman scald herself in the course of two weeks?

"That's how you start the conversation?" I asked. "Is there a possibility someone could get killed if the plan doesn't go right? Could that someone be my husband? Because if it is I say no. My children need their father. And you can't talk me out of it," I said.

"Answers to your questions. Yes and no."

"What the hell does that mean?"

"Yes, someone can get killed if it doesn't go as planned. No, that someone would not be your husband. It would be her. But as long as we follow the plan, she'll just get a little banged up," she laughed, "but not

267

killed or seriously injured."

"If it goes wrong, will we be caught?"

"No," she said, definitively.

Why not just mess up the plan and kill the bitch then?

Annihilationanddirtylinens.

Littlepiecesofskullmixedwithredhairandblood.

Annihilationanddirtylinens.

Littlepiecesofskullmixedwithredhairandblood.

Pins and needles spread happiness all over my face. The thoughts ran and repeated, then ran and repeated again. I could get high off the feeling it gave me.

"Cece, did you hear me?" she asked.

I licked my lips and clenched my eyes shut, willing the voices away.

"Okay, I'm going to need more details."

"I can't really give you a whole lot more, other than the fact Katelyn will disappear, your children will stay with you, and you'll have your old life back. Nikolay will have his summer plans demolished, he will be in complete financial ruin, and he and his fat pocketbook will return to me. I've been doing a little warming up to him on the side so…"

There went my coffee again.

"What the hell is your problem today? You drink like child."

"It was just what you said about warming up to him…it's nothing," I laughed down the scalding liquid, stifling the gurgle in my throat, trying to envision this woman warming up, like the day I tried to imagine her enjoying something sweet to eat. What was warming up considered for her—cracking a smile?

"Anyways, they vill suffer greatly and we'll both

be reinstated into our social clubs after the final act. All under one condition," she bartered.

"What is it?" I asked, fantasizing about the magnificence of her proposition.

"You can never, ever, tell anyone about me. Never. Long after I'm gone, even if you ever get the urge, you hold your tongue. If your conscience ever gets the better of you, forget it. It will ruin you."

"I can handle keeping my mouth shut. But if everything you say comes true and you are the one responsible for giving me my life back, I would like to keep in contact with you somehow, especially after all we've been through."

"No, it's not possible. We're partners, and once the deal is done, so are we. You don't speak of me. But it won't matter, we'll have our revenge and all the spoils, and you won't need me anymore and vice versa. I'm here because I serve a purpose to you right now. Like the bicycles. Once our common bond is gone, we're done too," Dinah explained.

She was so cutthroat.

"I would really like to know more details. When's this happening so I can arrange things for my children appropriately?" I asked.

"Two weeks from now. I will meet you on Saturday morning around eight a.m. Have your gas tank full. We'll be taking a little drive."

"More, Dinah, I need more."

"I can't tell you more and there is one other detail I need you to take care of to complete the mission. But you can't ask me why and you're not going to like it." She sighed.

"What is it?" I asked.

"Say yes first," she said.

"I can't tell you yes if I don't know what it is."

"It's important."

"I'm on board Dinah. If you can deliver everything you say, I will do my part too. You've done all the legwork so far."

"And, have I let you down?"

"No. And I think Mitchell's starting to see her for what she is—a demanding, gold-digging, high-maintenance woman who's incapable of co-parenting. I can tell she's wearing on him."

"I need a reason for Katelyn to pick-up Camdyn at your brother's."

"At Dominic's? Why?"

"Do you have another brother?"

"No, but I will not have my family, and especially not my children put into harm's way. Absolutely not," I said flatly.

Dinah opened her mouth to speak, but sat back in the booth instead with pursed lips. I could see her burning with frustration.

"Cece, this is not the part where anyone gets hurt. I need to place her there. She needs to have been at his apartment for my plan to work or the whole thing's a bust. *The Big Show,* will be when you meet me here two weeks from now."

"I don't know. I don't want them involved."

"All of our work has been for naught if you can't do this. And there's one more thing," she said, pinching her fingers together, and scrunching her small nose.

"What now?"

"I need you, if possible, to try to get Katelyn inside your brother's apartment," she said wistfully.

I sighed, throwing my hands up, a deep belly laugh rolling out. My scalp became hot just thinking about her in my brother's apartment with my child. It all seemed so fucked up. My head started pounding as my vision blurred. Dinah flickered like a holograph as I hit the side of my temple trying to steady my eyes and knock the picture back into focus, as the voices whispered to me.

Annihilationanddirtylinens.
Littlepiecesofskullmixedwithredhairandblood.

"Pull it together. Pull it together, Cece," I heard her yell from a faraway place.

"And how do you expect me to arrange this?" I asked, cross-eyed.

"Use your creativity. It's something I can't do for you, and so far I've thought of everything. Don't make it obvious, either. It has to seem like it makes sense."

"Well, I have the kids this weekend and I know Mitchell will be working to try to earn some extra bucks. I will think of something."

"Bravo," Dinah said with a deep exhale.

"Do I have to run it by you first?" I asked.

"No, just make it happen," she said gruffly.

****

My plan wasn't fool proof, but it was the best I could do on short notice. Josie had a luncheon/work session for the parents at her treatment facility on Saturday at noon and Camdyn had soccer practice at two o'clock. I asked Sam if I could pick up an extra shift Saturday morning to give me a reason to require a babysitter. Dom agreed to watch Camdyn while I was at work.

I trusted Dominic with Camdyn. Maybe I shouldn't

271

have, but I knew deep down he would launch every weapon in his apartment before he would let a hair be harmed on the boy's head. And with all the changes in our household, it was important for him to have someone to lean on.

"Well, sure I'll watch the little man," Dom said.

"And, could you take him to the Korean barbecue place around noon again for lunch? He really liked it," I said.

"Yes ma'am," he said.

****

I was all jitters and nerves at the coffee shop in the morning, praying everything would go as planned. We were really busy, which helped me keep my mind off things. I had no idea why this was so important, but Dinah said everything was a bust if it didn't happen. Being kept in the dark was frustrating, but I had to play by her rules if I wanted my life back. So far she had delivered on every promise and I could see Mitchell coming around, if only slightly. Katelyn was getting to him.

I wanted my scheme to seem natural and unplanned. The only snafu was how well Mitchell knew my obsessive behavior. There would be some pushback.

"No, I can't pick him up, Cece. The buyer in Tribeca is reconsidering the deal. The gas didn't permanently damage anything inside and I need this sale," he pleaded in a whisper.

I had a feeling the buyer was there right now by his hushed tone.

"I can't miss Josie's first parent/daughter conference, Mitchell. These sessions are important and

I didn't put it on my calendar with everything going on. I'm not letting Dom drive Camdyn to practice. Besides, Dom has to go into work soon anyway and he wouldn't make it back in time. And your parents will never make it from Jersey to Queens and back again in under an hour. What do you want me to do?" I asked.

"Cece, how in God's name did you forget about Josie's luncheon? You never forget anything. *Ever,*" he stressed.

"Mitchell, I'm out of my mind right now, okay? I took this shift today to try to earn extra money so I wouldn't be scraping bottom once you shut off my card and I never put her conference on my calendar. If it doesn't get inputted into the digital calendar, I don't get a reminder, and I'm screwed," I explained, hoping he'd believe me.

"Unbelievable. The one time in your life you actually need to be super-organized and you fall apart," he whispered with an edge to his voice which made me want to reach through the phone and strangle him.

"You're why I'm falling apart. Now, is there anyone else who can take him?"

"Anyone else? Are you asking for Kate's help?" he asked smugly.

"Would she be willing? I would let Camdyn hang out there and miss practice, but Dom has to go to work and he has enough weapons in his apartment to start World War III. It might be too much temptation for Camdyn not to toy with his firearms until Dom gets back," I said.

"Oh, dear Jesus. I will call her right now," he whispered and hung up.

Address and time please? He texted, ten seconds

later.

I texted him the address and a pick-up time of twelve-thirty p.m.

She'll do it. And you're welcome, Mitchell texted a few moments later.

I knew he was probably smiling, thinking I had decided to let her in to help with the kids. Little did he know I was setting her up for something. I only wish I knew what that something was. My blind faith in my Russian accomplice was draining me, but I only had a little bit longer to go.

****

Josie was all tight hugs and smiles when I walked through the door of the center. She looked a little better already, somehow calmer and more at peace, her brown hair resting softly on her shoulders, instead of pulled up in a tight bun as she often wore it to dance. Seeing her in yoga pants and a fitted t-shirt spoke volumes to me. Josie's casual wear was usually very loose-fitting, because she thought everything made her look fat. Costuming her for dance was always a struggle.

Also, Josie made a friend, Briana, another teenager with the same disorder, and someone with whom to commiserate. I was fully attentive at the session as they discussed unrealistic body image, seeing what we saw versus what our children saw. A few mothers broke down in tears, but I stayed strong for Josie, internally beating myself for the fact she had inherited her disease of compulsion from me. She used food to temper her demons while I used a sponge.

The girls talked about the things they did to hide their disorders. It broke my heart to hear Josie's story about her self-loathing after the night she ate my homemade spaghetti dinner. She said she'd filled up two mason jars that night.

Most of the other bulimics were *hiders*. Some girls left toilet paper in the bottom of the bowl after they threw up to hide any remnants leftover. Excessive use of air freshener, gum and mints were also a popular theme. It was quite alarming to see all these gorgeous girls starving themselves for beauty, trying desperately to fit into an unrealistic mold.

I was engrossed in Josie's healing process, but my palm was starting to get twitchy as it neared twelve-thirty p.m. I hadn't received a call yet. I needed to get a call from Mitchell or my plan had failed. What if Dom didn't take Camdyn to the Korean place like I'd asked him to? What if they started gaming, lost track of time, and decided to take a late lunch? What if they started gaming, didn't want to leave, and ate leftover pizza or something else breeding mold in Dom's refrigerator?

So many things could go wrong. Twelve-thirty came and went and I started to sweat, trying to concentrate on the counselor's words. I felt my skin grow hotter as every minute ticked past the target time. My hand flickered on my phone and I was now squeezing it in anticipation of a vibration.

"And we have to love our bodies for…" I heard a female counselor drone on in the background as my chest tightened. I started to get dizzy, finally noting I wasn't breathing. I let out an enormous puff of air and a few people took notice.

"You okay, Mom?" Josie whispered.

"Yes, honey, sorry. It's rough for me to hear this stuff. I'm sorry I didn't notice sooner."

"It's okay. You're here now."

But I wasn't. My mind was somewhere else. At twelve-forty-five, Mitchell texted me.

There's no one there, Cece! WTF. Kate has been parked out front for fifteen minutes waiting for someone to appear. Is his apartment blue? Wrong address? There are some shady characters lurking around and she said she doesn't want to hang there for much longer.

Whew! I let out another sigh, one of relief this time.

Key should be hidden in the dead plant on the porch. Tell her to use it. They probably went to Cam's favorite Korean place for lunch real quick, I texted back.

I watched the clock for a response. Five minutes, nothing. Ten minutes, nothing. Oh, come on.

Well? I texted Mitchell.

Oh sorry. She got in, but I don't think they're back yet, he texted.

Just as long as she gets him to his practice on time, I texted back.

Mission complete. Dinah would be so proud. I received a ring from Dom on my way out of the treatment facility.

"Why did you send his skank here?" he asked.

"I needed someone to get Cam, I had an emergency. I forgot about something I had to do for Josie," I said.

"You forgot?" he asked suspiciously.

"It didn't make it on my planner, I'm sorry. I'm a bit frazzled lately."

"I called her a whore and told her to get out."

"Dom? If she's going to be in the kids' life we need to be civil to her," I said, using Mitchell's words.

"Don't believe the bullshit he's feeding you. She stole your husband, Cece. Fuck her. I told her she was a home wrecker and to get out of my place."

"And what did she say?" I asked amused.

"She said okay and took Camdyn with her. And let me tell you something, your kid fucking hates her too."

"And how do you know?" I asked.

"We went to the Korean restaurant and he said, 'Uncle Dom, I fucking hate her.'"

"Well that's one way to know. And so glad your language is influencing him," I said, a smile unwillingly arriving on my lips.

"Fuck her."

"Okay, I got it. It won't happen again, okay?"

"Okay, better not."

"Get to work Dom, don't want you to be late."

"Work, blah. Okay, later sister."

"Thanks Dom, bye," I said.

****

After practice, Camdyn was more despondent than usual, and I worried Josie's hospitalization and Mitchell's gassing incident were throwing him into a dangerously dark place. It seemed everyday on the news there was another school shooting, and I secretly feared my son might be the next troubled kid to hit the headlines.

"Everything okay, bud?" I asked, fluffing his long hair out of his face. "Yeah," he said tossing his soccer cleats onto the doormat. I picked them up, opened the front door, knocked the dirt off them, and then placed them back on the mat. Camdyn definitely didn't share the perfectionist gene. This gave me comfort his fascination with explosives might be a passing phase,

277

not an obsession like my OCD and Josie's dance.

"Uncle Dom mentioned you weren't too happy with Katelyn," I mentioned.

Camdyn flinched. What had she done now?

"I don't like going over there," he revealed.

"Why, what's up?" I asked.

"Nothing," he deflected.

"Camdyn, I need to know what she's doing," I pleaded.

"I don't want to cause anymore fighting between you and dad," he said, covering his ears.

"I promise I won't say anything to him," I said. I might've been making promises I couldn't keep, but if what Dinah assured was true, Camdyn wouldn't be seeing anymore of Katelyn.

Camdyn made eye contact with me then, and it shook me how much he'd grown up in the last few months. He knew I wouldn't break my promise to him. "Dad's always working, because he has to make more money now, and I guess they had these routines on the weekends before, and now she acts all mad I'm there and she can't go to her coffee shop with Dad. Not like I want to be friends with her, but she doesn't even talk to me."

"I'm sorry honey. I don't think she knows how to relate to children. As long as she's not being mean," I said rather relieved. Ignoring him was better than name-calling, like what she'd done to Josie, although I was still far from pleased with her actions.

"She is mean, mom."

"How, honey?" I asked, panicked.

"When dad's there she's all over him, but when he's gone, she's either running or on the computer, downloading pictures to Facebook, and when she's not on Facebook she's writing her stupid novel. I interrupted her once to ask her where the peanut butter was and she threw a thesaurus at me."

"She what? Why?"

"She said not to disturb her while she was writing and to find it myself. She gets into these weird zones when she's writing, like she can't hear anything else around her, and it's creepy, and she hates me."

The few writers I knew were some of the most self-absorbed people I'd ever met. Katelyn was so busy creating imaginary people, she didn't have time to cater to the needs of the living, breathing ones right in front of her. Even her potential future stepchildren. Stupid twat.

"Well, hopefully your dad comes to his senses. But, in the mean time, don't be afraid to tell her she's being a jerk and you're going to tell your dad if she keeps it up."

"I don't want to tattle."

"Tattling's okay when people are being jerks."

"Really?"

"Yeah, I hate how mean she's been to you and Josie, you're sweet kids. Your dad needs to know about it. He doesn't see how she really is. Once he knows, he'll make her stop," I sniped.

"I sure hope so," Camdyn said and ran up the stairs to shower.

I watched my son's long body climb the stairs. He must've grown at least two inches in the last couple of months. He was going to be tall like his daddy. Hopefully, he wouldn't be as stupid.

Chapter 21
The Big Show

It was Camdyn's second weekend with Mitchell, and my last day with Dinah. Today Mitchell promised Camdyn he would take him to *The Bodies* exhibit in the city. *The Bodies* display showcased the preserved insides of actual human beings. I was skeptical of the graphic content of the adult display, but Mitchell thought it might spark Camdyn's interest in medicine. In any case, he was spending quality time with his father, away from Katelyn. Apparently, she didn't care to spend time with my son, as Mitchell had mentioned something about her going north again today.

The stillness of the morning air gave me an eerie feeling that Camdyn wouldn't be the only one to see human remains today. I met Dinah at our diner bright and early. We should've had a special drink or meal as our send off for our final escapade to get revenge on our husbands, a tribute dance or something, but then I remembered whom I was talking about—the woman who never smiled or ate.

I was very nervous for our trip and had doubled up on my migraine medication earlier in the morning. A full mug of coffee sat in my drink holder, my sippy cup of courage. I didn't know where we were going or what we were doing, but someone was getting hurt today. Someone could die today.

I saw Dinah lurking in the parking lot by the dumpsters, a black book bag slung over her shoulder. We gassed people the last time I saw her backpack. My gut wrenched already, the kind of bellyache you get when you're about to do something you're really going to regret. She wore her blonde hair back in her green scarf, big sunglasses, black tight jeans, and a leather motorcycle jacket. She was one smoking hot, badass, older woman. She reminded me of a Charlie's Angel, ready to add insult to injury with her good looks and deadly force.

I was a poor counterpart, not complimentary to her fierce, infiltrator look. Instead, I looked like a beat-up, stressed-out, middle-aged housewife trying to hold it together. My brown eyes had dark blue circles of blood pooled beneath them from a night of unrest.

"You look like shit," she said, as she climbed into the car.

"I didn't sleep much," I said.

"Well, I need you alert, so chug down your coffee and stop for more if you need to. You need nerves of steel. And you need to breathe. It all comes together today," she yelled, in her attempt to pump me up, but it only made me more nervous.

"No pressure."

"There will be pressure. Anticipate it. Embrace it," she said with her devilish grin.

"Where're we going?"

"I think you know," Dinah said.

I did know. I got on the freeway and headed toward Long Island. It's where *she* was and if she was going to be harmed today, it's where we were going.

"What do you have in your bag of tricks today?"

"Special surprise."

"Oh come on, please tell me. I've been sick to my stomach trying to figure out what's going on. I can't take it anymore," I admitted.

"You have to wait. I've come to know you better and if there's one thing I'm sure of, it's you have to wait."

I knew there was no arguing with her, so I drove, trying to ignore the bugger of a headache coming on, despite my medication which had stopped working about a month ago. There was no time to go to the doctor in the midst of my shit storm.

"You need to park at the beach," she said, as we got closer.

I hated to admit how much I loved the little, gray barn cottage. It was nestled back in the trees, without a neighbor for miles. I saw a white, colonial style home way up on a green, rolling hill from where we were. It was gorgeous and secluded as well, and their only neighbors.

The cottage was so quaint and private, and I could see how this special place might inspire a writer. It was only a short walk from the beach, which was on the opposite side of the street. It was pretty much their own private beach, since no one was within miles of it. What a find. I was jealous he would be spending the summer there with her. The kids were going to love it too, and I cringed at the thought of them enjoying their "new" family.

"Do you have kids?" I asked.

"No. I didn't want them," she answered.

Well, it didn't surprise me.

"Stop thinking that way, Cece. It all ends today.

There will be no summertime fun for them here," she said, so decisively I believed her.

It was nearly eleven a.m. and Camdyn and Mitchell would be leaving the expo soon. I'd wondered if they were coming up here afterward. I watched the waves crash into the shoreline, one rolling, frothy top over the other; the winter washing away into spring on the brink of each one; a rebirth, a new start. I could smell the emerging season in the air as I sat there with the windows rolled down, taking in deep breaths of the freshness to calm my nerves, as I hoped there could be a new start for me too.

"Some background information I wanted to share," she began.

"Yes."

"Katelyn wants Mitchell to buy this place. She doesn't want to be in the city anymore. She wants them to move here and start over. She moved the lease date to begin in April because she couldn't wait to get away from it all. Away from you," she went on.

"What? He can't be that far away from the kids," I said, "And Mitchell would never leave Manhattan, and his business is there. It's ridiculous."

"I believe those were his thoughts exactly. She's trying to talk him into the fact he could make a killing in The Hamptons, and it would just take a little groundwork to get started and she could help him," Dinah continued.

"He'd never ever go for it," I said, shaking my head, sipping my coffee.

"You're right. But I wanted you to know," she said.

"So, what're we waiting for?" I asked nervously. I

wanted to get it over with. Whatever *it* was.

"Are you ready? I'm waiting for you to be ready," Dinah said.

"Oh, I'm ready," I said, holding my breath.

"I'm going to need you to breathe, *dammit*. And not only right now, the whole day. I can't have you passing out on me."

"Okay," I said with a gasp, letting out the air, "Some of us aren't hardwired for this stuff, Dinah."

"This is your chance. Do you want revenge? Do you want to make him pay for all he's done to you and get rid of her once and for all? Badly enough to be brave for one day so you might live the rest of your days with your unshared family and friends?"

"Well, when you put it that way."

I waited as she fished around in her black bag. She pulled out a foiled wrapped plate.

"More information for you. Like myself, and any good woman, Katelyn has a sweet tooth. Every Saturday she and Mitchell go to the coffee shop in Brooklyn and she dips her chocolate biscotti in her coffee," Dinah said.

"You're a borderline stalker, aren't you? Were you a Russian spy? I have to ask, because I've been wondering it this whole time and if I'm never going to see you again, I was wondering if you might satisfy my curiosity."

Dinah's blue swords for eyes snapped my neck back into the headrest. I could almost hear her say the words *You are an Id-eee-ot,* in her strong accent.

"No, Cece. I was never a Russian spy. I'm just a very good observer," she said. Her words sounded strangely familiar to me.

"Well, then it makes two of us, but I'm pretty sure you have one up on me," I said, "So, what are those cookies laced with? Poison? How do you know she'll eat them for sure?"

"Not poison to most, but poison to her," she cackled.

Dinah pulled off the foil to reveal homemade cookies, the European ones with two vanilla wafers and chocolate filling inside.

"Those look like plain old cookies to me."

Dinah whipped out her own container of chocolate filling; the delicious kind with nuts mixed in, which was evident by the label. I smiled as I saw the genius on her plump, smirked lips.

"Okay, so what if she doesn't eat them?"

"She'll eat them. They don't have much food at the cottage yet. Mitchell is going to bring groceries up later with your son and she's used to eating a treat every Saturday," she said firmly.

"So, how are these cookies going to magically appear on her kitchen table? I can't very well deliver them."

She pointed to the big white house on the hill.

"And how're we going to persuade strangers to deliver cookies?" I asked becoming more flustered at the guessing game.

"You'll see," she said as she exited the car. She dug a note out of her bag and fastened it to the plate of cookies with two pieces of tape, taking special care the wind would not blow it off.

We tiptoed into the entrance of the gravel road. It was a serene setting, only the sound of woodland creatures chirping and snapping branches all around us.

It was a place made for lazy days by the beach and picnics in the forest, not acts of violence. I couldn't get my head in the game because I felt like I was on vacation; the ocean still making hushing sounds behind me, lulling me into peacefulness. And I couldn't hear our own footsteps, which was a good thing, because Dinah was moving fast and I had to keep up. As we got closer to the cottage, I spied a fleck of red from the front window and dove into a bush, my heart kicking in my chest. Vacation-mode was officially over.

"It's okay. She's at her desk, facing the backyard, writing," Dinah whispered.

I followed Dinah as she crept up the old, gray, wooden steps of the porch, placing the cookies on the doormat.

"This is where you have to be quick and not freeze. If you freeze, we're fucked," she whispered.

I heard the scraping of Katelyn's chair and my belly heaved. She heard us. To my dismay, Dinah also froze, her electric blue eyes lighting up. *Oh shit, that woman never showed fear.* A few minutes later we heard another door shut and realized Katelyn had gone to the bathroom—w*hew!*

"Perfect, more time to run. Okay, I'm going to ring the doorbell; as soon as I do, sprint to the line of trees over there as quickly as you can. There is an old, brown woodshed way back in the thick of the trees. I'll meet you there," she instructed.

I nodded, although I felt my knees starting to wobble like they did on the scaffolding in Tribeca. I couldn't mess up this time. I had to pull through. Dinah dropped the cookies, rang the bell and I was off. The doorbell was a gunshot for the race of my life.

My heart ricocheted in my throat as I sprinted as fast as my legs would carry me. I never looked back as the lithe, black-clad figure in front of me moved at warp speed. Dinah was super-fast. Of course she was. Totally out of breath, I made it to the woodshed. Dinah had already entered the dilapidated structure, its walls of rotting wood falling apart with uneven boards sticking out. A caved in ceiling made up its roof. A crowbar was slung haphazardly between the ground and the pull-out door, holding open the crumbling entrance. The damp, shredded pieces of wood where the upturned part of the metal bar crushed through the floorboards startled me in a way it shouldn't have. I'd seen similar splinters recently.

"It doesn't look safe in there," I said.

"Shh, and catch your breath, we have to run straight back," Dinah ordered.

Oh no, I didn't think I had another sprint in me. She should have told me this was part of the plan. I could have trained a little in the last couple weeks instead of sitting around in my bathrobe, waiting for my impending doom. Dinah emerged with a small, aluminum softball bat.

"What're you going to do with that, hit her over the head?" I asked jokingly.

She nodded, a pleasant smile on her face.

Jesus Christ.

Annihilation and dirty linens. Little pieces skull mixed with red hair and blood.

This is what the monster wanted. I tried to follow her as we made our way back to the cottage, but she was too damn fast. Dinah was moving at a speed too fast to be real, blurring my vision. Her blonde hair had come undone, and whipped wildly like the yellow fire of a superhero streaming behind her. Outside the cabin, she refastened her green scarf, its European fibers resilient and strong just like her. As she waited for me to catch up, she stalked closer with her bat, as if she couldn't bear to completely stop moving for my sake.

"You're slowing us down," she complained as I clung to a tree, panting and trying not to vomit.

"You could have mentioned this was part of it."

"Stop complaining, we're so close to the grand finale," she hissed.

"You make it sound like a fucking fireworks show," I said, in fast breaths.

"Because it will be," she said.

Dinah padded slowly toward the house and I followed her, fearful of what I might find. Did Katelyn bring her epi pen? Would she be gasping on the floor, begging for her life? Did she decide to pass on the cookies? Would she greet us at the door, only to have Dinah smack her over the head anyway? I was so nervous. My knees wobbled again, and I couldn't hold my breath to steady myself, because I was still fighting to catch it.

"Breathe Cecelia. This is it. The final act," she said.

Dinah approached the door and opened it with only the slightest click of the knob. It wasn't locked. I could hear Katelyn trying to sell Mitchell on the cottage, *"I want to live in a place where you don't have to lock your doors at night, like where I grew up,"* she would chime to him in her naïve, sing-songy voice.

We tiptoed into the house and immediately heard a choking sound from the bathroom. A plate of half-dozen cookies lay uneaten on the table. She had gotten through half of them before her throat started to close. I put my hands over my eyes and watched Dinah through parted fingers as she snuck over to the entrance of the small bathroom. I stood a distance away, but maneuvered myself so I could see through the crevice of the door. There was nothing like hitting someone when they were down.

Katelyn had administered the pen and was waiting for it to work when, *Whack!* Dinah thumped her over the head with the bat. I jumped at the sound, hoping she didn't split open her skull. It made me think of the fire extinguisher in her apartment: *Little pieces of skull mixed with red hair and blood.* It'd happened. Her skull had been cracked. The blood was there. My heart suddenly felt lighter as if I'd given the monster a large morsel it'd been craving. Was annihilation next? Was she dead?

Edging closer, I observed Dinah had knocked her out good. Katelyn sputtered slightly, rolling halfway over on her back. Dinah kicked her in the kidney with her boot, flipping her over on her face.

Whack!

I jumped again as Dinah clubbed her over the head once more. This time blood sprang from the left corner of her temple. Christ, I thought she might be surely dead now, but in either case, she was definitely unconscious.

"Come on, I need your help dragging her," Dinah said.

I reluctantly entered the scene of the crime. There was a lot of blood, spreading faster over the penny tile now. Katelyn lie there, her eyes rolled back in her head, her red curls spread over her face, along with her cherry-blood droplets casting a gnarly contrast against the white tiled floor.

The smell. It was metallic, just like I expected it to be.

"Get her arms, I'll get her feet," she ordered.

I did as I was told and once again felt out of my body; the combination of trance-like shock and the floaty feeling that often accompanied one of Dinah's missions. It was as if I knew I was performing the physical action, but didn't quite feel in control of my own body; like moving around in a dream, or a nightmare in this case. I strained to support the weight of her limp body, as Dinah seemed to carry her with ease. I half-dragged Katelyn as Dinah shouldered most of the weight. Dinah then single-handedly tossed Katelyn facedown on the front porch, the heavy thud of her dead weight hitting the porch, making me jump and shut my eyes. And then, Dinah started running for the car.

"Where're you going?" I scream-whispered.

"Stay there."

"What?"

"Stay there, I'll be right back," she said as she sprinted in her little ninja pants back to the car.

I stared at Katelyn's young, incoherent body spread out over the porch. She looked so comfy in her gray sweats, like her eyes were just shut because she was sleeping. But she wasn't sleeping. She was severely concussed or dead. The trickle from her forehead had grown into a small puddle, turning the gray barn wood into a sickly brown pool beneath her. I didn't try to find a pulse on her body, fearing my suspicions were true.

I was shaking uncontrollably, my knees rubbing together, my hands twitching, my head throbbing. I really hoped it was almost over. As much as I wanted my life back, I couldn't stomach physically hurting people, and this was too much for me. Maybe Dinah would drive us home again like she did the night of the gassing. I had a sinking feeling she wasn't returning at all. Maybe she'd taken off to call the police? I started to get nervous.

Fourteen minutes later she returned with her black backpack. I knew something else had to be in there besides cookies. Cookies were far too innocent sounding for Dinah's grand finale. Dinah's gloved fingers pulled out the jar of Nutella, the wafers, and a butter knife. Then, she pressed Katelyn's hands to all of the items. The knife was dirty with a thick crust of old chocolate spread matted to the blade. In a manner I could only describe as disgustingly seductive, Dinah lowered the knife into her mouth and sucked the metal with such delight, I thought she might swallow it whole. She was a circus creature, submerging the sword deep into her throat and then removing it with the greatest of ease. Like Mitchell, Dinah's husband must've truly loved his mistress to give up *Ole Deep Throat* over there.

It was the first time I'd seen Dinah eat anything. She then proceeded to take a sanitary wipe from her bag and rub the knife clean, and then re-administer it into the jar of Nutella to place a fresh swath of brown delight on the blade.

"What in the world are you doing?" I asked, dumbfounded.

"I told you I loved sweets," she said creepily. "I

have to go inside for a moment and clean up ze' mess. Hold on," she continued, still catching her breath.

Dinah forced Katelyn's fingers into a better grip around the handle of the knife before she dropped her dead palms to the ground with a bang. The crashing plummet of Katelyn's corpse-hands didn't disturb me nearly as much as Dinah taking an extra minute in the middle of our assault to lick her dessert knife clean.

And there I was, left with the body again. I felt so awkward staring at the poor girl—face down, unmoving like a homicide victim on a crime scene investigation show. *Like whistling through the graveyard,* I'd heard my mother's words echo. It was her saying for when you're guilty by association, but act none the wiser. The irony of her words stabbed at me, at the idea I might indeed be whistling through this young lady's graveyard very soon.

I'd loathed Katelyn for all those months and she had almost beaten me. But it seemed the tables were turned at this particular moment.

"Okay, are you ready for the grand finale?" Dinah asked, barreling outside breathlessly.

I nodded, not sure if I was.

"Are you ready to run again?" Dinah asked.

Oh God, not again.

"I don't have much steam left," I whimpered.

"Pull it together. This is it, Cece, one more mile sprint between you and freedom. You'll never have to see her again," she said.

"Okay, I'm ready then," I announced, trying to invoke some courage.

Dinah dug at her bag, peeking into it and then slowly extracting something as if she were carefully removing a snake. It wasn't a snake. It was far worse—it was a hand grenade. Dominic's hand grenade. The pineapple-looking one I had seen at his apartment. I took a big leap away from her.

"Do you know what this is?" she asked.

"Yeah, it's a fucking grenade." I yelled.

"Keep your voice down. You don't want to wake sleeping beauty," she said, pointing downward.

"Please tell me we aren't going to use it," I said.

"Why would I bring it if we weren't?" she said, as if I had asked the dumbest question she'd ever heard. "This is a MK.II post World War II grenade."

"I don't care about its history, just tell me what we're doing with it," I said taking another step backward.

"This is a fragmentation hand grenade designed to destroy everything in its path, which spans about thirty yards or so. There is a five second delay before detonation," she went on.

"And, what're we blowing up? And how is she not dying if we're leaving her here?" I asked, moving back some more, trembling this time, falling onto the bottom step, and then catching myself on the railing.

"We're blowing up the pool house and she will be far enough away not to get hurt. It's a bonus if she gets debris on her and is not killed."

"And what if she dies? Does the plan die with her?"

"No, but it's better for you if she lives."

"I see. And why the pool house again?" I asked, confused and petrified, now on the ground level, ready to run.

"You will find out soon enough," she said.

A downright scary grimace crossed Dinah's face. Her malicious smile was wide, her eyebrows scrunched downward in mischief. She enjoyed this shit. *Psychopath!* I thought if things didn't work out with Nikolay, I could always introduce her to Dominic. Any gal who got her rocks off throwing grenades was his type of woman. Dinah pranced off the steps onto the yard getting into good firing position.

"Are you ready for the grand finale?" she announced with excitement.

"Ready," I said, shaky legs on their haunches, positioned for take-off.

I watched in disbelief as she removed the pin and threw it with the precision of a professional baseball player right through the window of the pool house. We both took off, racing each other to the car. Even though I had a head start, her fast legs passed me up in seconds. I counted in my head, breathlessly, 1, 2, 3, 4, *BOOM*!

Oh My God.

I stopped, jumping right out of my body. I knew it was going to go off, but I didn't think it would be so loud. My headache exploded into excruciating, mind numbing ringing. It was as if my brain split in half, sending a ripple of alarms from temple to temple. I imagined my brain, a ping-pong ball jarred loose, bouncing around to the new siren in my head.

I looked for Dinah and all I saw was her silent mouth telling me to "move", since I had lost the ability to hear. How could she not be disturbed by the sound? It was deafening. I was sure my eardrum was punctured. It took all of my strength to keep going. I looked back to see flames and smoke billowing behind us. My heart was in my esophagus as I tried to charge forward again, seriously lagging behind the warrior princess.

Dinah was already in the car and had the ignition roaring before I reached the embankment to the beach. She could have taken off and left me there, but she waited for me, just like when I almost fell off the scaffolding in Tribeca. She was a good comrade. *Oh Thelma.*

I had my hands clenched to my ears sure they must be bleeding. I jumped in the passenger seat and let her speed away. There was no one in sight to see us leave the scene of the crime. I was worried Katelyn might catch on fire before Mitchell or the police could discover her, but I was in so much pain and disorientation, I couldn't process the thought properly. I cushioned my throbbing skull into the headrest and closed my eyes, my whole body fighting the uncontrollable shakes.

"Lay back and enjoy the ride. Operation complete. Relax now and wait. Don't do anything else but wait and see. It will all come together and make sense eventually, I promise," she chimed happily.

I nodded, still not able to speak, straining to hear her through the ringing.

"It will dissipate. The ringing. Give it some time," she told me as she went about thirty miles over the speed limit down the coast.

Fifteen minutes later, as we were getting on the expressway, I heard the sirens of multiple police cars and fire engines. The whole time I was waiting for my head to stop throbbing I imagined Katelyn's limp body burning to death on the front porch. I imagined her waking up to her flesh burning, wondering how she'd gone from death by allergic reaction to death by raging fire. Dinah was sure we moved her far enough away. Then, what was the motivation to leaving her on the wooden steps where she could catch fire? And, why was it a bad thing if she did burn to death?

I was going to pass out. I couldn't hold it together any longer. I was breathing in long, jagged breaths, trying to calm myself, but it wasn't working.

****

When I awoke I was in the parking lot of the diner and she was gone. Not a note or a trace of her to be found. Dinah was totally gone, and I knew I would never see her again.

My reflection in the mirror showed no signs of immediate distress, only a blank slate of whiteness and dark eyes staring back. When I tried to move my mouth to speak nothing happened. I slowly ran my hand over my face, pulling at the tingly, hot flesh to make sure I wasn't paralyzed. My palm grazed a dollop of something mushy on my cheek. It was chocolate. I flinched as I wiped the inch-long smudge on a tissue. Dinah must have flung some of the Nutella spread my way when she was mouth-fucking the knife. What other traces of evidence had she left clumsily behind?

The red numbers on the digital clock in my car shocked me back to the present. It was already four p.m. My shift at *The Coffee Bean* started in one hour. I had enough time to go home, hop in the shower and get to my alibi—I mean my job.

As I drove to my empty house, I had a sinking feeling Katelyn didn't survive the blast. Other anxieties swirled in my brain as I patiently waited for all the pieces to come together like Dinah said they would.

What was in the pool house and why did we blow it up? Had Mitchell made it there in time? Would the blast traumatize Camdyn or would it fascinate him, like watching a twisted video game? And how was this all going to blow back on Dominic? Dinah told me just to wait and see. I was waiting and seeing as patiently as I could. I arrived at the coffee shop completely distracted and didn't even greet Sam as I put on my apron.

"Well, hello to you too," Sam said.

"Sorry, tired today," I said, not lying after my mini-marathon.

"It's tiring playing mommy and daddy, I'm sure," he said.

"This is true," I replied.

I scoured the stainless steel of the machines to refocus my energy. My reflection peeked back at me and I thought of one word—*murderer*. Did I really kill her? No, Dinah killed her. I didn't kill her. But I was definitely involved. There was a distant ringing still in my ears and I couldn't hear Sam very well, but I couldn't miss his question as he came in from taking out the trash.

"Were you at the beach today?"

My body halted in mid-scrub. I slowly turned to face him.

"Why do you ask?"

"There's sand on your tires and the underside of your car. Little early to be going to the shore. What happened? You go into *cougar-mode* and start stalking young juiceheads down there?" he joked.

Oh no.

"Went through a construction area today, only thing I can think of," I said, casually turning back

297

around.

"Yeah, sure," he joked.

I received the frantic phone call from Mitchell at five thirty p.m. Finally.

"Mitchell, I'm at work, what is it, we're slammed," I lied.

Sam's right eyebrow arched up as he overheard me and motioned to the completely empty coffee shop with both of his hands and a quirky smile. I winked back, and my response seemed to appease his curiosity for the moment.

"Cece, there's been an accident," Mitchell said panicked. I thought he might have been crying.

"Is Camdyn okay? In the city, at the convention?" I asked, playing dumb.

"No, he's fine. It's Kate, she's been hurt. We're at the hospital," he said.

Whew. Hurt meant not dead.

"Oh, my. What happened? Is she going to be okay? Are you at University?" I asked.

"No, I'm not at University," he sighed, "I'm at Southampton Hospital."

"What? Where's that?" I played dumb again.

"It's in well, South Hampton. Long Island, yeah know?"

"What the hell are you doing there?"

"Kate and I. We sort of. Well, we were renting a vacation spot, thought it would be nice for the kids this summer and she likes to write up there," he said reluctantly.

"Say what now? You have a summer home too? You have a house in Montclair, an apartment in Brooklyn, *and* a summer home in the fucking

Hamptons? And I'm working on a Saturday night in a coffee shop so I might have the luxury of a manicure. Are you kidding me, Mitchell?" I asked.

"Cece, please," he started, "I knew you would be mad if I told you. It's something she really wanted, but some things have surfaced about her that, that are really bad," he stammered.

Mitchell didn't sound so good. In fact, he sounded shell shocked, *no pun intended.*

"What is it?"

"There was an explosion and they found things at our cottage. I haven't been up there since we rented the place, but she's been going up on her own," he said, his voice trailing off, trying to figure things out as he went along.

"An explosion? Was Camdyn anywhere near it? Are you sure he's okay?" I asked.

"Yes, yes. It happened before we got there, but they found things, Cece. Katelyn is handcuffed to her hospital bed right now and I need you to come get Camdyn until I can figure this out," he said desperately.

"What? Mitchell, what kind of things?"

"Body parts. Doll body parts mixed with expensive jewels, a safe full of money, and our wedding pictures," he blurted out in one incoherent sentence.

"What're you saying?" I asked.

"They think Kate stole Robin's jewels, Monte's safe, and she maimed and stole your dolls," Mitchell whispered.

"What? Why? And how did she even know who Robin and Maeve were?"

"I-I took her to meet them once over dinner. It didn't go well. Oh God, Cece, can you drive here and get Camdyn? I'm sorry to pull you away from work, but I-I think you were right," he said, crying.

As he said the words, it was as if the four separate corners of the universe pulled together before me to form one cohesive square. It all made sense now. Dinah had planted the stolen items in the unfinished pool house. Katelyn would be pronounced a kleptomaniac, stealing from all those who had shown her disfavor. There was one common theme of all the people she'd taken things from—none of them liked her. She had done that part all on her own.

It was a dirty shame Dinah had to destroy my dolls, but I guessed she felt it was important to make it more believable, and steer any blame away from me. My heart sank at the fact I would never see my beloved dolls again. I had a small sliver of hope they might resurface when this was all over.

"You said an explosion. Is Katelyn all right?" I asked, trying to divulge more information about the state of Katelyn's injuries. As long as she wasn't fatally injured, and she received a minimum sentence for her crimes, enough to make Mitchell hate her forever, but not enough to destroy her life completely, I'd be very pleased with this outcome. It seemed justified for all of the pain she'd caused my family.

"Cece, they found a grenade to be the source of the explosion," Mitchell said shocked.

"Who would do that?" I asked.

"Camdyn said Dom was missing a grenade after Katelyn came to pick him up last week, and he blamed Camdyn, threatening to tell us if Cam didn't fess up. Camdyn swore up and down to your brother he didn't do it, and pleaded with him not to tell us after the incident he'd had with the last grenade. Dom caved and chucked it up to misplacement of inventory." Mitchell sighed.

Ah ha. Placing Katelyn in Dom's apartment. It was Dinah's coup de gras to tie Katelyn to the crime.

Bravo Dinah. Bravo.

"Wow," I said in amazement.

"I know. I—I think I might have made a big mistake. All of it. The whole thing. Her. I think, I. I think, I made a mistake. Do you think you can come down here? I need you, Cece," Mitchell blubbered into the phone.

Those are the coveted words every woman who has ever been cheated on wants to hear. Even if she never gets back with the cheater, she still wants to hear those words. The corners of my mouth perked up as I realized—I had won.

"I'm on my way," I said and hung up the phone.

Wasn't that just like a man? Girlfriend gets carted off to jail and he's already running back to his wife begging for mercy, like a bad, white-trash country song.

"Leaving so soon?" Sam asked.

"I'm sorry, Sam. There's been an accident, something with Mitchell's girlfriend. I'm not sure of the details, but he wants me to go pickup my son at the hospital in South Hampton."

"South Hampton, well La-De-Da. Isn't he the high roller," Sam said, as he turned up the television.

"Not really," I said as I tossed off my apron.

"Oh well, looky here," he said to my back as I exited.

I heard the television blare: *U.S. and Russian leaders hail nuclear arms treaty.*

301

I had my hand on the front door to the empty coffee shop when I heard Sam playfully yell over the TV.

"See, Cece. The U.S. is back in cahoots with the Russians. Russians, Cece, you love Russians," he laughed, and I was immobilized for the second time that morning in the shop.

"What do you mean?" I asked, not turning around.

"Oh, you know, just call me 'Dinah', Sam," he said, erupting into laughter.

My gut wrenched and did backflips. *How did he know her?*

"What did you just say?" I gasped.

"Okay, we're still playing this game. You know how hard this is for me, right? You keep your dirty secrets and your little blonde wig all to yourself and I won't say a word. You could loosen up about the weed though. You have to admit it helped with your headaches, right?" he chirped.

Chapter 22
The Big Reveal

Oh Sweet Jesus. I had to drive and pick up Camdyn, but I couldn't stop hyperventilating long enough to decipher Sam's words. I managed my way into my vehicle and drove across the street to the car wash to clean off the sand and attempt to breathe again. It couldn't be true. Someone was playing a sick joke on me.

I reached into my glove box, searching for something, but I wasn't sure what. Somehow I knew the blonde wig would be there. I pulled it out, along with the Kelly green scarf and oversized black sunglasses. Dinah's scarf. Dinah's sunglasses.

"What is happening?" I screamed out loud as the rollers pushed my car through the wash. No one could hear me, so I squealed some more, as loud as I could. Full-out shrieks escaped from my lungs like the deranged person I was. I watched bubbles splash all over my windshield, pouring water over the glass with the same force as the liquid falling from my eyes.

There was a letter addressed to me in the glove box. Strangest thing was—it was in my handwriting.
Dear Cece,

If you're reading this, you've figured it out. Congratulations, you won! I wouldn't try to think too hard about all of this right now. All of the pieces will come together over time. To give you some peace of mind (if that's possible) I first appeared at the company Christmas party where you first learned you had a pest problem in your marriage. You needed me because you couldn't get rid of it on your own. You weren't strong enough to pull it off. Your mind created a more beautiful, resilient, smarter version of yourself. There were times I had to come out without you there (like when I had to destroy your dolls) and that's when you would black out. Your headache was me knocking on the door to come out and play.

And sorry about Sam. You know you always wanted to do it, and it will make the tables seem more even if you decide to patch things up with Mitchell. Think of it as a little bit of leverage in the back of your mind to give you some solace as you rebuild your life.

If you play your cards right, you won't see me again. Let's hope nothing else happens to make me reappear.

The last part of my letter is instructions on covering your tracks. This part's important. Don't fall apart before you read it:

1. Destroy this letter—burn it, preferably

2. Erase the Supra app on your phone with all of Mitchell's contacts—ASAP

3. Destroy the wig and sunglasses

And last but not least...

*4. There is a treasure for you hidden in the place where Josie hid her demons. Find it and you will be handsomely rewarded. (You know I had to leave one little item of suspense on here for you *smile*)*

Sincerely,

D

Holy, Mother, Mary and Joseph. I was Dinah? Dinah was me? I slept with Sam? Fuck!

Well, that would explain the unusual stinging when I urinated the other morning. It wasn't a bladder infection, but the distinct recognizable sensation, which occurs after intercourse. And then there was my cotton candy mouth. It wasn't cotton candy mouth; it was cotton mouth—from smoking weed—with Sam, right after I screwed him. Or was it before? Did I need a little something to take the edge off first? Good God, who was I?

The scarf in my hand was shaking in green waves of beautiful silk. Was it a green scarf, or was it a babushka? A babushka—like the one belonging to my prized Russian Minsk doll.

And then, like the forceful blow of Dinah's aluminum bat to Katelyn's skull, the connection hit me hard—Dinah was a Minsk. I was Dinah. I was a Minsk?

The car wash ended and I pulled up to the overhead dryer, watching the water flicker off the car like the pieces of my brain pulling apart from my mind. The tears had stopped, replaced by hiccup-induced gulps for air. My stomach twisted as I fought the vomit building up in my throat. I sat there and watched the water pool in the corners of my windshield; obsessively irked the dryer couldn't get to every single spot.

Dinah's wig still sat on my lap, its platinum blondeness glaring at me, laughing at me in a Russian accent. Russian, like my espionage informant Minsk dolls. My super-female conjured from all of my vast novel-reading, movie-watching influences, made the doll come to life. My Minsk doll was my pint-size idea of perfection. Of course, I'd modeled my super-hero version of myself after her. After all, she was super-sexy, highly intelligent, and cutthroat. Oh my, I was having a nervous breakdown. I wasn't going to make it to pick up my son. He probably shouldn't ride in the car with a lunatic anyway.

I remembered then, the first time I saw Dinah in the ladies room, during the peak of my terrible migraine, also apparently the first time my mind broke. She was wearing her signature 1950's red and black swing dress. She'd startled me, materializing out of nowhere, like at the lawyer's office, because ghosts don't need to open doors to appear.

As my breaths started to erupt into rapid huffs and puffs again, I noticed a litany of parking tickets sticking out of the glove box. I left the lid hanging open at the sight of the blonde wig, and there they were, dangling at me, like a brutal reminder of my time spent in the dark. *Wait a second. It was the night I was blacked out the longest. Clues to my lost past?*

I snatched the tickets out of the box and flipped through them in horror. It was like a trail of breadcrumbs leading to all the buildings we assaulted in the city. I'd assumed when I awoke in Tribeca, all of the tickets were from the same parking spot. But upon closer inspection, I discovered one or two tickets from each and every one of Mitchell's sabotaged listings. She must have driven around without taking them off the windshield, leading me to believe they were all from one location.

Damn it, you didn't think of everything now did you, Dinah?

What else had she overlooked? I was going to have to pay these before Mitchell saw them and caught on.

Or before the police caught on. The police. I couldn't give them a reason to suspect me.

I needed to get to South Hampton or my absence would look suspicious. There was nothing like a good scare to motivate me into action. Maybe she'd left the parking tickets in there on purpose for that reason. She was one smart bitch. Wait—I was one smart bitch.

At the honking of the frustrated motorist behind me waiting to pull into the carwash bay, I put my car into drive and took off for the freeway. I might have been crazy, but I wasn't stupid.

I had a long drive to wrap my fucked up head around all the clues pointing to the fact Dinah wasn't real. She was a figment of my imagination, a character my disturbed mind created to help me accomplish a single goal. I was determined to win my private war and my secret subconscious super-being had figured out a way to do it. I felt like I was brilliant-scary, like Albert Einstein or Leonardo DaVinci, only with multiple personality disorder or schizophrenia.

But it wasn't like there were multiple people in my head, only her, right? What do you call it when you just have one special friend? Everyone else was real— right? But what were the other voices all about—the bad ones?

Oh, dear. I would be seeing Dr. Gibbs very soon. Tomorrow if possible.

Even the name, Dinah, didn't sound right now when I thought about it. It wasn't even Russian. While at a red light, I used my voice recognition option on my smartphone to do a search on Dinah. The automated voice told me it was a Hebrew name meaning "Avenged." My eyes popped at the uncanny connection, frightening me, my brain trying to grasp how I had picked out this piece of information from one of its far, buried corners. I must have known what her name meant deep down somewhere and chose it as my superhero name.

Dinah the Avenger. Good God, I might skip the Southampton Hospital and drive directly to the insane asylum and commit myself.

Concentrating on the road was difficult, when all I could picture in my head was the beautiful woman who led me into battle over the last few months. I remembered thinking how familiar she seemed the first time I met her. It was because she was a phantasmagorical version of my favorite doll.

Women always admired and wanted what they didn't have. Dinah had gorgeous blonde locks, bright blue eyes, and a more chiseled version of my own already high cheekbones. Her face was a bit rounder and her lips, the chemically filled version I'd always envisioned for my shriveled, forty-year old ones. She had large, perky breasts, which sat up nicely on their own, as opposed to mine which had the life sucked out of them two children ago. She was also super-thin, fit, and as agile as a jungle cat. How I fabricated those last two traits was beyond me.

The part that made everything solidify and come together perfectly was her steadfastness to carry out a plan. Her unwavering confidence to see through whatever cockamamie strategy she created without a doubt. I was a great planner, but all of the ballsy ingenuity I would have needed to carry this out, I pulled from her.

Dinah also had the ability to toughen me up when

I'd go soft, transposing my wimpy disposition into courage. And, Dinah was so much smarter than me. To take everything I knew about my husband and spin this delicious plot was something my simple mind could never create by itself.

It was like the intelligence center of my brain teamed up with my bravery epicenter, turning it on full blast; all the while fine-tuning my motor skills, making them able to do extraordinary tasks (my spidey-senses), creating the most fantastic version of myself. Every capacity in my mind and body came together to accomplish one very important task. It was amazing and terrifying at the same time.

And then there was the great battle between my mental disorders. My OCD would have never allowed me to welcome a vagrant into my car, but Dinah made it possible. I tugged on my hair so hard I thought I might rip it out, as I pondered the wish-washy thoughts, skipping over one another like skittish pebbles across a lake. Some skipped, whereas the big, dark ones sank to the bottom, waiting to be discovered at a later date.

The long drive to the Hamptons gave me plenty of time to think about it all. Dinah never gave me any contact information. No cell, no email, no address. I never saw her with her own car. I never saw her talk to anyone else but me. I remembered the waitress at the diner looking at me like I was mad when I insisted my imaginary friend didn't need anything.

And then there was Dinah's omission to liking sweets. Flashes of abandoned ice cream bowls and dollops of fudgy spread on my cheek surfaced as I tried to navigate through my distorted brain cloud. Forks stuck like daggers in the middle of uneaten pieces of chocolate cake.

It was like sifting through a dream world, trying to decipher reality from fantasy, steering through the hazy planets that exist between awake and asleep, none of it seeming tangible enough yet to make it real or instill guilt.

And then there were the voices; they seemed to have faded away.

Muddy boots and empty ice cream bowls.

Annihilation and dirty linens

Little pieces of skull mixed with red hair and blood.

What a cracked woman I must have looked like, running around the city talking to myself. Surely, someone had to have seen me. As I threw everything back into my glove box, I reached across the seat, remembering how cold it felt the night she was sitting there. It was too cold, icy almost, because there had never been a body there. The items in the glove box, the excessive scarf wearing, the fact our scarves were the same color, was making my head hurt now, because there was only one scarf—mine.

And when the "shits really started to hits the fan," as my mind made her say, (boy I was funny too), I got a headache and her image flickered. I remembered her whole body fading in and out like a faulty, old-fashioned television screen. I thought it was my vision, but it was my brain short-circuiting. Probably from sensory overload. How she obtained all of her information or did some of the things she did, I'll never know. And I didn't want to know. But if her plot actually worked, I would be grateful to her. She may not be real, but she'd always be real to me.

Chapter 23
The Party

The white lights in my backyard sparkled like iridescent butterfly wings, reminding me of the little floaters, which graced the inside of my car the day I'd passed out in Brooklyn. I swatted at the butterflies. Everyday started out a little like this one.

In the wake of the accident, my memory began coming back from my time spent in the dark. I was like a criminal amnesic, my secret transgressions coming back piece-by-piece. It was as disturbing as it was comforting.

There were flashbacks of breaking and entering, blonde wigs and arson, streaming back to me randomly in the middle of grocery stores, medical buildings and nail salons.

Paraffin wax treatments created images of homemade bombs, and recollections of Internet searches on how to construct military weapons. The horror, when I'd realized I'd blamed all of the computer research on my son.

Even though I'd come undone, there'd been a reassuring calming effect, which had occurred since the final toss of the grenade. I'd appeased the monster. When Dinah disappeared, *it* retreated back into its black, grimy hole. But, I'd been left with this. They called it post-traumatic stress disorder, according to my shrink. My flashbacks were my mind's way of recovering the memories I'd lost. Sometimes I wished it would stop trying so hard to remember. There were things I didn't need to know.

Every last bit of my energy had been invested in starting my new interior design business. It was literally the only thing keeping me sane. If I could channel my nervous energy into something productive I could keep my mind off the fact I had another person living inside my head.

Recently, I'd picked up a job for the owner of a white colonial home in West Orange, New Jersey. It wasn't until my first day on the new jobsite when, I'd remembered breaking into the white colonial overlooking the gray barn cottage in East Hampton.

The large white house on the hill was owned by a couple named Reachers, who had since moved to the South of France, renting out their home for the last five years. No one was due to arrive until June. There was no couple by the name of Reacher living there during the grenade attack. Katelyn claimed they'd delivered her cookies. A story the police had chalked up to yet another one of her lies.

Even though Dinah had left a mountain of evidence against Katelyn, my daily fears of getting caught by the authorities was intense. However, Katelyn was the one who had access to all of Mitchell's properties. It only made sense she'd been the one to sabotage them.

Later, when I'd driven to the brownstone in Brooklyn to help Mitchell move out, I remembered the open kitchen window. The one I'd used to break in during my early days as Dinah. The information I'd gathered on one covert escapade would later be the decided motive for Katelyn's destruction to her boyfriend's business. A motive Mitchell would back up with 100% certainty.

She'd been scheming to move Mitchell to The Hamptons permanently. Away from me. Away from the burden of his children. Coaxing him into the idea they could start anew there. She'd help him build his business. She'd write the great American novel. They'd live the dream.

Mitchell's marvel explanation for her motive to the cops was presented in his stellar salesman voice, leaving no room for doubt.

"She wanted us to move out of the city. She wanted to start over on Long Island, in East Hampton, leaving the big city life behind. At first it was only for the summer, but she changed her mind and decided she wanted to pick up and move there permanently. It became this idea she brought up once a week and then every day until she was pretty insistent she wanted to sell our brownstone in Brooklyn and move here."

Then, I remembered Dinah telling me outside of the divorce attorney's office about the open window. She was giving me a clue for later, maybe? It was so hard to tell these days.

Even though I was the one who should be committed to the psychiatric ward, Katelyn had been the one deemed insane. The best part was when the crazy factor started to make up where any of the other evidence lacked. When one thing pointed to *crazy*, it could encompass all other things. Like, *well, why did she use human fecal matter to destroy the apartment— because she was crazy. Who knowingly makes cookies from a spread with nuts in it, when you're allergic to nuts—a crazy person. Who steals from people, simply because they don't like you—Dunno—Bitch be crazy.*

Tonight, I would need to gather all of my marbles and put on my best sane face. Tonight, Mitchell would be throwing me a party to celebrate my new business. It wasn't necessarily true I wanted to take Mitchell back, it's that I was left with no other choice. I wasn't mentally fit enough to stand on my own yet. Our children needed one stable parent in the home. Of course, I wouldn't tell him about my issues, but until every single puzzle piece snapped back into place, and all of the flashbacks stopped, I wasn't comfortable being on my own. So, I was stuck with Mitchell. It was my punishment for all of the crimes I'd committed, I supposed.

Although, I was stunned and pleasantly surprised by Mitchell's work on the party. Our backyard was covered with pillowy white tents, bright white lights, ice sculptures, catered serving stations, a stage with a band, and two open bars. It was gorgeous. Every party needed a grand purpose and this one would be to advertise and celebrate my new business. The invitations read, *Cece Designs Preview Party.*

Cece Designs.

Oh, how I loved the sound.

Mitchell had made great efforts to repair the damage, although like any breach of trust in a marriage, it could never be undone. His retribution for his indiscretions included but was not limited to: scheduling our weekly marriage counseling appointments, rebuilding my doll room, and arranging a sixteen year anniversary trip back to our honeymoon spot in Aruba to rekindle our flame, as he had put it.

As for my friends, Mitchell decided it was time for our reinstatement back into the "club." There was no better way to do it in my crowd than with an extravagant party. People might not want to be there, but they would want to attend to see how the event was orchestrated. Mitchell told me not to worry about the details, because it was something he wanted to do for me. Mitchell had never organized a personal dinner, so I was both curious and scared to see his handiwork. Being a broker, I knew he had arranged many large-scale events for clients, but trying to host a huge shebang out of your home was another story.

After Mitchell finished refurbishing the Ivory Tower he further impressed me by having contractors build my very own home interior design studio in our basement.

He'd invited my clientele and asked them to bring friends. My reputation for fine design coupled with my friends' desperate attempts to stagger back onto my good side, resulted in my business picking up right away. With all of the referrals I received, by the time we headed to Aruba, I had to turn a few jobs down to accommodate my vacation. It was thrilling—all of my nervy energy finally being used for something constructive.

The elaborate display of my work is what took my breath away. In the four corners of the tent were large white boards featuring professional photos of my designs, along with samples of the actual high grade materials used to make them. My samples were divine, and Mitchell's marketing was genius.

The party was Mitchell's way of saying he was sorry to me, and all of our friends who were affected by his wacko, convict, ex-girlfriend. We were welcoming them back into our fucked up life.

I could hear the great debate among our friends.

Please welcome The Laramie's back into your circle, you know the ones with the philandering husband, obsessive-compulsive wife, bulimic daughter, and introverted son who tried to blow up the school.

If they didn't show, we knew it was too much for them to handle, and if they did, we knew we had our friends back.

Mitchell fretted over the party for weeks. I had laboriously pored over the cleanliness of the house and although I'd been in contact with the girls for my business, we hadn't all gotten together in a social setting since our unofficial breakup. I was just as nervous as Mitchell about the people who wouldn't show. I wanted my friends back and after all the faith I'd put into Dinah's promises, this was the one part I wasn't sure would actually come to fruition. Even though some of my girlfriends were traitors, I still desired to have the whole picture back.

My family arrived first. Natalie actually got there before the event to setup her elaborate array of yummy desserts.

"Oh yes, you are creamy, puffy, and delicious," Natalie cooed as she continued to sculpt her lady lock cookie tower. The rolls of soft crème were arranged in a delicate pyramid, the top locks frosted with tiny pink flowers.

"Beautiful," I gushed.

"Just like you, sister." She waved a powdered finger in my face and did a childlike spin away from me to tinker with the lovely fruit-filled arrangement on the opposite side of the table.

To my wild surprise, Dom was the second person to arrive. He was still livid with Mitchell. Even though the tear gas and grenade used in the incidents was his, he was not charged with any crimes. In Dom's over capacitated militia-center-of-an-apartment he'd actually forgotten he had the tear gas, until it surfaced Katelyn had stolen his grenade. Then, he put two and two together and Katelyn was indefinitely linked to the most serious of all crimes on the list: the gassing of civilians with a military weapon. Dom had something called a FEL, or a Federal Explosives License, and was somehow registered with the ATF as a licensed explosives dealer.

Since being investigated by the ATF, Dom's license had been revoked. He was irate and insisted Mitchell supplement his income, but Mitchell wasn't having it. Although Mitchell did apologize many times for his weapons being stolen and used in the manner they were, he would not concede to making monthly payments to my brother.

This was actually the part of the whole mess that bothered me the most. I would figure out a way to compensate my brother. Mitchell was putty in my hands, and my master manipulator skills had never been stronger.

"You showed," I said as I slung my arms around Dom's shoulders.

"I had to be here for you, Sis. Stressful, waiting to see who's gonna walk through the front door."

"Well, it means a lot to me you're here."

"Of course. Now where is that rat bastard husband of yours?" he said, grabbing a beer off the bar.

"Please, don't start trouble. I appreciate you being here, but if you can't control yourself maybe you shouldn't be," I said through gritted teeth.

"Don't worry, I won't do nothing," he said.

Dom dressed up for the occasion, which I found so adorable. He was a jeans and t-shirt kind of guy, but wore pressed gray slacks tonight and a white button-down shirt. He let his hair grow out over an inch from his scalp, which was a nice change, and I could smell his fresh aftershave. I gave his clean-shaven cheek a light pat.

"This is nice," I commented.

"I thought you might have some single, rich friends," he whispered in my ear.

"Dom, behave!" I yelled as I ran over to fuss with a tablecloth.

"Hey, hands off the linens," I heard a voice say. Familiar hands slid around my waist. They were warm and comforting, which is all I needed at the moment. Once the shock wore off and I stopped taking my meds, I'd probably be revolted by Mitchell's touch again. But, for now I'd use him to soothe my frazzled nerves.

"Only trying to tidy up," I said to my husband, whose mouth was trailing light kisses down my neck. I wiggled away from him. It was too soon.

"They'll show. Don't be nervous, Cece."

"You're the one who sounds nervous," I said.

"Really, because I was using my best 'I'm nervous but trying to project confidence voice,'" he said laughing.

"I think you're losing it. Must be old age," I joked.

"Just as long as I never lose you again," he said.

I turned to look at my husband. He was back. He

was so back. It was like he'd never left. And, I didn't understand how someone could just flip a switch like that. He was in love with someone else not two months ago, preparing to divorce me, and now he couldn't stand to lose me? I didn't believe anyone, even a man, could be so fickle. He just didn't want to be alone.

I half-smiled at him. No matter how hard he tried, there would always be the fact he had cheated on me and it would jab at me like an annoying hangnail I couldn't rip off.

Nikolay and Luka were next to join us. My stomach still jumped when I saw Nikolay. To me, he was still Dinah's husband, and I half-expected to see the fabricated, gap-toothed Lucy on his arm, but instead my mind flashed to the cottage.

I'd stopped by the cottage on my way back to Jersey to take in the fruits of my labor the day of the assault. I'd remained in the car with my window down listening to Nikolay lament over his destroyed property.

"Ah," he'd gasped to the detective, *"This was supposed to be my vacation home for me and my partner."*

By partner, I didn't think he was referring to Mitchell. Nikolay had stood there with his hand perched on his hip, kicking debris off his fine leather loafers. Similar to the ones he wore tonight.

It was clear to me after hearing Nikolay say one sentence, combined with his proud-as-a-peacock hip mount, he was as queer as a two dollar bill. He wasn't married to Dinah. He wasn't married to any woman. If I would've heard him speak, I would have picked up on it right away, but we never got close enough to him. Sure, his name was Russian, but he was one hundred percent American. American and gay. I remembered thinking he had a too sweet smile on those pouty cherub lips, and Mitchell had described him as *flamboyant.*

Nikolay and his "friend" were the other couple sharing the cottage. It's why Dinah wanted to blow it up, because in her mind, it was Lucy he was shacking up with. Going forward my life would be a giant jigsaw and I hoped eventually I'd be able to see the big picture of what happened in its entirety.

"Darling," he'd said as he kissed my cheek. Luka shook my hand, and I blushed. "Thanks so much for coming," I said.

"Your work is stunning," Luka commented. Luka was stunning. Hot, blond, tall, and fabulously dressed.

"Thank you, please tell your friends."

"Don't worry, we will." Luka exclaimed, heading for the dessert table. I left Mitchell to talk to his business partner for a bit. They had plenty to celebrate. They'd landed the Tribeca deal after all, which ended up affording me a lovely workspace.

It was a gorgeous evening with a gentle welcoming breeze ruffling the tent after a hot, musty day. Every time a person entered, Mitchell and I both cocked our heads to see if it was our old pals, and I kept myself busy entertaining guests and prospective clients until they arrived.

For this evening, Mitchell told me, I could buy whatever dress I wanted, because it was my big night. To his surprise, I donned an older, yet fabulous designer red dress and heels. Lord knew I had enough dresses hanging in the closet, which I'd only worn once. I always loved the red one with its deep, plunging neckline, belted middle, and flowy bottom. Its swishy material made me want to twirl around, especially with my mind so topsy-turvy.

A secret part of me wore it as a tribute to Katelyn, but I would keep that part all to myself. It was funny how her story ended. She'd connived a man into trading everything for her so she could turn around and destroy the business she'd helped him build. Stealing from his friends and family, all so she could feed a secret vengeance and manipulate him into moving to a place he had no desire to go. I hated how this story started, but I loved how it was ending. I wondered if she might be able to add—*In Jail* to her Facebook status update.

"No new dress for tonight?" Mitchell asked me suspiciously.

"I've been too busy working to go shopping and this one seemed just right," I answered.

His eyes lit up with delight. I wasn't faking it either. I had found my modesty in all we'd been through and I wanted him to see I wasn't going back to my old superficial ways.

"Well, it looks absolutely stunning. You know I always loved this one," he complimented.

I smiled back at him, thinking that was the plan.

A half hour into our meet and greet, they appeared in groups of two. Robin and Marcus and Maeve and Monte made their way through the tent, big smiles plastered on their faces, friendly waves as if no time had passed at all.

"I told you they would show," Mitchell said.

We walked hand and hand over to our old entourage. The cool breeze tickled my open-toed shoes and exhilaration of happiness raced up my spine. There were lots of tight squeezes and cheek-kisses. The men sauntered off to the bar as I was left to face my backstabbing besties.

"I knew you guys would pull through," Maeve said in her gentle voice.

"Thank you. It's been rough, but we're making it work," I said.

"Look Cece, we're sorry for not being there for you. It was our husbands, yeah know?" Robin said, fidgeting with her jewel-studded purse, grabbing two glasses of champagne off the tray from the waiter.

My eyes fixated on her jewels and my flashback interrupted my spiteful thoughts with images of charred remains. Dinah had left on the open gas line in the pool house to allot for a grander blast. My mind flashed to the burnt cottage, scattered limbs and sparkly rocks littering the lawn like a twisted fantasy. The cottage still mostly intact, with some shattered glass and a few straggly wooden pieces on the front porch. One piece would later be the one they'd decided caused the contusions on Katelyn's head.

The air smelled of sulfur. Men walked in hazmat suits placing doll parts and jewelry in evidence baggies. I observed a stray doll leg lying near the porch and had to laugh to myself at the bizarre scene. I had witnessed their maimed and dismembered bodies in my own home and now I had to look at their burnt remains. It felt like I really had been to war.

"Cece, say something," Robin said fretfully.

I'd completely blanked out into her rubies and diamonds. It happened so easily.

"No, I don't know. Your husbands?" I asked, trying to recall the question.

"I'm sure you don't want to drudge up that awful

time period, Darling. Our husbands still remaining friends made it terribly difficult for us to choose sides, and while we love you dearly, the man you sleep with, will ultimately win out," Maeve defended.

What a cop-out. As if they didn't have minds of their own and were solely controlled by their domineering husbands. Robin could tell Marcus to run down the street naked and jump in a lake and he would do it.

"I see," I said.

They were relieved of their awkward moment when Julie and Callie made a loud entrance with their husbands. Ahmet looked like a damn runway model in his tapered black pants, gray blazer, white, pointy-collared shirt. His sexy, brown-almost-black, almond-shaped eyes screamed—sex. It made me grin how I'd noticed Luka noticing him.

Julie's husband, Stan, a quiet dermatologist, appeared just the opposite in his plain navy blazer, white frumpy shirt, and khaki pants. Her little sister was always one-upping her.

"Cece," Ahmet ran over kissing me on both cheeks, and grasping me a little too tightly.

"Good to see you, Ahmet," I said.

"No, good to see you," he said, spinning me around into a dip, as Callie snatched him back and grabbed him a beer.

"This is why I don't take him anywhere. I have to fight them off with a stick," she joked.

I could teach her a thing or two about that.

Julie strode right over embracing me awkwardly. She was drunk already. "It's been way too long," she said.

"Yes, yes it has," I agreed.

"Let's cheers to new beginnings," Maeve said as she brought me over a glass of champagne, rounding us up in a circle.

We toasted our glasses and I was reminded of the last time we saluted each other—at the fashion show. A frown emerged as I remembered the last moment before I saw him with her for the first time. She would always be the woman who tore my world apart, but she was paying for it with her freedom. I took one tiny sip of the cocktail and put the rest on a nearby table.

"Where's your drink, Love?" Maeve asked, flipping her long blonde hair down the center of her black, curve-hugging dress.

"Trying not to drink too much. I have a lot of prospective clients here," I whispered. Really, the alcohol didn't mix too well with my meds. One more reason I couldn't adequately surmise the guilt I should be feeling. But truly, as far as I was considered, Dinah had committed those acts, not me.

"Right," she said, blowing me off a bit.

Our meet and greet was over and Mitchell got on stage to address our guests. He looked so handsome, decked out in one of his many expensive black suits, blue shirt casually gracing his chin as he cocked his head down to adjust the microphone. I knew he was nervous from the partial smile on his face and I could have bitten the cute dimple right off his cheek, he looked so delicious.

"Good evening everyone. Thank you all so much for coming to celebrate, *Cece Designs*," he said as the crowd roared with applause, making me light up my own shade of red. I should've known how to take a compliment at age forty, but this was a bit overwhelming for even me.

"I thank you all for joining us tonight, for what I can say has been a long time coming. Cece is one of the most brilliant and talented women I know and anyone who has had the pleasure of knowing her will tell you she puts her whole heart and soul into any project she takes on and doesn't let up until it's as damn near as perfect as it can be. I've had the great fortune of living with this woman, my own personal decorator, for years, and now I'm able to share her genius with all of you. Please take a look around at the tables for some of the stunning work she's already done. Our home has decades of craftsmanship if you'd like to take a look inside, and I hope if you are considering an interior decorator you give the job to Cece, because She.Is.The.Best," he said, embarrassing me a little. The crowd erupted with applause again.

"I'd like to also make a toast on a personal note. If everyone wouldn't mind raising their glasses again, we've had a tough year here in the Laramie household and I wanted to say thank you to my wonderful family for continuing to support me when things were tough and for pulling together when we really needed each other. And most of all, I wanted to thank the love of my life. A wonderful mother whose dedication to her children is unwavering. A person who has always been able to see the good in me, even when I couldn't see it myself, and to a woman who I know affirmatively, with one hundred percent certainty, I could never, ever live without. To my wife—Cecelia Laramie," he finished, his eyes going dewy as did the rest of the crowd as they exploded into another ripple of clapping.

I was beaming like a newlywed when he approached the table throwing his arms around me in a huge hug. He spun me around in the air, kissed me hard for everyone to see, and once more our adoring fans put their hands together. The attention was nice. I could play this game for tonight. Everything was still a bit fuzzy, and emotions were uncertain, but I acted in a way I thought might be expected.

The Ginnifer McIntyre way.

The band started to play and we watched in glee as our guests took the floor. We were about to dance as well when Mitchell was beckoned by the wait staff to address a shortage of something in the kitchen. I saw his face scrunch together. I told him to let me take a look at the menu, but he wanted me hands-off. It was so hard for me to not be part of an organized event at my own home, but I restrained to appease him. He had worked so hard on this party to make me happy and it was lovely.

If Dinah were there I would have loved to have clinked glasses with her in a victory drink. I wondered what her poison of choice would be—vodka, probably.

"Here's to you, D," I muttered under my breath, raising my full glass of champagne in the air.

The girls walked up to give me hugs, complimenting Mitchell's warm speech. He really did a stellar job this time. And, what a way to end it. A private sentiment only he and I shared. Robin's loud, carrying voice broke my dreamy stream of consciousness.

"Cece, is the dress you have on the same one you wore to Maeve's Save-a-Child charity a few years ago?" Robin asked.

"Yes. One of my favorites," I said giving it a whip around.

"Mitchell still hanging onto the purse strings, eh?" Julie asked from behind her.

"No. Actually he told me to do it up for tonight, but I've been so busy with my new business, I haven't had time to shop. City shop, at least. So I pulled this little baby out," I said, giving it another playful twirl. Everything still seemed like a warped fantasy to me.

One thing for certain was my friends were seething with jealousy over my business, so I let them take their cuts. I understood. They didn't have an accomplishment to call their own in two decades. It must have been hard seeing me thrive doing something I loved while they were navigating their same boring lives. I'd just gotten back into the club and I was already doing things to compromise my affiliation, but I didn't care. If anything, I was passing them up, not slowing them down. *Eat my dust on my hot new bike—bitches!*

In fact, something happened after *Cece Designs* took off which spurred their own professional awakenings. Over the course of the next few years, each one of them would come up with their own enterprises. They all pulled themselves up by their proverbial stiletto straps and did something with themselves. Maeve created her own makeup line, marketing it to the New York City model scene with all of her connections. Robin opened up a virtual *Mommy and Me and Friends* website, which linked stay at home moms with other mothers in their community. Julie and Callie started their own wine business. They had the *whine* part down perfectly. Pretty soon, our coffee chats were about our new ventures, instead of our husbands' accomplishments.

By far, my business was the most successful. All of the nervous energy I'd been harboring over my own home and family, I poured into my business instead. My family was better for it too. I wasn't living vicariously through them anymore and I was more enjoyable to be around, or so they told me. In a way, we were all better for Mitchell having met Katelyn. Everyone was better off—except her.

Hopefully, Dinah would remain locked away like Katelyn in her cell. Katelyn hadn't been sentenced yet, and until then I refused to envision the woman in an actual prison, or feel any real remorse.

I shivered at the thought of people finding out about all I'd done. My mother's words were like an echo in my ear now—d*on't let her come out*. It spooked me every time I thought about the fact she saw Dinah before I did. She saw my mind begin to splinter as hers had. My only hope was I could stop it or at least slow it down so I didn't end up like her; a near-vegetable spending my golden years in a nursing home.

Sorry mom, I couldn't keep my cuckoo it its clock. Apparently, it had a mind of its own.

There was only one person who could leak my secret identity—Sam. He was also my little bit of leverage against Mitchell, something to keep in my back pocket if we ever did reconcile. Sam knew things that could condemn me. Although, the beautiful thing about Sam was he wouldn't say a word. But if I were to tell people we'd slept together, he'd dance on top of the tabletops and shout, "Hell yes, I did her."

When thinking about my options, two women came to mind: Anita Botson and Ginnifer with-a-smiley-G McIntyre. If I had to pick between which of the two women I'd rather be, the answer was easy— Ginnifer. In this ugly, evil world, she was definitely the lesser of the two. Maybe there was a place for divorced women in other suburbs, but in our world they were put out to pasture until they coupled up again or died.

So, she's who I'd be for now. But, someday, I'd be known as Cece—the ex-wife of Mitchell Laramie who started her own successful company and kicked her cheating, groveling husband to the curb.

My work here was done. I'd made Mitchell hurt like I'd hurt. And, I'd made Katelyn hurt more than anyone should hurt. My children would remain safely with me, and all would be well again in my old dream house.

As long as *She* didn't come back out again.

Epilogue

The day after *The Big Show*, I burned the letter, wig, scarf and sunglasses in a fire pit in my backyard. I watched the embers burn down until the scarf fibers were ashes and the plastic of the sunglasses melded around the wood in a gooey mess. Instead of erasing the Supra app, I drove to my cell provider and bought a whole new phone. I was sure there was some tech guy somewhere who could have pulled my history off the old one, so I got rid of the damn thing, and traded it in for a new one.

I waited a couple of months and let the world around me settle before I put the last piece of the puzzle together. I had figured out most of the events from the last months in question, but there was one mystery remaining. I waited until the ground was nice and thawed and ready to be unearthed. But mostly, I was afraid, of what I might uncover upon Dinah's final request:

4. There is a treasure for you hidden in the place where Josie hid her demons. Find it and you will be handsomely rewarded. (You know I had to leave one little item of suspense on here for you *smile*)

Well, Josie hid her demons all over the backyard, so this would be taxing. Dinah couldn't make it easy on me. It wasn't her style. So, one late day in May, after I dropped Camdyn off at soccer and Josie at dance practice, I'd stared at the tool shed, knowing what I had to do. As I removed the shovel out of the shed with purpose, I had no idea what I would find. Dinah had not tried to make a reappearance; but I wanted to put her to rest for good, and to put her away I had to fulfill her last request. Otherwise, she would haunt me forever, and I'd worry she'd be so displeased she'd come back to punish me.

I strode over to the line of bushes where Mitchell discovered most of Josie's jars. I was looking for a place to start. The bushes covered a forty-foot span across the length of our yard. I walked back and forth across the hedge line, frustrated, not knowing where to begin. Surely, if I had really come up with this plan there had to be a rhyme or reason to where I buried this treasure of which she spoke. It wasn't like me to not be meticulous in my planning and I wouldn't have just thrown it anywhere.

My eyes scanned the dirt near the bushes, looking for a spot recently disturbed. Then my eyes caught it as I drew in a sharp breath. Why had she been so careless? Mitchell could have seen it trimming the hedges and I couldn't imagine what he might have thought. There, in the far right corner of the yard was a foot sticking out of the earth. It wasn't a human foot, well it was, just not a flesh and bone human foot. It was a black stiletto attached to a slim doll leg. One of the victims in the cottage attack. X marked the spot.

I pulled the dismembered leg out of the earth and started digging. I didn't have to go very far before I hit a metal box. As I pulled it out of the ground, I realized it was one of the same metal boxes I'd seen at Dom's apartment—an old-fashioned military gun safe. Jesus

Christ, I hope she didn't leave me a gun. Or a bomb. Would it blow up, killing us both? I stood there staring at it not really wanting to open it, but I knew I had to. I picked up the safe and put it up to my ear. There wasn't any obvious ticking, but she was never into the obvious approach. I shook it gently like a mystery Christmas present, and heard a light rattle, but not a heavy one indicating weaponry. It was actually very lightweight.

There was no escaping it. I needed to open the damn thing. I unfastened the metal latch and it easily clicked open. What I saw in there threw me back on my ass in laughter. The clever bitch. Instead of a gun there was one pristine, boxed number one Minsk doll. Even as my deranged, alter-ego, I couldn't bear to part with her. So, in the end, Mitchell got the one amazing woman he couldn't live without and so did I.

A word from the author…

Cara Reinard is an author of women's fiction and domestic suspense. While attending college, she was an editor for her student newspaper and sold advertising space for the publication. Cara is employed in the pharmaceutical industry and currently lives in the Pittsburgh Area with her husband, two children and fluffy Bernese Mountain dog. When she's not hustling or chasing tiny footsteps—she's writing.

http:// www.carareinard.com

CPSIA information can be obtained
at www.ICGtesting.com
Printed in the USA
LVHW080229020421
683296LV00024B/320